Long Range's mind raced; then as he entered the pass, he wheeled his machine about, stopping for a moment to wipe his hand across his dusty face and red-rimmed eyes. He jerked the shotgun from his saddlebag and, holding it in his left hand, nosed his bike back down the narrow trail. As he approached the bend he could hear the sound of motors laboring up the mountain toward him. He cocked the shotgun with his thumb, feeling completely cold but fiercely elated.

The oncoming machines appeared, closer than he had calculated and coming fast. He leveled the shotgun at Bad Hand. Bad Hand saw it, ducked, wobbled, stamped instinctively on the rear brake. His rear wheel locked and his bike slewed sideways, and suddenly machine and rider shot off the path and disappeared, plummeting screaming over the edge. . . .

THE LOST TRAVELER

"Unquestionably the best, most mature, most honest, fairest, and most wise piece of fiction ever written about the Hell's Angel's."

Norman Spinrad

STEVE WILSON
"A talent to watch."

W9-AYC-820

The Kirkus Reviews

Also by Steve Wilson
Published by Ballantine Books:

13

THE LOST TRAVELER

A Motorcycle Grail Quest Epic
and Science Fiction Western

Steve Wilson

BALLANTINE BOOKS • NEW YORK

ISBN 0-345-34113-9

This edition published by arrangement with St. Martin's Press, Inc.

Manufactured in the United States of America

First Ballantine Books Edition: July 1987

"Adventure" . . . represents the random, the gratuitous, the unpredictable element in life. . . . To accept an adventure is to accept an encounter with a force which is in the proper sense of the word supernatural. . . .

—P. M. Matarasso
The Quest of the Holy Grail, notes

the wildest cock-blowing
gang-fucking foul-tongued
head chick
thus the most so—

—Gary Snyder
"Hymn to the Goddess
San Francisco in Paradise"

Apples and pears with right good corn
Come in plenty to everyone
Eat and drink good cake and hot ale
GIVE EARTH TO DRINK AND SHE'LL NOT FAIL

—Traditional English song accompanying Apple Howling,
Twelfth Night libation to orchard and meadow

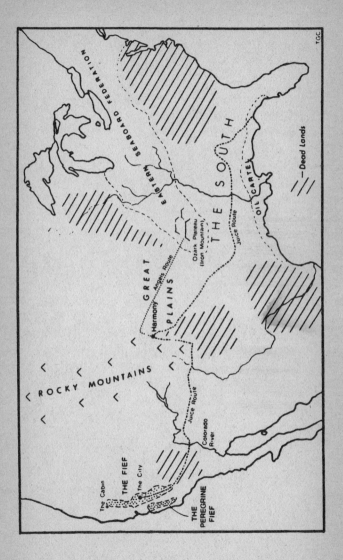

PROLOGUE I

IN THE THIRD YEAR OF THE LAST DECADE OF THE TWENtieth century, the civilization then current in the world came to an abrupt end.

For reasons we can only guess at, one of the major powers launched an all-out attack on another. From then on, the outcome was inevitable; the moves for the most part were preprogrammed into electronic machinery. Nuclear, drug and chemical attacks crippled each of the major powers, and their effects dispersed to cover the entire globe.

This was the crisis in world affairs known to future times by the simple synonym BLAM. . . .

. . . THE HELL'S ANGELS MOTORCYCLE CLUB OF CALIfornia survived.

In the lottery of nuclear offense and defense and of the winds, much of the west coast of America was spared the effects of radiation for a time. A potent cocktail of poison and drugs had been unleashed on the cities; but the Angels were already accustomed to facing a hostile world while under the influence of every known combination of nar-

1

cotics; and their strong sense of corporate identity and loyalty to the group survived at a time when soldiers tore off their uniforms and executives danced naked in the ashes of their corporation buildings. In the shattered streets their kingdom had manifestly come; the world was hell.

And an extraordinary piece of good fortune ensured their survival. On the second day after the attack, a large party riding out in search of beer, led by their President, clashed with a group of looters. When these had been beaten and disposed of, the Angels discovered that they had inadvertently rescued no less a person than the President of the United States; caught while traveling by the attacks, he had been making his drug-fuddled way to the White House West when his car had struck and killed one of the looters, whose friends were attempting to return the compliment when the Angels had arrived.

President embraced President, and the Angels' services (as bodyguards) were offered and accepted by the bemused but grateful Head of State. From then on they would be by his side throughout the efforts to reorganize whatever was left of men, materials and unpoisoned territory on the West Coast. The Angels' future was assured. . . .

TIME PASSED.

The Fief, whose center was the City, and whose territory then consisted primarily of what had been the San Joaquin Valley, called itself simply the Fief—as its originators conceived it, a territory and an idea held in fief for the unborn, the future.

This title also served to remind the world at large, and especially its neighbors the Peregrine Fief, that it was *the* Fief, the original state on the West Coast that had emerged from the confusion of BLAM and post-BLAM days; masterminded by Californian academics, and alternately bolstered and confounded by the presence of the increasingly eccentric President and his Praetorian Guard of Hell's Angels. But after a while the Angels were established in their own camp, on a bend of the river some distance away from the City, setting up as slave traders, cattlemen and Cos-

2

sacks to the Fief, which supplied them in return with mechanical artifacts and fuel. Not guns, however; as time went on, and barrels rusted, firing pins bent, and cached ammunition became unreliable, the Fief artfully replaced it with spring-operated crossbows, or bolt-guns. For the farmers and Angels, that is; they kept making enough guns to supply their own small army.

Although it was the Angels who really defended the Fief. Across the hills of the coast ranges, in the Salinas Valley, some time after the Fief had begun to build and to lay down its carefully thought-out system of society and culture, another township had come together. This was a very different affair. Its leaders were the remnants and offspring of the military-industrial complex, and although it adopted the superficial style of the Fief, calling itself the Peregrine Fief and collecting another gang of motorcycle outriders around the remnants of the old Gypsy Jokers, its ideals were different indeed. Basically, while the Fief did its best to lead a rational and harmonious existence, the Peregrines were out for advantage. The coast's supply of oil was diminishing. By their position the Peregrines dominated what there was. The Fief tolerated this; the newcomers as yet did nothing to stem the flow, and made no aggressive moves; and further, the Fief knew it was strong enough to retake the oilfields and destroy the Peregrines if necessary. And further still, it knew the coast deposits were diminishing fast, so the real problem lay in another area.

TIME PASSED.

While the Peregrine Gypsies probed their strength and were dealt with by the Angels, the two Fiefs officially cooperated to renew and maintain the highway south and east, all the way to the oilfields of Texas and the Gulf Coast. These were already being efficiently worked by an oil cartel, the one stable element in the otherwise incoherent moil of statelets, estates and counties known merely as the South. The Fiefs traded hides, minerals, small manufactured goods and the like for oil and gas. The Cartel was prosperous, for it also supplied the far coast, where a large state with

3

a more rigid organization had prevailed, under the title of the Eastern Seaboard Federation.

Why all the emphasis on oil and gas? The economy of these surviving fragments was concentrated almost exclusively on agriculture, and the land had had to be worked intensively to support the populations that survived the initial slaughter, the dip soon afterwards due to further deaths from dominant lethal mutations caused by atomic radiation, and the continuing toll as recessive mutation made itself evident in those born mentally deficient, physically malformed, or both. For there was only a limited amount of land available; the cataclysm had also left a large portion of the country as radioactive wasteland, where nothing would grow; the Dead Lands, they were called. In the struggle to keep their little societies alive, the people had neither time nor resources to invent new means. The workhorse remained, in pump or tractor, truck or motorcycle, the good old internal combustion engine; and it was as thirsty as ever.

A pipeline east to the oilfields would have been too vulnerable to the nomad bandits who flourished and perished on the edge of the societies. So the big tankers with their freight trains of trailers plied back and forth on the Juice Route, as the road east was known. And the Fief continued to be regulated by the unobtrusive élite called Literates; and the Peregrine Fief plotted; and the South stagnated; and the East was an unknown factor; and time, according to the various clocks in the various organisms, set by the common rhythmic geophysical environment of the planet, passed.

—*Fief Known History*, Vol. 2

PROLOGUE II

Over two hundred summers had passed.

It was winter, deep winter, in a remote corner of the country to the north of the Fief. The wind had dropped and the white trees were turning ghostly in the dusk. A gray-bearded man in a tattered leather coat stood quietly in the shadows under the trees, scanning the cleared, snow-covered space of a gentle rise. On top lay a dwelling large and low like an upturned boat, with a single light shining from down in its dark shape.

The man's gray eyes quartered the bare snow, shining under early moonlight, which lay between him and the fence surrounding the cabin; he was searching for foot-prints. When satisfied, he moved forward across the un-tracked snow and trudged steadily up the slope toward the fence. The smell of cows and wood smoke came to him. A dog began to bark. At the gate he stopped, his boots in mud. All the dogs were barking now.

The light inside became a single diamond-shaped point as heavy shutters were swung to, and he heard the dull chunk of a bolt-gun placed in the firing-loop. A man's voice called out:

"Who's there?"

"I'm an old man. I'm on my own and I need shelter," he cried back in a querulous voice, leaning bent and huddled over a stick.

"Where's your party?" called the rough voice.

"I got separated from them—look, you've got to let me in or I'm finished," pleaded the old man, sounding exhausted and desperate.

There was silence, then the voice shouted, "Step to the light," as a panel slid open and a shaft of light illuminated the packed snow in front of the big door. The old man stumbled forward and stood panting, his breath showing in small steamy clouds.

"Why should I let you in?" said the voice at last.

"Please," the old man quavered back, "I've got a little coin."

Almost immediately the bolts slid back.

The old man stumbled forward into the warmth and light of the cabin and stood there blinking as a rough-looking bearded man in an apron wedged the door with a thick bar of timber, and, easing the spring on his cocked bolt-gun, leaned it under the shutters. None of the people in the room, or the kitchen adjoining, helped or stopped the old man as he moved across to the fire, where he stood warming his hands and looking around him dully.

It was a poor place. True, there were hams, cheeses, onions in strings and bunches of herbs hanging from the cross beams of the next room, and the woman bending over the stove there was red-faced and plump. The board floor was scrubbed, and the smell of meat stewing, candlewax and grease, wood smoke and the beasts in the byres adjoining, compounded with human and animal leavings and the many smells of a long winter, was not unpleasant. But it was a poor place. The two young men sitting at one of the tables on each side of the fire had pulled off their boots after the alarm and got back to glasses of liquor and cob pipes without a word to him. There was no guitar propped

6

anywhere he could see, and no bright woven rugs or dyed hides decorated the log walls, promising the bright colors of other seasons. These people were interested in keeping themselves alive and comfortable, and not much else.

"And what the hell is an old crow's dropping like you doing up here in the back end of the world?" said the aproned man when he had finished locking up and came over to stare at the visitor. "The settlement's three days south and you don't tell me you stopped out nights as you are."

"Wolves wouldn't mess with him—there ain't enough meat there," called one young man with a snigger as thin as his face.

"No, no—I was out hunting with my neighbor, and we got split up this morning."

"Out hunting with no guns or blankets?" said the aproned man.

"My nephew had the gear, and I lost my gun as I was running—"

"Running from an angry rabbit," shouted the thin one, and shrieked with laughter while the old man looked down and stood shuffling his feet and rubbing his grizzled beard.

"Well that might be," said the father, "but you ain't getting back to the settlement till the mail party comes through next week. And you don't stay here getting outside our victuals till I see some of that coin you told about out there."

The traveler fumbled under his tattered coat, produced a small pouch and with trembling hands shook out a pair of small gold coins. The bearded man picked them from his hands, bit them and tucked them beneath his apron.

"That'll serve for tonight. Same for every day from now," he said. "I'm Jessie Calder, that in there's my wife Martha, and these are my boys Lew and Matt."

"I'm obliged, Mr. Calder, and I don't wish to impose on you longer than I need. Are there no other travelers that pass through here?"

"You're the first since the fall."

So he's not here yet.

7

Lew was shrieking, "And you ain't properly a traveler, you're more like some damn thing the dog brought in."

There was fresh commotion from the next room; a skinny boy in tattered clothes was being simultaneously held by one ear and booted round the kitchen in a flurry of skirts by the surprisingly agile Mrs. Calder; from her angry shouts it seemed that he had dropped a pail of milk. Lew, the thin son, went to join in punishing him. The old man sat down quietly opposite Matt at the end of the table nearest the fire.

When supper was ready he rose and shuffled into the kitchen to help carry the dishes through. While he was in the other room, fat Matt asked his father in an audible whisper why they didn't finish him off and take all the coin? As this idea was being vetoed in the hopes that his nephew might prove generous, the old man fussed about the earthenware pot of potatoes and the wooden bowl of curds.

They ate in silence around the table lit by a hanging lamp, and the lighted circle shifted slightly as the lamp swayed in the draft. From the dark outside the circle came the sound of the orphan boy in the kitchen whimpering, and the wind whining and singing through the chinks in the walls; in the corners, by the larger gaps, snow lay where it had blown in, in neat lines, as if it had been poured from a sack. Logs burning in the fire steamed, and sometimes suddenly they cracked and sparks flew up. The old man took no potatoes and declined the curds.

When they had done the woman cleared away, but on her second trip to the kitchen she dropped a dish; she stared in silence as it rolled away across the wooden floor. Coming to the table again she plumped down heavily on a bench and rested her head on her arms. In the kitchen the boy wordlessly scrabbled with his fingers at the food that was left over, finishing by drinking the curds down from the wooden bowl. The men had poured drinks but these too were unfinished before they began to nod.

Outside the wind howled higher and whipped up the first light snow that was falling into flurries and spirals, blurring the outlines of the snowy earth with the night sky. The boy curled up on some sacking in the kitchen and fell asleep.

The old man sat quietly by the fire till the sound of the family's snuffling and snoring filled the cabin. He leaned forward to throw on fresh logs, then rose, standing at his full height for the first time since he had entered. He looked around at the sleeping forms, grunted and moved forward.

THUMPS AND BANGS PENETRATED THE BLACKNESS IN which Jessie Calder's head was immersed as if in a barrel of molasses. The pain the bangs produced suggested that a band of tiny creatures was endeavoring by violent means to break into his head and get at the molasses. His head was grateful as the fiery circles their blows produced subsided back into rings on the molasses, and faded away.

It was a smell, wafting like a sprite, a shred of mist, through the wire thickets of his moustache, up into the caverns of his nostrils, as soon to be exhaled, but quickly asked back in, deeper, the rhythm of sleep's breathing now broken; a smell, subtly dissatisfying as a promise of "later," as smells will be, which nudged his other senses in pursuit of it.

Since it was a smell of beer, this process did not take long with Jessie. His eyes bleared open, fluttering in protest against the light. He tried to push himself up from the table he had slumped over, but was arrested by a number of factors; a blinding pain in his head; the sight that presented itself opposite; and the fact that a large iron staple had been driven into the table and his left wrist was clamped down firmly under it. The pain passed, and the staple hurt his hand when he tugged at it, so he looked back at the sight opposite.

The old man, no longer looking very old, sat on a bench tilted backwards, leaning his back against the opposite wall. By the light of the fire Jessie saw that his hair had been combed straight back, and it fell, thick and silver, almost to his shoulders. His old coat lay folded under his sack on the bench, and he was wearing a denim jacket with the sleeves cut off and small cloth badges stitched to it. On the

9

table before him four bolt-guns lay neatly arranged in a row, as well as a two-gallon cask of Jessie's best beer, stove in at one end with a hatchet, standing next to Jessie's own drinking-bowl.

Jessie was suddenly terrified; he turned his head this way and that, to find Lew on one side of him, and Matt on the other, also stapled to the table and still out cold. He tried to call but no sound came. Finally he managed to croak, "Martha!"

The old man looked up, as though noticing for the first time that Jessie had revived; smiled at him; and gestured with the bowl. Jessie looked, and on the floor by the fire saw his wife. She was naked, and the firelight burnished her limbs as she lay on her dress, with one leg drawn up under her, and her long dark hair loose about her face. For an instant Jessie wondered why she had hardly ever seemed so beautiful before, all those nights climbing in beside him in a night-shirt. In the midst of his terror he felt a softer anguish, a regret.

"Funny how you see 'em different after some other feller's been there, ain't it?" said the old man with a chuckle, and the deeps of that voice, its richness and assurance, everything that separated it from the old man's previous whine, plunged Jessie back into terror.

"Well, now, jackass, let's see what we can do for the boys there," said the old man, getting up and coming round the table with a bowl of beer in each hand. As he approached, Jessie, without thinking, lunged out with his right hand, surging forward to overturn the table. But the table had been nailed to the floor, and Jessie crashed forward on to it, bruising his ribs, while the old man danced away from his flailing hand. None of the beer spilled. He set the bowls down by the slumped young men, then turned away to throw more logs on the fire. With his back to them a large winged death's-head-and-wheel patch could be seen on the back of his jacket.

Jessie was a big man, and bold enough, but his helplessness, his hangover, the humiliation of Martha and now the shock of knowing his captor was a Hell's Angel for

10

sure, caused him to cover his face with his free hand and emit a long succession of small sobs, no louder than a quiet hen clucking. It was as he drew a tearing breath for more of the same that the old man turned and saw what was happening.

"Now, Jessie," he said, and paused to drink, "don't be upsetting yourself that way. You know you could be dead now if I'd wanted it like that; couple more drops of what went into the grub and you'd be all quiet for a spell. Likewise could of cut your throats laying on the table. Or I could let you up and still kill you quick—wouldn't be so much for an Angel.

"No," he went on expansively, "I'm a crazy old bastard, just want someone to talk to that ain't always *wandering off* somewhere. Old friend of mine's calling here sometime soon, and I got to wait up on him, but that's no cause to kill you. Course *he* may kill you, but while you're living you can hope, ain't that right?"

He settled back on his bench, and noticing Jessie glancing at Martha, went on, "Now dry up, the boys are coming round. And don't worry too much about your old lady," he cackled, "she won't die, it's not poison."

So the family revived, the young men whimpering when he called Matt a fat scum-sucker for thinking to kill him, and said he should maybe fix the pig so there would be no more like him. Martha tried to scramble away, but she discovered her ankle was tethered securely to the table; so she pulled her dress over her head, and sat with her face turned, looking at the fire. The old man fetched the boy from the kitchen and sat him down, with some bread and cold meat, next to Martha by the fire. They all gulped greedily at the bowls of beer to moisten their parched throats. And when they were all more or less settled, the old man began, as he had promised, to talk to them; to tell them, in fact, a story. . . .

I THE SPRING FAIR

Jesters clowns and jugglers
Wine and knives for sale
Dancing in the meadow
Angels on the hill.

　　　—Spring fair song

To THE SOUTH OF THE CITY A GREEN FIVE-ACRE MEADOW
fell away to the river, and there, every year on the morning
of the spring equinox, a fair was held. On one side of the
meadow there rose a small hummock with a circle of trees
at the crown. Every year the Angels rode in from their
camp and gathered on the top of the hill to attend the fair.

Long Range John looked round as bikes snarled leaping
up the hillside, skidding round on the crest to join the others banked under the shady eucalyptus tree. It was a sunny
early morning and already warm. Up on the knoll the Angel banners ruffled on their poles in a fresh breeze, which
shook the figurines hanging from the lower branches of the
rustling trees; corn dollies and Mothers of rush, brought
by the citizens the night before, and carved wooden long-
horns and animals hung there by the Angels. Both paid
homage to the forces that fed them. On the trunk of the
biggest tree, looking down on the field below as it filled
with the colors of the crowd, hung the horned bull's mask
of the President, and the cougar mask, wolf skin and hawk
feathers of the officers of the chapters.

12

Long Range John reached up and tied a thong to a bough above him, the sun glinting in his eyes in diamonds of brilliance as the leaves above him rustled and swayed in the wind. A wooden carving of Glitch, an Angel favorite, the godlet of hang-ups, danced grinning on the end of the cord. Long Range had whittled the little figure in the winter, horns, imp's grin, left leg cocked behind the right. He had held pretty well to the shape that had come to him first. He lifted it up now and left it for the sun, hoping for a good summer.

Looking up at it he stepped back, a tall thin young figure dressed in jeans, a dark blue woolen shirt with his chapter's emblem—a bird on the wing—woven in natural wool on the chest, and a prospect's sleeveless denim jacket with no patches. He looked about. Angels stood or squatted around under the trees. Their talk was sometimes rather over-earnest. The generations in the empty land had left their mark on the Angels. They were generally more taciturn than their twentieth-century forebears, and less flamboyant. As with all lonely men, the thought of a social gathering both attracted and unnerved them. Further, one strong impulse told them to lash out and stomp what made them nervous; there had been murderous brawls at fairs before then. This was one of the central events of the year, but it was just as open to chaos as any other part of their lives. Yet the Fief's great gift of regularity conveyed itself, and underneath also they all knew of the band's dependence on the Fief; and besides, everyone had their favorite story of fine partying and compliant City women at the fair. So it could go either way, and the mood among them held a certain tension. Long Range felt it too.

An old truck pulled in below at the foot of the hill, and some Angel women and children jumped out and began scrambling up the slope. Long Range got breathless as he saw a small blond figure among them.

Lila came on, her green robe and golden hair flowing out behind her in the wind. Her face was pale and elfin, mischievous, the lips a shade thin, the chin somewhat pointed, green eyes sparkling. Long Range was standing at the top of the slope when she reached it, stood there laughing at her own breathlessness, recovered and said, "Hi, Long Range," a touch mockingly, and went on to talk to some other Angels before he could get himself to say anything.

Jamming his fists in his pockets he clenched his teeth and swore furiously to himself. The same old song.

Around him Angels and their people began to move down the hill, toward the tents and banners flapping in the wind, and the music.

IN THE CENTER OF THE CITY, IN THE FIEF'S COUNCIL tower, Frank III, President of the Hell's Angels, lay with his boots up on a council stool, eating grapes and waiting on the head Literate. While it was not the Angel way to think things out in advance, Frank, for all his I-own-the-joint-and-I'll-spit-if-I-choose manner (and indeed, grape seeds were pinging off ornaments and littering rich rugs), Frank was getting himself together for this annual encounter. As President it was his business to screw as much as possible in the way of parts, gas, tires and artifacts from the Fief in return for as little as possible in the way of furs, captives, cattle and duties for his people; and to minimize whatever little incidents had occurred during the year between them and the Fief, such as rape, abduction, theft, murder and brawls, for instance.

Not a hell of a lot of that this year, but why was he being treated so well? The old fuckers must want something, was his conclusion, and he settled himself to extract the highest price for it.

The Literate cleared his throat and bustled in. His order's concession to their continuity with pre-BLAM times was a tie and collar; time and comfort had modified this into a floppy arrangement lurking among the blue robes. Frank was struck as usual by the Literates' restlessness, their apparent preoccupation with something that wasn't actually there. This one called himself Eliot, and Frank didn't underrate him. Also he liked him better than his

14

predecessor, Wordsworth, the melancholy bastard who had once had ideas about destroying his people.

"Greetings, Frank, sit yourself," said Eliot, the Ss coming out with a high-pitched whistle; dentistry had not been one of the surviving sciences.

Frank stayed standing and mumbled something about some more wine.

"Certainly, to be sure, festival day that it is," said Eliot, and, biting his beard a couple of times by way of a windup, he shouted to the guards outside for wine.

" 'In the rigging,' as my man would have said," he chuckled, looking up to see Frank's stare on him direct as an animal. "Well, Frank, well. I see the skins are not so numerous this year. Hard winter you've had of it."

No you don't, you bastard, thought Frank.

"Cattle didn't suffer though," he said with the air of a satisfied man. It was true the winter had hit them hard and everything was a little ragged at the edges this year, but catch him owning to that so the old turd could screw them over whatever it was he wanted.

The wine arrived, in large goblets of coarse metal: Angels had been known to push the annual prevailing atmosphere of good will on these occasions to the extent of walking off with the precious ones.

Frank went to the curved window and stood looking down over the town wall and ditch at the meadows below and the river sparkling beneath the mild silvery air. He looked across at the Angels' hill and then at the river again, meandering by. He wished he was down there with his brothers, turning on, setting up some little town piece. Hey ho.

"A great day for it, Frank, I know, so I shall endeavor to be brief."

Frank turned. The old boy was standing by his heavy chair, looking directly at him.

"I know you've had a hard winter, and the Peregrine Gypsies will be pushing any time now. You need gasoline and all the rest of it, you need it badly, and you're in no position to barter for much. I know, I know, a lame Angel can trash ten Gypsies, but you still need these things.''

"Why not say what you want," said Frank.

"In return for what we're offering it's ridiculously little," said Eliot; a little too quickly, thought Frank, though the old man was already taking a drink to give himself pause. Then he went on.

"We want an outfit to make a modest journey, on our behalf.''

"You want a party out now, when you've just said the fucking Gypsies'll be up our ass any minute? And you don't want much?''

"Not a party, Frank. Three.''

LONG RANGE JOHN FELT TIGHT IN HIS CHEST FROM EXcitement. Down among the tents in the meadow there was so much to see, after the long, drab, hard winter at the Angels' camp. No one had hassled him yet, even though he was on his own and the City boys went about together in their club or college jackets. Some of them were all right, he had even talked with one or two who asked him about life up at the camp, and his bike, and the Gypsies and whatever, and though you couldn't really talk, one of them had shared some wine. Then an unbroken white mare had got loose from the sale ring and bolted through the tents, collapsing some and causing some fine confusion. Then he had met a young girl with a beautiful tame fawn stumbling big-eyed and awkward behind her and he had talked with her but hadn't felt quite right about it because of Lila. He had walked on, the coin his foster father had given him after the sales in the auction shed jingling in his pocket, and a raven-haired whore in a shiny dress had called to him from the tent with hung flowers, her face painted with a colored spider's web, her breasts hypnotic, but not for him, so he had gone on to the braziers, where Fief sellers plied their people and the Angels with the unfamiliar rich food, and had a pasty full of spiced beef and vegetables and a tumbler of the cool, sharp, white wine.

He walked on a little way. Music pounded everywhere;

16

there was nowhere you could go where the drum's pulse, and tambourine and guitar, and keen shrill of the flutes and fiddles couldn't reach you. Some of the troops of dancers from the outlying villages had begun to dance already, and would dance from now till dawn, or until they dropped. They had started already, and still it was only morning. Long Range John was usually rather a melancholy person, but at this moment he felt differently. He half-closed his eyes, looking to the sun, and felt the music pulsing in his blood in the orange light.

"Spread your wings, man," said a familiar nasal whine, and Long Range opened his eyes to see his friend Milt, scraggly beard and high forehead, his lanky frame in knots, knees bent, arms crooked, hands flapping, acting out Long Range's spirit taking flight.

Long Range fell upon him, kicking his feet away from under him, and they rolled about on the grass between the tents, fighting, roaring, Citizens scattering like poultry. Finally Long Range pinned him down and cuffed him about a bit, until he realized Citizens were watching, for whose benefit they exchanged a juicy French kiss and then, getting up together, looked around stony-faced for reactions. Finding only tactfully averted faces they walked away, laughing haw haw haw in contempt, to a slope nearby where they sat down under a pine tree.

Milt fished out a little box and produced a small cheroot wrapped in dried leaf; he was fumbling with tinder when Long Range produced a box of Fief matches and lit up. Milt handed him the reefer and he took a couple of hits. The grass had been dried and prepared by Milt's mother; it was good stuff. In an inattentive way he noted the shift in the music of the fair and other sounds, and felt the blades of grass stroking his hand, rasping but soft. He took another toke and handed it back to Milt, who gestured down to the walk between the pavilions. Two Fief girls in flowing holiday silk were walking linked, heads on the swivel, though trying to keep up their adult unconcern; especially the blond one who had silver bracelets, and so presumably rich parents, and thought she was proud. But even at this distance her chubby little dark friend was clearly nothing but hot meat.

"Make 'em?" grunted Milt, with a lungful of smoke.

Long Range shook his head.

"Lila?" sighed Milt, letting the smoke out at last.

Long Range looked down at the girls again; their unconcern was dissolved in stares, whispering and giggles as three Angels, Half-Lugs, Rexit and Belial, came down the pavilion walk. Half-Lugs and Rexit were already clowning obscenely, aping an excruciating lust for the girls, offering their bottle of wine in one capacity or another, Half-Lugs working forward on his knees, wringing his hands, tongue lapping and eyes out on stalks, till the dark girl swung her shoulder-bag into his face and knocked him sprawling. But the blond girl ignored it all, her brown eyes fixed on the third Angel.

Belial came last, his pale head slightly tilted, looking back at her with small pale eyes strangely defined by delicate lashes, his light red hair cropped closer than the others, his body expressing nothing but a relaxed alertness. Sitting quite close but not involved, his attention like smoke drifting around the scene, Long Range saw Belial's face and the girl's as tied each on one end of an invisible but perfectly real connecting line. Her brown eyes were looking tenderly, but her lip was quivering, unconsciously, frightened of what she was feeling.

Belial's face settled into an expression of complete calm. Without thinking, Long Range was reminded of the day Belial had first come to the Angel camp, as a young newly orphaned boy from the far pastures; standing outside the stockade, surrounded by a ring of hostile older boys, he had stared that absent stare for a while as they insulted and pushed him. Then in a moment he had kicked sideways and broken somebody's leg below the knee. He had hurt three of them badly, and after a terrible beating had lain looking up at his hard-breathing captors and, as one bent down over him, spat bits of his broken teeth up at him. For which he had been instantly accepted.

What the hell reminded me of that, thought Long Range.

He looked down again. Half-Lugs and Rexit, with the plump dark girl between them giggling helplessly, were aping a furtive, conspiratorial departure, as a knot of Fief steelmen and truckers stared and muttered nearby. Belial and the other girl were gone.

"THREE?" SAID FRANK BLANKLY. "WHAT THE FUCK GOOD is three? They'd be wasted before they got south of the Bend."

"But they will not be going by the Bend, Frank, nor will they be going in that direction at all. They will set out on the, ah, Juice Route."

"Then they get hit even sooner. Your tankers can do it, but did you ever hear of Angels getting to stick their noses on the Route?"

"Frank, let me explain. This is a very special party. Things will be done that never were done before. Normally we would use the army, but for this thing only your people, tough, quick and irregular, will do. If it comes off people everywhere are going to know about Angels because of it. Frank, this will make one of the greatest songs."

"What would you know about our songs?" said Frank quietly.

"We know that to an Angel his true song is more important than his life. Not many of us in the City have or encourage the qualities of soul that are necessary for the songs to come to us. This is perhaps why we feel that Angels may succeed where our people would not, in this case."

"All right, all right, but don't go blowing off about stuff like that. It's secret, right? Any Angel thinks you're on to his song and he'll kill you and know he's done right. Right?"

"I understand, Frank, and I only mentioned it to let you know that this thing is important in your terms as well as our own."

"Right, now, how the hell would we get on the Juice Route? Tankers only on the Juice Route."

"You'd be in a tanker, Frank."

"With my bike up in the cab with me? Sure, fucking ay."

"That is correct, Frank, in a way. Three men and three machines. But not in the cab; in a compartment within the tanker itself."

"Route checks?" said Frank, interested.

"Have been cursory for many years. The Peregrine Fief and the oil cartel thinking, as we have done, that no benefit we could get from such small-scale smuggling could be worth the loss to us of fuel and trade, were it discovered. The guards are there more to keep unauthorized trade off the Route and protect the tankers from bandits than to check the tankers themselves. At any rate, we shall construct false panels."

"So what happens when a half-empty tanker with false panels gets to the far end?"

"It will not. It will be attacked by 'bandits' and destroyed. The driver will survive to tell the tale."

"Fine," said Frank, "now you tell me one thing, what the hell is all this worth? Why should you take a chance like that to get three brothers south? None of my people are getting into this till I know the whole scene."

"Certainly, Frank, certainly. But first let me provide you with a little further stimulation. Would you care to smoke?"

Frank was surprised. "Didn't think you dudes were into that."

"Certainly, we in government forgo all stimulants, and though you may find it hard to believe, are not sorry to do so. But we have found medical uses for sativa and developed a strain which I think you may find interesting."

He called and a maid came with a wrought-metal tray, a small pipe with a brass bowl, and a carved wooden box full of grass. Frank said he might find her interesting too and lunged at the girl. Eliot watched calmly as he missed and fell off his stool on to the floor, the girl swept out and Frank, sitting up, filled the pipe and lit up, settling himself with his back to the low window. Watching this figure in soiled jeans with colors over his bare chest, soft boots, a

20

necklace of bear's teeth, a big brass-bound knife stuck in his belt behind his back, his beard streaked with gray and his ratty hair swept back and secured with a thin knotted headband of leather cord, sprawling on the rich dark carpet among the heavy furniture, and sniffing and sighing over the grass, Eliot permitted himself an ironical reflection on the unexpected tools of statecraft; although he admonished himself instantly for belittling the Angel leader on account of his appearance, or assuming that Frank high would be any less acute than otherwise.

"Nice," said Frank after they had stayed quiet for a while, listening to the music rising faintly from the meadow, watching flags on buildings flapping red and white in the wind.

"Suppose," began Eliot, "our party was caught in the tanker, and the Peregrine Fief claimed an abuse of the Route running through their territory sufficient to justify closing it down?"

"We'd have to go down on the Peregrines—us and your soldier boys together."

"Suppose we did so successfully, and took over their Fief?"

"We could waste the Gypsies, there'd be nothing between you and the Juice Route east—good times."

"Conceivably not, Frank. Perhaps the first thing that would happen would be that the Southern States would march in on us, while we were still weak from dealing with the Peregrines. That is if the Eastern Seaboard Federation failed to do so first. You can't know, Frank, but you may have guessed, just how much they are waiting for an excuse like that."

Frank waved his hand ambiguously, exhaled smoke and said, "Then why do a dumb fucking thing like go down the Route?"

"No, Frank, what I'm saying is not why we should avoid doing so; it represents why we cannot afford not to. I wanted to demonstrate for a moment how precarious our position, and yours too, really is. The Peregrines don't cut off our juice anyway simply because they know the same thing applies to them. If the South becomes even a little stronger they may push west, cut the Route and starve us both out."

"So what are you going to do, like, what are our three heroes going to do? Off the South?"

"I'll tell you, Frank. Somewhere on the far side of the mountains, there's a man named Sangria. . . . ."

"Sangria? Isn't that some kind of drink?"

Eliot muttered, " 'Give earth to drink and she'll not fail.' " Then he said, "No, Frank, this Sangria is a man."

LONG RANGE SPRANG INTO THE AIR, TWISTING HIS HEAD, hair lashing his shoulders, long legs stiffened to thrust up a few more inches, ecstatic. For a moment he seemed to hang there, arms extended, hands cupped, toes pointed, his turquoise beads floating in front of his face. He was up in the blue, his head felt the same size, felt as brilliant as the sun; the right motion with his arms and he felt he could hang there forever, hover like a hawk off over the festival and the river, the town walls and the trees.

As his feet hit the ground the music began again with a great crash, and next to him Milt spun up screaming into the air. Down the line of leapers the high point went, like the ripple in a cracked whip. Lila and the Angel girls stood opposite, their robes shifting and snaking, the drums working their feet, working their feet, an endless pivot, a soft bounce, the high music tearing leaping figures up through their sea, the sea receives them as they slide back down.

A crowd of Citizens surrounded the dancers and the band. It was no scheduled event, just that at a certain point in the afternoon, the heat, excitement, wine, dope and good times had gathered most of the Hawk chapter down by the music. Belial was there, and caused a mild sensation in the line by wiping his face with a pair of fine lace panties, then wordlessly tossing them back to the proud blond girl, who ran sobbing from the crowd. A little dog ran after her yapping. The leapers' screams rose, and the dust.

Lila's father Fork stood in the crowd, a wife on either side of him, in his belt an ax, a wooden drinking-bowl

22

clanking on a chain attached to his wrist. He was very drunk, and being an officer of the Wolf chapter, he was screaming, "Chickens!" at the Hawk dancers and flailing at them with the chain if any came close to him. The front of his buckskin trousers was open and his wives were trying to arouse him, but without success. His bleared eyes were trying to focus on Long Range, who danced turned away from him, in front of Lila, his eyes on her. Fork nodded his head to a slow private rhythm; all eyes were on the dancers and not even his wives seemed to notice his rage slowly growing. He had contempt for Long Range as a Hawk, an orphan, a prospect, and now the little prick was well known to be making cow's eyes at his daughter Lila. Fucker! With a shout of "Chicken fuckers!" he flung his wives away from him and lurched forward, groping for his ax.

He was brought up short as Belial, twisting in his leap, landed right in front of him, so that they stood with their faces close, Fork blocked from the other dancers. The music wheezed to a halt.

"That's not true, Fork," said Belial. The crowd around them in a wide circle listened intently. A fight between Hawks and Wolves would be bloodier than a brawl with the Citizens; no Fief cops could stop it.

Fork was brought up short for a moment: everyone was a little uneasy of Belial. Then he shook his head and put his arm up to push Belial aside; but Belial's knife was already in his hand.

Fork stepped back a pace. Belial said, "I'll show you, Fork," and as Fork crouched, Belial extended his bare left arm. The crowd started, as his knife slashed down quickly across his own forearm. As the blood welled out of the cut and dribbled down his fingers he tossed the knife to Fork.

"Your turn."

Fork was off balance, unprepared to undergo the ritual showing of indifference to pain, but unable to back down. He grunted as he cut his scarred forearm, and, grinning at the blood, tossed the knife back to Belial. The latter paused, but neither Fork nor anyone else in the crowd took this for hesitation. Somebody gasped as he cut his arm again, above the first wound, and tossed the red blade back to Fork.

Fork fumbled the catch. His skinful of beer had helped with the first pain, but now he felt sick and confused. With a hard face he cut himself again, sighed, and said, "Eh, Belial," as he tossed the knife back again.

Belial raised his eyebrows, waited a pause, a second, a third. Then still looking into Fork's eyes, the knife slashed across again, and blood ran.

"Eh, Belial," roared Fork, and lumbered up to him. The young Angel stood without expression, the knife dangling loose by his side in his right hand as Fork's greasy bearded face thrust right up to his, and with spectacularly ripe breath bellowed for the third time.

"BELIAL!"

There was dead silence. Then Fork grabbed the young Angel's left arm, and pressing his own to it so that their blood smeared and mingled, hugged him close with his good arm.

"You're too much! Beautiful!" he yelled.

The crowd roared approval. Fork's hairy bulk swung Belial around with him, but the young Angel's right arm stuck straight out above them in the air, the bloody knife like a red flag.

The music began again. Fork was yelling.

"Take a wife. C'mon, take one." One of his dark-haired wives came up and stood with her hands spread on her hips, grinning. Belial disentangled himself from Fork, went toward her, and as she came forward, tossed her the knife and skipped spinning back into the line of dancers.

Long Range and Milt looked at each other and walked off. Higher up the slope Long Range looked back. Belial was dancing in front of Lila.

FRANK DIDN'T SEE IT TO BEGIN WITH.

"So this guy, Sangria, he can make stuff grow in the Dead Lands. That's cool, more to eat is always good, but what makes it so important?"

Eliot sighed inwardly. How could he miss it?

24

"The only thing that is stopping any one of our states from becoming powerful enough to overrun the others is lack of the wherewithal to support a larger population and expand their industries and armies. If this man can do what our reports imply, within a generation whoever has the use of his discovery will be in a position of strength, or, in the case of the two larger states, overwhelming superiority."

"So you have to get him first," supplied Frank.

"For our own defense," nodded Eliot.

"Right, right, whenever there's something really shitty going down it's always, like, for our defense." Frank was on his feet now, waving the pipe about and glaring at Eliot, who was watching him carefully.

"Listen," shouted Frank, "you know only two of us have ever been beyond the mountains. Me and Brawl's the only ones been beyond the mountains, and we're lucky mothers to be back, and you know it. If we *got* beyond the mountains we'd never get back, not with a prisoner, not any way. You think I'm such a stoned crazy fuck-out I'm going to send my brothers into *that*? Come on, Eliot, come on!"

They both stood in silence, admiring his performance. At length Eliot replied.

"What we had in mind was an arrangement that you might find yourself able to accept, Frank. First, reward. We will give you last year's sum for skins and captives, though this year's numbers are far inferior. We will ignore the incident with the women in the middle meadow last July, and the dead trader, Mathews, whose body we discovered earlier this month. If you hand me the list of parts and supplies you have prepared, it will be met in full and immediately, without arguments, and it will be supplemented by everything necessary for the matter under discussion.

"Second, feasibility. For the very reason that few of you have been beyond the mountains, it may be easier for you to go there; one must never, as you know, underestimate the power of surprise. We have a certain amount of friends, of one kind and another, in some of the places you will

25

have to go; the people who got us the information, for instance. You will have calculated already that the party must pass through the South's middle-town, Harmony, and that rules out sending anyone such as yourself or the older brothers who might be known to travelers there; though naturally your experience would qualify you best for the job. But the people I am going to propose that you send, you may find it more acceptable to part with. So, third, personnel.

"I suggest the lad who has spent some time with us, Milt Travers, as he will be able to communicate in sign and his other languages with the people they will have to contact. We will also need a first-class warrior; normally you would quibble about risking one for us, but this time we would have had him anyway, over the trader's murder, and I think you will not be sorry to lose him for a while."

"You mean that little bastard Belial," muttered Frank.

"Correct," replied Eliot. "For the third man we are less particular, but I have a suggestion, Milt's friend Long Range John. They fought together against the Gypsies last year; and it might be that his reputed dream-sight will be useful to them."

"I don't know," said Frank doubtfully. "That was only one time really. Him and Milt don't even have their colors yet."

"Would you care to tell me about that time?" asked Eliot. "I heard a rumor, nothing more."

"Well," said Frank, "it was our fire feast three winters back, and the brothers were all in the hall getting wrecked. You remember old Sockeye? Well he was really wiped out that night, really bad. He strips off and climbs in the water-trough, dancing about and singing, doesn't matter to him there's snow outside, he's really out of his mind, you know?

"Long Range is sitting with the Hulk, his foster father, and he starts looking queer, so Hulk says, what's up? Long Range says he's remembering he's had a dream about Sockeye dancing in the trough. Hulk says what happens next, he drowns? Long Range says no, it was weird, he gets a bolt in the guts from the Gypsies.

"Well Old Bull is sitting next to them, also double bad, and all he hears is something about Gypsies. So he jumps up yelling, 'GYPSIES? YAA-AH-AH, GET THE FUCKING GYPSIES,' and he grabs a carving-knife and runs out swinging his blade and yelling. Of course some guys start running after him to stop him, and then other brothers further off see them and hear all this yelling about the Gypsies, so they grab their gear and run out too.

"And sure enough there *are* the fucking Gypsies, sneaking up to try and block the doors and fire the hall. I don't know which is more surprised, us or them, but we were so stoned we didn't care, just tore into them. Even Sockeye runs out, still bare-ass naked, clubbing them with a stool until wouldn't you know, zap, a bolt gets him right in the guts. Well, you know, we beat them off, only lost three brothers and we gave fourteen of them to the crows. But Sockeye was a good brother gone."

Eliot thought it was a good story. Frank went on.

"To start with no one much knew about Long Range saying that, they just thought someone had spotted the fuckers outside. But Hulk starts calling him Long Range from then on, and when anyone asks why, he says because he's got good vision, and tells the story, so in a couple of days everybody knows. But it's never happened again that I know of. So it's not like the doctor, not a lot of use that I can see."

"As I thought," said Eliot, "so you won't mind parting with him. If the three of them leave soon it will look like a run to the summer pasture. When they get back, glory for the Angels."

"If they get back," sniffed Frank. "Anyway first we have to think about some coin for the poor old Pres?"

"Some coin for whom?" inquired Eliot.

"Me," said Frank, grinning beatifically.

IT WAS DARK. FIRES FLARED ABOUT THE MEADOW, SHOUTS and music and drunken laughter rose above the hum of the people's voices, conversing across the cooking fires, toasting in horn goblets, murmuring under the trees. Cloaked figures, walking, seemed larger than themselves, or crouched close to the fires, smaller. Unseen waves passed across the field and among the people, meat smells, sounds, rumors, movements; the invisible breeze made the torches outside the larger tents flare out sideways, dragon's breath, flickering and snapping like shining fabric, whipping on the night.

At the foot of the Angels' hill a giant bonfire blazed. Frank lolled with the officers, drinking beer. Someone had butchered the little fawn Long Range had seen earlier in the day, and the Angels gorged on the meat, grease dribbling in their beards. In the shadows nearby another group squatted about a City girl who lay helplessly drunk, naked from the waist down, her body jerking. Frank, undistracted, was saying quietly:

"So it's a big deal, and the Fief creeps think we give 'em three Angels and then forget it. Who the fuck they think we are? Now listen, here's what we do. We watch 'em. We watch the Route, we watch the Fief. And all the time we're ready to go. Now you can dig it—that way we GET THERE FIRST. So we get the professor which everybody wants so bad."

"So then they got to give us everything we ask for?" supplied the Sergeant-at-Arms.

"Right, right," answered Frank with emphatic, secretive enthusiasm. He tossed down his beer and crouched looking round conspiratorially at the others, until suddenly they all burst out laughing. Frank roared, "Got 'er warmed up yet, boys?" leaped to his feet and ran to the group of young Angels; ripping down his pants and knocking the others aside, he fell onto the groaning girl like a thunderbolt.

In the darkness of a far corner of the meadow, away from the people, Fork lay where he had fallen in the long grass, a vast mound of fur-covered flesh.

Late in the night his eyes fluttered open and he saw, a foot from his face, the grinning muzzle of a black dog,

28

gnawing and gnawing at the meat bone that had dropped from his drunken hand as he fell. He saw the bubbles of saliva between its teeth, the freckles on its glistening gums. With a sideways glance at his slight movement of waking, the dog clamped the bone in its jaws and made off into the night.

Fork's mouth was parched and he was ravenous, but he was too drunk to move. He made sounds, wanting his wives to come and comfort him, but they were gone into the night. His body began to shake. He lay in the long grass, crying like a baby.

A crescent quarter-moon hung in the night sky above him, small and glowing.

DOWN BY THE RIVER LONG RANGE STOOD IN SHADOWS under a willow tree. Where the moon shone through the swaying leaves his figure was stippled with shreds of shifting silvery light. In front of him the river ran, ripples of blue silver gleaming against the dark invisibly moving waters. Before him on a spit of sand Lila, her golden hair around her face, lay on her back as Belial mounted her. Half-Lugs and Rexit squatted at the edge of the sand in silence, watching. The only sound came across a mile of meadow—vague snatches of chant. "Fair is fire, fire is fair," and the drums throbbing.

Long Range had wandered there earlier, stoned and solitary, through damp rustling grass, to stand beneath the tree. Hearing people approach he had waited; a joke, a wraith, a watcher. When he saw who they were it was too late to move. By the moonlight he could see Lila was very high; her face seemed thinner than ever, rinsed out, glowing, somehow windswept. They stood still on the sand, Belial facing her and the other two on either side of them. They stood in silence for a minute, the drums pulsing in the distance. Belial was staring into her face, Lila was looking back, things going backwards and forwards between them, the tension building up, buttressed and contained by the two hulking figures that flanked them.

Belial reached out with both hands to her neck and unfastened the green robe. It fell to her ankles; beneath she was naked. Long Range's hand went to his knife. By Angel law, wives and unmarried daughters were to be respected. It was a rigidly observed taboo; he couldn't believe Lila would consent in violating it.

But unbidden, she dropped to her knees and hugged Belial's legs, nuzzling her head into his crotch. He pushed her away and went to sit and watch as the other two stripped off and began to fondle her.

"Did you like it how Belial handled your old man today?" said Rexit, flicking her nipples with his thumbs. She nodded. Half-Lugs lay down on his back in the sand and told her to get on down. She got on her hands and knees and crawled between his legs, lowering her head to take his erect cock in her mouth so that her hair fell around her face and spilled over his belly. Rexit crawled on top of her from behind.

Long Range heard her chortling with her mouth full. "O Glitch, not there, Rexit, I was sore for a week last time," she mumbled.

"I got some bike grease. Anyway Belial don't like no sloppy seconds," Rexit laughed, straining and thrusting forward. She gasped and slid forward so her body lay between Half-Lugs' legs, her face buried in his crotch. Rexit got his hand in front of her and for a while there was silence broken by squelching and slapping as Rexit humped up and down, until he was finished. He sat back then and watched her work on Half-Lugs, her head bobbing up and down faster and faster until Half-Lugs' hips rose and he grunted.

She rolled off him on to her back brushing sand from her belly, and said, gurgling slightly, "Your turn." Belial rose, slim and muscular, crossed to her and knelt between her legs for a moment, naked, very close to her but not quite touching. After a pause he swiftly thrust himself forward up between her spread legs. Her legs rose and parted still further and she cried out and then groaned as he withdrew, only to slide forward again more slowly.

Belial moved, his hard bare buttocks flashing white in

30

the moonlight between her legs, undulating, gathering momentum irresistibly, grinding in, slamming down on her, Lila groaning continuously now, their movements faster and faster until the moment of convulsion when her back arched and only her shoulders and heels touched the ground, and Belial grabbed her bottom, grunted, ripped his body up into her, rearing up, lifting her screaming for a moment as they came.

After a while Belial rolled off and she lay on her side with her legs curled up, softly stroking his scarred arm as he lay for a minute half-covering her. She shivered and he rose and picked up her robe, tossed it to her and began pulling on his own clothes. She held it to her as he straightened, complete, and looked down at her. The look between them was now frank and amused; she also seemed grateful, but when she started to say something he turned on his heel, and the three Angels walked back toward the fire.

Lila sat for a while, her head turned so that her features were averted from Long Range's sight. Then she walked to the riverside, laid her dress down and, crouching, splashed water on her face. It must have felt strange, for she did it again and again, pausing to look at the drops of water on her hands. Then she squatted, splashed water between her legs and over her body. She dried herself with the hem of her robe and, taking a comb from a pocket in the garment, combed her long hair as best she could. Last she knelt over the low river bank and, holding her hair back from her face, peered down at her reflection in the dark water. Then she stood up, looked about, and pulled the robe on and fastened it. She looked about her again, at the spit of sand and up at the new moon, patted her hair and wandered off slowly toward the fires.

Long Range stood still for some time. The frantic thumping of his heart began to subside; the sick feeling still came in waves. His eyes stared. After he stepped from behind the tree he whirled around, suddenly, then cursed himself for his sudden fear that someone might have seen him watching and doing nothing.

He was very confused. As an orphan he had struck an

inner bargain with himself that whatever pain he met, the one thing that was useless was to complain of it to anyone, or to himself. But now from his confusion and pain there struggled out the feeling of injustice, that after his summers of devotion and gentleness, this was unfair. The warm spring night and the trees and the moon mocked him with memories of the direction they had seemed to tend to, the things they had seemed to promise. A deep-seated bitterness took root in his heart. He ran through the grass toward the dark hill and the bikes.

ELIOT THE LITERATE SAT AT HIS CARVED DESK, HIS LEFT arm gently rubbing at the arm of his massive wooden chair, his hand cupped over the dark carved head of a Citizen whose nose was almost gone, now, from the accidents of time and the gentle rubbing of previous Literates. Outside beneath the high narrow windows the fires glowed in the meadow, but Eliot, business over, preferred, even on such a night, lamplight and his papers.

He considered the sheets before him, his commentaries on the *Fief Known History,* both pre- and post-BLAM. He had returned, now as often, to the moment itself. He read

A convulsion, a climax of the energy dance. Necessary in terms of the preceding frenzy; perhaps. Our librarians assure us, and our own readings confirm, that the Event was universally predicted; they knew, as we know when heavy weather is on the way. The records of the sensitive discover them mistaking a red sunrise for the great bomb flowering in silence, or the rumble of a machine for apocalypse in another quarter. Although, ironically, these prescient fears diminished from a weary familiarity, as the Event itself approached.

However, no government, or alliance of governments, was able to do anything to stop it. This is the most striking feature, perhaps: even with their technological mastery, their wealth inconceivable by our standards, they were powerless. Why?

As survivors, our every impulse is to consider that the event was intended, inevitable. Our religious thought conceives it so—"Our seed led from the flames." And as we consider the behavior of these people, the talk without meaning, the willful gestures, for us the overwhelming impression is of trance, of a people high and low, deprived by their social structures, by historical development, perhaps ultimately by, yes, divine intervention, of some essential dimension of will.

Or was there some visible point at which they *chose* to be so deprived—say when they discovered an identity derived not from creation but from their conquests?

The mind turns also to regret. Like one of the many poor nations in the pre-BLAM world, though separated not by affluence but by time, we gaze at the wonders; instant communication for all, the endless stream of artifacts effortlessly produced by the nearly automatic factories, the mastery of the air, the colors and lights all around. Our noses to the window of their world, we can ignore for a time what our historians and priests have been so assiduous in pointing out, the population pressures and the breakdown of coherent philosophies, that led to the crime and emptiness at all levels in the times before BLAM.

He finished reading, reached for his pen, and, opening his leather-bound personal journal on top of the commentary, began to write again.

"Doing an unsatisfactory gloss on BLAM motives. A joke—as I fumble with conclusions that a predatory attitude might have been at the root of it, the Sangria business forces the Fief to begin what could be our first major offensive action. No other way if the information is correct. I remember a conversation with the Angel leader Frank; bothered by some small threat to his leadership, ranting as usual, threatening to settle it violently. I finally expressed puzzlement at all this bluster, uncertainty; why did they not first settle the correct Rule, then apply it in all cases? F. became quite eloquent. All this Rule crap was just like us, he said. Things change. Everything changes except Angels. At all times, Angels are themselves. Therefore can't be dealt with by rules.

"I felt obliged to point out that without Rule, its step-by-step application, there would be no social organization or art in the Fief, not enough to eat, not to mention no industry, which provided, incidentally, Angels with their machines. F. interpreted this as allusion to their dependence—growled that anyone can make bikes—(a veiled threat re Peregrine overtures?)—only Angels can make Angels. With occasional assistance from our women, I could have pointed out.

"Despite the irony of the sometimes murderously self-willed President labeling *us* authoritarian—for myself, I admire aspects of their existence—the warrior-ethos—to live with presence of death—not accidental death, but death sought out, confronted, again and again. Feel your brothers about you, knowing they really share this. Objectively too, they're useful to us—flanking the Fief, providing irregular military vs. their counterparts. No match for regularly equipped and trained soldiers, but an excellent buffer.

"But recall that talk with Frank because, muddled as he was, if we, the Fief, had as strong, as timeless, an idea of ourselves as they do—would we initiate this attempt on Sangria—which if successful means, inevitably, end of Fief as we know it—i.e., a reasonably sized, more or less self-supporting, self-determining state. Answer is, no alternative; ignore it and it will *not* go away. Question for us is same question I should ask pre-BLAM times—did they do all they could?"

He blotted the page and closed the journal.

34

II THE RUN

See how from far upon the eastern road
The star-led wizards haste with odours sweet!

—Milton: "On the Morning
of Christ's Nativity"

WORD CAME FROM FRANK III TO THE HAWK CHAPTER
that it was time Long Range and Milt went for their colors.
Milt was roused in the middle of the night, dragged to a
stockade hut and flung in the filthy unlit interior. Long
Range could not be found. Next day when he rode in, he
was pulled off his bike by the Sergeant-at-Arms, clubbed
unconscious and put in the hut with Milt. For two days
they lay without food, drinking the puddles on the floor or
the rainwater as it trickled through the roof. None of the
prospects knew what happened when they went for their
colors. Since they were young they had only seen the new
Angels come out from the barred Hall, some badly beaten,
but always proud and high, except for the one who had
been carried out head down between his brothers, dead.

On the third evening, across the river from their camp,
a bank of flat black cloud covered the sky from north to
south, dark, unbroken, slowly rising. The sun had sunk
into it and now rose light rose, like a fire behind a hill; not
just light to the dark cloud's gloom, but flying above its

leaden flatness with dimension, tiers of cloud with rosy bellies spreading out into the blue evening sky, where single dabs of dove-gray cloud hung. Every branch and twig and blossom of the trees in the meadow stood out, black, fibrillous, petrified, against the radiant sky above the dark cloud's rim.

The doctor stood leaning on the door-frame of his cabin, watching until the light went and night had fallen. He shivered and turned away, then turned again to watch as a group of torches moved across the center of the camp and stopped with a shout outside the stockade hut. Soon they moved off again, coming close to his cabin, and he saw Long Range and Milt stumbling and splashing in the muddy puddles, being shoved along toward the Hall. Spots of rain began to break up the reflections in the puddles as the Hall gates closed behind them and from inside a muffled roar went up.

The doctor wiped his hand across his grizzled beard and closed the door. By lamplight he worked on a herb brew, poppies and caraway, with the rain drumming on the cabin roof. His dog would not settle; her nails clicked on the floorboards and she wandered about. In exasperation he turned her out of doors, and as he did so, saw through the rain a group assembling silently outside the Hall.

"Be over soon," he thought, uneasy himself, and turned to fan the flames under his retort once more. The noise from the Hall suddenly rose again. It continued, mingled with the falling rain.

A minute later his door burst open and a group of dripping Angels stumbled in. Long Range was dragged in by his foster-father the Hulk. Milt and Belial took up stations by the door, looking back toward the Hall.

"He's half-drowned," said Hulk, laying the vomit- and shit-covered figure on the floor.

"Well thank God the rain washed the worst of it off," said the doctor testily as he knelt over the body and began pumping the back of the shoulders. "What the hell happened, anyway?"

"Fork tried to kill him," said Milt from the door, slurring through broken lips. "They gave us that to drink and then they shoved us and pissed over us and beat up on us and kept shouting the laws and 'One on all and all on one' and there were no Hawks there but we were high, it was all right, and I was on the floor by the officers' table and, shit, I saw Fork had Long head down in the beer barrel and he kept on holding him under, and Long broke up once and yelled and the officers saw it and tried to get over to stop it, but Fork's brothers were blocking them, they were in it too. Long got up again but then Fork had him right. I was knocked down trying but there was this roar and I got up and there's the Hawks coming through the gates and Belial, beautiful! Walking on the Wolves' heads to get to Long. He came down on top of Fork and stomped him till he got Long's head up and we got out while we could, Frank gave me our patches and tried to break it up, but the Wolves are pretty mad. Hey, I just realized, we got them! We got our fucking colors! Shit I feel weird! Is he all right? It was wrong, something was wrong, I know. Why'd Fork do that? Hot shit, was I glad to see the Hawks!"

"That's how it's meant to go, son," interrupted the doctor, hauling Long Range upright and dragging him to the bed, "your brothers get you out of it and you don't forget that; but it sounds to have got a little too real this time. Belial, get this madman Milt to his brothers—after what they poured down him in there he'll be high till morning so he better be in good company. Get the Sergeant-at-Arms over here on your way. Hulk, stay till he comes, in case the Wolves get funny. My bolt-gun's in the corner there. Long Range will be all right; just get me a woman to clean up all this *crap* he's brought up. And where's my goddam dog? Never there when you need her. . . ."

The doctor held Long Range's head and forced down a sleeping draft. He woke hours later crying out, saw the doctor by his bed.

"It's all right, son, all right. Don't touch your head like that, I patched it. Here, drink some of this."

Long Range drank. The skin was stretched tight on his pale exhausted face, the blue eyes sunken and staring, his habitual brooding expression settled into a visionary air. He spoke in a hoarse voice.

"I had a dream. I was chasing Lila, running, and I was wearing a mask that I had to keep on till I caught her. I got close enough almost to touch her and whipped off my mask and she turned; but her face was a mask too, and I couldn't go on. She moved away and as she moved she was taking her mask off, but just before I could see her real face she had turned away.

"Then I was in a big room, as big as the Hall only with more chairs, and men were moving in on me. I knew they were Gypsies, I tried to get ready to fight but I was cursing Lila too much, I felt helpless; then I woke up."

He laid his bruised head with the bloodstained bandage back on the pillow. After a while he asked, "Who got me out of the Hall?"

"Belial."

Long Range closed his eyes. But after a minute he said, "Fork might come."

"The Hawks are about, don't you worry, son," replied the doctor. Long Range slept again.

Hours later he woke. The darkened room was the same, but pale stripes of light fell from chinks in the shuttered windows. He smelled the sweet musty smell of herbs, and lay in the shadows listening to the birds sing.

The doctor nodded on a stool by the bed until he sensed Long Range's eyes on him. He rose stiffly and fetched some broth warming over the embers, and fed the youth in silence. Long Range ate ravenously for the first time in three days.

When he had finished he asked, "Who got me out of the Hall?"

"Belial," said the doctor, unsurprised, as he examined the cut on his head. Mild concussion probably.

Long Range groaned. Then he asked, "What about Fork? Why did he do that?"

"His daughter's knocked up. He thinks you did it."

"It wasn't me. How did he find out about her?"

"Her mother knew when she missed her time, of course.

38

He beat the girl but she wouldn't say. They all knew you were sniffing around her.''

"It wasn't me."

"But you know who it was. Look, just say and you're off the hook. You know it's against our law; do what you like with captives or Fief women but don't touch an Angel's old lady or his daughters. That way stuff like this doesn't happen." He paused for a while. "Not going to tell, eh? Well there's one thing more, brother. If you know I guess you saw it and you're still sick from imagining it. Maybe one reason Fork got you in the Hall was because you were feeling so sorry for yourself. But next time you could get your brothers killed as well."

"Screw them."

"Funny talk when they just saved your life. 'An Angel on his own is a dead Angel,' and you'd better believe it now."

"Look, doc, they saved my life, fact. But I don't have to like it. They don't know the things I've thought and felt, they never could. Never. They'd despise them. Them saving me just makes it more complicated."

"What things do you know?"

"All right, things I thought I knew."

"You believed in women," said the doctor, "and now you've found out what we all do—women aren't where it's at for a man. It's your brothers—stick by your brothers and they'll stick by you and you'll have all the women you want, maybe a wife or two someday, and you'll forget about Lila. Hell, that's not what I mean. What I mean is, it isn't right for a man to rely on women for so much of himself. You must know that most young guys feel that way about a girl for a time. With you there's more to it, all the feeling for your mother that you never knew came into it too." Long Range looked away. "I'm sorry to put it so plain," the doctor went on, "but if you lay so much on that feeling and then get disappointed like you have over Lila, you'd be hurting so bad you're bound to get yourself killed one way or another, sooner or later. Remember this. There's always another lay. I know it hurts, but pain is

39

real, it's a good way to learn things. It's like instead of what you've been doing, seeing the world through the feeling you have inside you, the world snaps back—'I'm like this!' And you *know* it.''

"No, doc, you're wrong. It's true my ma came into that feeling, but it was like, I don't know, she and what I felt for Lila were part of it, it wasn't all to do with them. It was right, I tell you. All you're trying to do is get me to think about myself the way the rest of the people think of themselves—the mighty Angel, fighting, taking women, getting drunk and lying about themselves without even knowing it.''

"There's more to it than that, boy," the doctor said. "When you're older you'll find out, when you don't just owe your brothers, when you've shared with them. Hell, getting half-killed last night you were supposed to learn something—I say it again—if you're on your own, you're dead.''

"There's more than one way to be on your own, doc," said Long Range. "I've been on my own as an orphan ever since I can remember, good as they've all been. My whole thing was not letting anyone know. But underneath that, I guess, what I felt for Lila made me think it was a warm world. You and this over Lila, you're trying to break that down, tell me the world's another way.''

The doctor groaned. "I'm trying to tell you the world is no one way, the world is what you make it. For an Angel the world is double free because he invents it; but he can't do it alone.''

"No," said Long Range, "you're trying to lay your idea of freedom on me. That's not the same. I want to be an Angel but I don't want it to mean that all I can feel for is my own kind—that's like loving myself. At times like that night, I want to know everything that's different from myself, mysterious.''

The doctor laughed and shook his head. "You sure like to think you're right. Well it's too deep for me, son. All I wanted to do was tell you some stuff to keep you alive. Still, I got something for you. There's no other way. You'll be gone pretty soon, and I said I'd do it when you got the colors.''

"Do what?"

The doctor didn't answer, but rose and unlocked a chest standing by the chimney. From the bottom he pulled out a package and handed it to Long Range.

"Your ma gave me this for you when you were born," said the doctor.

There was silence. At length Long Range said:

"Who is she?"

"She's been dead a while now, I'm afraid, son. She was a Literate from the Fief. Your pa was a young Angel, much like you, didn't have no kin either. They met at the fair. She came here in the dead of winter, long gone with you— her husband had sent her away. She had coin, and she was all right, so I looked after her well and kept the people away; but your pa was already dead, missing in a raid in the summer. Midwinter you came. That spring she took you and went to live at the far pastures; only the captive shepherds knew about her. A couple of years later word came from her husband: he would have her back, but without you. There was nothing for her here, being a Literate and all. But don't ever think it was easy for her. She brought you back to me. I'll never forget her crying when she left you, trying to stop it, because like I said, she was all right, but she couldn't help herself, crying and crying and looking round at you. She didn't live long; there was a sickness at the City a couple of years later and she went down with it.''

"What was her name?"

"Anna. Like I say, she gave me that for you. Said if you died I was to bury it.''

Long Range undid the strips of rag securing the bundle and unwrapped the cloth package. There was a knife in it, and underneath a piece of paper. The knife was beautifully forged with a lightly oiled angular blade of dull steel, a large brass cross-piece, handles of polished walnut set with brass bolts and a small brass pommel. The lines of the weapon flowed and swelled pleasingly, and it balanced well in the hand.

"Hey," said the doctor, "I remember, she gave your pa one the same."

He picked up the paper. It felt strange. It was one of the few times he had ever touched a sheet of paper; there was none at the camp. He handed it to the doctor, who read slowly:

"The son of Morn in weary Night's decline,
The lost Traveler's Dream under the Hill."

"What's 'decline'?" asked Long Range.

"Going down," said the doctor; "it means the end of the night."

"Was it her song?" asked Long Range.

"I don't know. Maybe she hoped it might be yours."

He turned the paper over. In the same neat script he read the words: "Unfasten the handle."

They both looked puzzled, until the doctor fetched a set of screwdrivers and Long Range unfastened the bolts in the handle. The wooden panels fell away. The steel shaft of the handle was inlaid on one side. To the left of the panel, a crescent moon of silver sank into etched trees. On the right at the base of the smooth curve of a hill, a figure inset in bronze lay curled like an animal asleep. A sheen of bronze flecks outlined the hill with brightness. The moon's curve and the figure sleeping balanced one another, and the way the scene had been composed suggested large spaces and tranquillity. They both thought it a beautiful work.

" 'The son of Morn in weary Night's decline,' " said the doctor. "Maybe it and the other one were in her family for a while. Well, you'd better get some sleep. I've been forgetting, you've got to go soon. Frank was going to send you and Milt and Belial out on a run before all this blew up. He'll probably get you out of here as soon as you're fit to travel, to try and cool things with Fork. He told me about this run after the fair, and I did a couple of things for you. Now you see, as well as the package, your ma

42

left some coin for you. So I took some and made nice to the Heifer in the workshop. While you've been inside he's been working on your bike. It'll look the same, but it's been balanced and geared different, and he re-bored it and put in new rings, don't worry, he's run it in too. Couple of other things as well. A clean machine like that gives you a little edge, which you might need."

"Where are we going? What about the other two?"

"Frank will tell you all about it, tonight most likely. If you mean their bikes, Belial will take the Shadow he borrowed from the Gypsies last fall, and Milt's drawn the side-hack."

"The side-hack? Then it's a long run?"

"It sure is," laughed the doctor. "Now get some more sleep. Doctor's orders."

OUTSIDE IT BEGAN TO RAIN AGAIN, THE DROPS TAPPING ON the cabin roof.

In Long Range's dream he lay face down on the earth by the side of a river. It was not their river, in the valley; this one ran between trees. When he turned his head he could see, nearby, lying on the ground, a horse. It was dying. Pitifully thin, with sunken eyes and wispy mane, it rose, collapsed, wavered to its feet again, only to collapse once more. It was so sad; but it was no good grieving. He had no strength any more. He lay watching the river run between brown rocks; the sun sparkled on it, and warmed his back. There was nothing more to do, he knew that he had done all he could. It was so peaceful, and he felt so good at last.

Then he felt something nudging his arm, nuzzling him, warm sweet breath on his cheek. It was his horse, his horse!

He sobbed with joy, and awoke crying gently. He turned his head and on the chair by the bed saw the shape of the package, the weapon his mother had left him.

THE EVENING OF THE NEXT DAY, LONG RANGE SLIPPED out of the doctor's cabin at dusk and made his way through the muddy camp to the covered practice yard where the others had assembled with Frank and the Sergeant-at-Arms. Normally a party leaving for the pastures or raiding passed the night before with their own chapter and the principal officers in the camp, and there was feasting, drinking and smoking with their friends before they set out. In this case the empty practice yard was the last they would see of the camp until they slipped away before dawn to avoid the angry Wolves.

Frank explained the other reason for the precaution and began to speak of the true purpose of their raid, but Long Range did not fully understand the implications, the danger and the immense distances involved. Milt was by him, gazing with great interest at the map Frank had spread on the trestle table before them. His time studying at the Fief had familiarized him a little with the geography of the continent. To the other two, anything further than the Salinas Valley had been irrelevant, until now.

They watched as Frank's long finger traced the red line of the Juice Route, south of the Rocky barrier, swinging right into the white of the Mojave and across the rivers to Harmony.

"You get a ride up to there. After that some brothers pick you up and head on out north"—the finger slid up over mountains and began moving right again—"then east to cross the Plains and these rivers, all the way to here"—the finger stopped at a small patch of brown. "In there's the Iron Mountain and the guy you want."

Belial, standing just outside the circle of lamplight, voiced what all three were thinking. "What about juice?"

"These pals of ours have cached juice every two hundred miles from Harmony on. If you don't get to meet them or if you lose them, you'd better know where the caches are." He handed them each a sheet of detailed maps.

"Now there's one thing," said Frank. "If you grab this guy and run back along the caches, hole up when you get to the Route outside Harmony. There's a cloth panel with the rest of the stuff in the chair; spread it when one of our tankers comes, they'll know it's you and the Prof; then sit tight and we'll come for you. You can't stick your noses

44

on the Route, and if you could, there's no juice between here and Harmony.''

He let that sink in. "That's right, once the tanker gets you to Harmony, there's no way back.

"Now I should lay a crock of crap on you about how you can't lose because you're Hell's Angels, but even you punks aren't dumb enough to go for that. You don't always have to come on like a winner to win. But you have to be tricky, you have to have more twists than an earhole, more twists than a fart in tight pants. No one knows how much we practice here, not till it's too late for them. We. . . .''

At that moment someone rapped on the door. Frank motioned the three young men back into the shadows as the Sergeant-at-Arms went to see who it was. There was a muttered conversation by the door, then the Sergeant came back, looking worried.

"It was one of the scouts we've had out west. A bunch of Gypsies are about. Crow snatched one of them and made him talk. They're heading east, looking out for a party of Angels which they know will be making for Harmony. If they ran into the party they had to capture them and find out who they're meeting in Harmony.''

"Shit," said Frank.

"That ain't all," said the Sergeant-at-Arms. "You know who's leading these Gypsies?''

"Probably Glitch himself," muttered Frank.

"Next best thing. Bad Hand.''

"Oh hell," snarled Frank. Bad Hand was a legendary figure, a hideously scarred Gypsy warrior with a crippled right hand who had walked half-mad out of the woods one day to join the Gypsies and harry the Angels. Captured Angels had been tortured and humiliated, flayed and dismembered by him and returned piece by piece to their people. What made it worse was that no one had ever seen Bad Hand and lived long enough to take a shot at him, or get a clear description.

"She-it!" said Frank. "Where are the bastards now?''

" 'Bout fifteen miles west and south," said the Sergeant.

"They won't move at night," said Frank. "Right. Get the Wolves together and ready to move on them at dawn. I'll go along too. You three take off right now—down the main track east a way, then hide out till first light and cut across country to the Route. Put the cloth panel out wherever you are, then hide up and the tanker train'll stop for you: should be about two hours after sun-up. You got that straight about the caches, you know what's in the chair and your bags? Oh yeah, I forgot; your colors."

"What?" said Belial.

"Gimme your colors, dummy. You're heading east, where Hell's Angel is a very dirty word. Remember, in Harmony you're three hired hands who just got paid, three bravos on the prod; there'll be a hundred like you, believe me, just don't try and stomp them all at once."

They handed him the denim cut-offs in silence, and buttoned their leather coats, fishing out gloves and helmets of soft hide from the pockets. Long Range touched the Glitch hanging under his shirt.

Belial said, "Just one thing, Frank. How did these Gypsies get to hear about our party?"

"I've been thinking, Belial, and I see it this way. There'd be no sense in Eliot double-crossing us, not before he's got what he wants. So it has to be that either the Gypsies snatched whoever talked to him, or. . . ."

"Or what?" said Belial, as the older Angel hesitated.

"Or the Professor don't care who he goes with. He just wants out, so he's telling everyone he's up for grabs."

"Then we'd better get going," said Milt.

"Shut up," said Frank, suddenly serious and fierce. "Now listen. You're never going to do this by racing. You have to feel what I feel, that you're *meant* to do this. You don't hurry and you don't stop, any more than the hawk stops when he dives after the hover. Your lives up till now have been your hover. Now go."

They none of them moved, but stood in a loose circle with their heads bent. Outside the shed the wind rose to a roar.

46

After a minute Frank chanted softly:

> "Sing my song
> Blood and dust
> Hawks fly on."

Then Belial sang:

> "Rivers run
> Gypsy blood
> Hawks fly on."

Then Milt:

> "Go lightly
> The mind's free
> Hawks fly on."

Then Long Range:

> "Reach the end
> Fly beyond
> Hawks fly on."

Finally Frank again:

> "Sing my song
> Blood and dust.
> Hawks fly on."

They stood in silence once more. At last Frank crossed to the table and blew out the lamp, and they filed outside into the windy night. Rounding a corner they came on their bikes; the dark shapes of Frank's guards dispersed silently into the night.

They climbed on, and switched on gas taps and ignition; there were no lights on their machines. Just before they fired up Frank leaned forward and said, "You know what they say about Bad Hand? That he thinks he can't be beat except by his own kin?" This had been discovered from a Gypsy prisoner. "Well, if you meet up with him there's just one thing to do."

"What's that?" said Milt.

"Don't forget to call him daddy," said Frank. They chuckled, and then Belial kicked over his motor and with a subdued roar they fired up. When Milt, cursing and straining, had finally got his engine to catch, they moved steadily down the darkened tracks and out through the timber stockade, without a backward look.

They edged down the rutted track, Milt's machine with the sidecar leading and the other two following as best they could. After about half an hour they pulled off the track into a grove of eucalyptus, dismounted and lay down in silence by their machines, the sweet familiar smell of the warm oil mingling with the damp grass, to wait for first light.

In the silence they soon heard the rumble of motors. They guessed it was Frank and the Wolves edging out of camp to get within striking distance of the Gypsies before dawn.

They lay quietly, glancing up at the sky. The stars were obscured by blowing clouds.

Later in the night a strange sound came to their ears, a faint creaking, hollow sound mingled with a distant gabble that their eyes and minds strained to make sense of. The answer came to them at once, and they strained their eyes overhead, but there was nothing to be seen, just the faint sound of the migrant barnacle geese, beating steadily northwards through the night.

THE TRUCK DRIVER WAS IMMENSE. HE STOOD AGAINST THE vast bulk of the tanker he drove and there was a distinct correspondence between them, the swell of the tires and the oval curve of the tanker's body finding its echo in the way the driver's bulk forced his arms out from his sides in a permanent gesture of involuntary supplication, a kind of waddling peace symbol.

The road stretched away empty and silent to a distance that shimmered in the morning sun. The three young bikers were sweating and straining to push the last of their machines, with the heavily laden chair attached, up a ramp into the hollow interior of the trailer that the tanker towed. Behind them in the distance the snowy peaks rose. The truck driver was crying.

"Please, please, move it up. They'll come, I know it. This is how it was. Oh God. We stopped. One minute there was nothing, the next they firebombed the escort truck. The soldiers were on fire, they were screaming, they were on fire. You could smell it. Oh God. Hurry. Please, please hurry."

He wrung his pudgy hands in anguish, his body streaming moisture, and ran swaying to the bottom of the ramp. Still muttering "Hurry," he flung his bulk at the back of the sidecar. The machine shot up the ramp and into the interior where Milt and Belial leapt on it and lashed it down. The fat trucker fell over and rolled down the ramp. Long Range hauled at him helplessly until he had got back on his feet and they stowed the ramp in the slots for it beneath the trailer. Nothing seemed to fit. They kept glancing back along the road. The trucker's panic was infectious.

Finally they were done. Milt and Belial stood at the door as Long Range struggled into trucker's overalls; while they had lain by the road waiting for the truck they had drawn grasses to decide who should ride first with the driver, and who remain in the secret compartment with the machines.

The compartment had been carefully designed; there were benches bolted to the sides, ventilation holes and a light, and the door, which from the outside was a false panel with gas gauges and levers in it, also opened from the inside; the handle inside had been painted luminous in case the lights failed. There was also an alternative exit, a hinged trapdoor in the floor that let you out beneath the truck.

The driver had already started the truck's mighty diesel, and its roar struck Long Range in the chest. Belial tossed him his bolt-gun and he shrieked, "See you guys later," as the compartment's door swung shut, and he sprinted to the front of the truck, hauled himself up into the cab, the

49

truck already beginning to roll forward, the brakes hissing, the fat trucker clashing the gears in his haste. Painfully slowly they picked up speed.

Long Range glanced into the long mirror on his side but could discern nothing in the truck's dusty wake. He looked around him at the bare desolate land under the profound blue sky. If he looked across the driver he could see the mountains off to their left. Anyway they were rolling, he thought; heading south.

Driving seemed to settle the fat trucker somewhat. He mopped at his tear-stained face with a red bandanna, then put a straw sombrero on his dome-shaped head, tossing a battered peaked cap to Long Range.

"You're the co-driver, right? What's your name, boy?" he shouted across the drone of the engine, suddenly arrogant now his tears had stopped.

"Long Range John. What's yours?"

"They call me the Barrel," he said, patting his enormous belly and grinning automatically.

"What happened back there?" asked Long Range.

The Barrel's expression became sober again. "It was about an hour before I got to you. We stopped, me and the escort, I guess because we were ahead of time, wanted to make sure you'd be there. We heard some bikes coming. They must have seen us and split up. Four came along the road. No colors. Might have been you. The lieutenant was shouting at them, then, wham, the rest of them come up from behind, lobbing bottles full of gas. I was still in the cab and when I saw the first one go off in the soldier-boys' truck, I pulled out."

"How come they didn't catch you?"

"I dunno. I figure I outran them. Unloaded, this heap does ninety-five, see, once we get going. Some of the soldiers were still shooting when I pulled out. If they kept at it for ten, fifteen minutes I got enough start for a while. But who the hell were they?"

"Gypsies. Under Bad Hand. They know about us."

"What the hell is all this? You little bastards are nothing but trouble. You nearly got me killed," the Barrel blustered. Long Range looked at him without speaking and he subsided, and went on talking normally.

"Well, we got a fair chance. It's not many miles to the bridge on the Stanislaus, by my reckoning. There's a Cartel post there. If we get beyond that, we've stopped them. They might give us an escort. You see anything behind?"

"Nothing," said Long Range. He hesitated and then said, "This is about the furthest south I've been. Is it all bare and dusty like this?"

The Barrel turned arrogant again. "You're a know-nothing, ain't you, kid? This is Dead Lands, where nothing will grow. In the old days they say it was all orchards and pastures like around the City, and they ran water down from the mountains and kept it in lakes they made themselves. But even if we could do that, nothing would grow now. Dead Lands, see?" He shook his head in wonder. "You guys. . . ."

Long Range was fumbling behind inside the back of his overalls, and the Barrel stopped talking as he pulled out his knife from behind his back. The young Angel stuck it, scabbard and all, in his boot, where he could get at it handily.

They roared on in silence along the unwavering road.

THERE WAS NO ESCORT FOR THEM AT THE RIVER. LONG Range stood quietly as the Barrel told his story to the Oil Cartel troopers who knew him; he omitted any mention of his passengers or of the attackers' identity. A patrol of troopers was sent up the road to try and find the "bandits," and after leaving sacks of supplies and mail he drove the tanker on across the high clattering wooden bridge, looking down on the shanties of the gangs of men who worked on the road and the bridges. There were women pounding clothes on stones by the riverside below. There had been no search; the empty tankers were sometimes loaded with cases of goods for trade on the way south, which were taxed at the Cartel checkpoints, but the Barrel had said they were empty and no one had checked. It all seemed to be routine.

The Barrel was elated by what he took to be the end of the real danger. Even without an escort, the chances of attack by the ragged bands who lived outside the settlements were remote. The Barrel pulled out a tin box from under the seat, unwrapped the contents and began eating fat sandwiches as they drove along. He told Long Range what was in each different one—there was pork meat and cheese, tomatoes, onion and lettuce, cream cheese with walnuts, ham and pickles, and cookies and milk. Long Range's food was out of reach in his saddlebags in the compartment. The Barrel finished his meal, belched and swept the crumbs off his mountainous stomach and, commenting that his mother "Sure could cook," offered Long Range a drink of water.

All afternoon they roared south through the unusually barren land. There were two more big bridges with Cartel posts, but the Barrel did not get down at either, merely explaining the absence of escort and being waved through, dropping sacks of mail and supplies as before. Even around the posts there were no flocks or herds, no animals foraging. Nothing would grow to support them.

Long Range sat in silence for the most part. His natural eagerness at the new sights was blunted by both the monotony of the wasted landscape and the truck driver's company. The Barrel seemed strange to him. None of his talk had to do with things that were familiar to Long Range, or touched his feelings. He talked of the coin he was earning for this special work, the things he would buy with it for the home his mother kept: in the heat of afternoon he began to talk about the women at the Cartel posts who would do it with the truckers, even with him, for food or presents. Long Range guessed it was the only subject that would keep him awake.

Long Range, for all his fatigue, was nervously alert; more from the events of the past weeks and the agonizing questions they raised than from the uncertainty ahead, the bare land, the strange town and the unknown contact. Everything suggested that he should kill Belial; the awful

52

moonlit scene, the violation of their law, even his disgust at his own inaction, all demanded violent retribution.

Yet Belial had also saved his life in the Hall, when he had reached the end of his strength and felt the wet darkness deepen about him, by smashing Fork down and wrenching Long Range's head out of the barrel up into the dazzling light.

A wave of self-hatred flushed through him. Better to die! But he was too honest, still, not to know that he didn't really feel that, sick with self-loathing though he was. The same honesty made him stop himself dwelling on the scene by the river, for he knew that a part of himself was fascinated and excited by it.

Another Angel would have killed Belial for breaking that particular law, but the doubts Long Range felt and had expressed to the doctor about the Angel way would not allow him to resort to that excuse.

It was not that it was easier to be inactive. It was that he found that, after all, he did not hate Belial yet, nor feel anything particular towards him. It was just Belial. He had grown up with Belial, seen a hundred instances of his cruel solitary animal nature.

Only this time it had destroyed something Long Range valued. But the something had been an illusion, Lila, beloved, golden-hair, lying spread out on the ground. . . .

There was no strength in him to do anything, no reason, nothing to make it even important. A weird weightlessness possessed him, as desolate as the wastelands drifting by.

The Barrel was urinating into a bottle. "Barrel ain't stopping for nothing," he chuckled. "You know what that girl I told you about, back at the Purgatoire, you know what she called this?" He shook his flaccid penis, which lay, puckered and snail-like, in his pudgy palm. "The mutton dagger, that's what she called it." He chortled, corked the bottle, and drove on, not bothering to button up again. The windows were closed against the dust and the heavy smell of urine remained.

Toward the future Long Range had no expectations. If he had weighed up their chances of returning alive he must

53

have concluded that they were not good, but he had caught some of the feeling that Frank had wished to convey, and felt some force rolling them toward Harmony and the plains beyond. He felt detached from their situation. The strangeness, the monotony of the journey was hypnotic. Glancing across at the mountains again he saw them, through the dust, as if he was dreaming the scene.

The truck smashed across a hole in the road, flinging him forward against the dashboard.

Towards evening the road swung gradually east, through an area of hummocks and mounds, where the blowing soil of the desolate countryside had covered the ruins of a town. The rays of the setting sun slanted behind and the shadows seemed to point their way on into the night.

A little further on the Barrel stopped. Long Range's ears rang in the silence as he clambered down and stood swaying, waiting for the Barrel to slide down on the other side. He stretched, then noticed for the first time that ragged sagebrush was growing by the roadside. The evening was rosy and golden, softened by the dust; the air seemed formed from big soft particles that had come together to make up a veil or curtain with the scene around them painted languidly upon it, like the faded tapestries he had seen once in the City. To their left and ahead the mountains lay, in hues of gray, sepia, lavender, fusing in the distance to a dull blue.

The Barrel saw him gazing ahead. "We go up there," he said, "thirty miles or so there's a pass. Then it's descent, but things grow again—yucca, old oaks, stuff like that. The air is better too—hot enough, but not like that hell we came through today. Well, let's see to your buddies." He waddled to the back of the trailer and banged the side of it once with the flat of his hand.

In a moment the panel swung open and Milt let himself down and stood swaying on the road, looking pale and ill. They waited for Belial to get down but there was no movement. Long Range stepped forward to peer inside the compartment, when there was a strangled squawk from the

54

Barrel, who had turned round to find Belial standing beside him.

"He went through the trapdoor," Milt explained.

"Best to be careful," said Belial quietly, then stretched and yawned mightily, in silence. Milt stood still, looking around him with delight, at the desert and the hills in the evening light.

AFTER A SHORT BREAK THEY GOT IN AGAIN, BELIAL RIDING with the driver, Long Range in the compartment sitting on a bench across from Milt, who swung the door shut and fastened it. As the truck picked up speed they were bumped and rattled ceaselessly and with no warning, but for Long Range Milt's company made up for the discomfort. His friend's bony face and scraggly hair were accentuated by the harsh light from the solitary bulb in a wire cage bolted to the ceiling. The road hummed beneath them, and gas splashed about in the tanks of the lashed bikes. Long Range dug out bread and meat from his saddlebags and ate ravenously.

"That driver toad wouldn't share his grub," he said with his mouth full.

"He looks like he never has," said Milt.

"How was it in here?"

"Well it was hot as a bitch all day, and I tell you being inside like this really gets to you after a while."

"How was Belial?"

"Oh, most of the time he was asleep. But I'll say one thing, that bastard's got a good idea of what's going down. I mean, I don't know how it is with you, but for me this has all been pretty sudden, and then sweating in this tank all day, I tell you when we got out I didn't know if it was going to be night or day, let alone where we were going, or why.

"But old Belial, you know how he is, he doesn't say much, but quite early on he leans over and says he hopes I don't mind but he'd like to run over what Frank said again, because our only chance of getting what we're after is to do things exactly right. Well it passes the time. So

55

we go over the maps again and then start getting our story straight, what we're going to say in Harmony. He says he's heard there's a market there where the truckers bring stuff from the Fief to trade. Now the story is, we were working with an outfit down south, working sheep, and we bought the bikes off some guys down there who said they'd picked 'em up at this market. Which they might have done. And then when we got paid it was all in Fief coin because our *padron* said he'd sold the last lot of hides to the truckers. So that's how come we've got all Fief gear and coin. Neat, huh?

"But now get this. He sticks that red head even closer to mine and looks at me with the pale eyes and says there's another thing he reckons he should tell me, because it might get in the way otherwise." Milt stopped talking to take a sip from his wineskin.

Long Range took it, numb and waiting, expecting that Belial had told about Lila. Milt went on.

"He says that ever since he can remember he has known, I mean *known*, that he couldn't get beat in a fight, if he stood his ground. I wasn't about to ask him how he knew it, I tell you; he was really serious. Then he said that went for everyone except one man, he could beat them all except this one guy. And that guy is Bad Hand."

Long Range stared across at his friend under the harsh light. Something he had dreamed flickered on the edge of consciousness, and before he lost it altogether he was aware that, for some reason he did not wish to remember, the knowledge the dream had carried was dark and fearful. Then Milt spoke again and he lost it.

"He said he's heard a Gypsy captive sing a song about Bad Hand, how Bad Hand couldn't be killed either, except by his own kin, and he didn't have any kin. And when he'd heard it he'd known he couldn't stand up against that guy."

"I don't know, I don't know," said Long Range wearily. "We'll just have to hope we've outrun them. The way I feel right now I couldn't handle a drunken midget, much less Bad Hand. I have to crash, brother, I really do."

Milt turned off the light and they sat in the darkness with only a few chinks in the compartment appearing, the bikes between them, the tires humming beneath them, all around the muffled roar of the engine and the intermittent jolting rattle of the truck and trailer ploughing over the rough road through the night.

Long Range dozed, drowsy from the wine, jerking awake as he nodded forward and each fresh jolt threatened to smash him forward into the bikes. His mouth began to dry up; he thrust his head deeper down into the collar of his coat and tried to sleep. Vague scenes appeared before his closed eyes—the kitchen table in the Hulk's house, a favorite slope on the hills behind their camp, a crack at the exercise yard. He half-slept, tossed about on the bench, his face gritty, the nerves jiggling.

He awoke early at what he guessed to be two or three in the morning. He had never been so cold in his life. His hand, touching the metal bench, almost stuck to it. But there was something good about the breathtaking intense cold, cold as iron, that bit through the blanket and his clothes. There was no defense against it, and nowhere to go. Aching with hunger again and freezing cold, he felt a chill exhilaration.

He considered his situation once more and for some reason recalled the doctor's words, how his self-pity might get himself and his brothers killed. Staring in the dark he knew now he could do what was necessary. He felt no less hopeless, but stronger. It was a grim comfort.

When he awoke again, chinks of light filtered down the ventilation channels. He shivered and rubbed his face with his hands, peering across at Milt who was hunched up opposite, his hair at wild angles. Long Range found the covered bucket clamped beneath the seat and urinated into it, the chemical odor from inside cutting sharply in the fetid air of the compartment.

Milt stretched, yawned mightily and scratched himself. Long Range drank some water and chewed on a piece of dried bread.

"You know what that mother up front's got in his

bread?'' he asked Milt. "Cream cheese and walnuts. Pork meat and pickle.''

Milt surveyed their cold meat and bread gloomily.

"What time do you reckon we'll get into Harmony?''

"Should be sometime tonight, I guess.''

"Should be good eats there. Southern cooking. Southern women too.''

"I'll settle for the eats first,'' said Long Range. Then, "What's that?''

They felt a bumping under the trailer, and the compartment dipped rhythmically.

"Flat, I guess,'' said Milt. Then they both stiffened. Above the noise of the truck came the roar of bikes.

They stuffed the food back in the saddlebags, and Milt cocked his bolt-gun as they felt the tanker slowing. Long Range looked around and then hissed:

"I left my fucking gun up front.''

Milt was tugging at the trapdoor.

"When we get outside,'' he whispered, "you stay underneath the truck. I'll try and get on top and when I loose off, you hit them too. O.K. . . . ?''

The trapdoor swung up and they saw the pale road below moving slower and slower. They looked at each other for a moment; then the truck rolled to a halt and Long Range, not giving himself time to think, slipped through the hole and dropped quietly onto the road.

The truck had pulled over onto the right; and lifting his head on the hard road, Long Range saw the wheels of two bikes and a truck on their left. He sensed Milt slipping away behind him as he crawled to one of the trailer's big wheels and looked round it in time to get a glimpse of a thick-set black-bearded man wearing Gypsy colors over a Fief army uniform, with a bolt-gun leveled in front of him, striding toward the truck's cabin. There was something wrong with the way he walked; just before the Gypsy passed from his field of vision, he realized that the man was a hunchback.

"Come down, you,'' Long Range heard him shouting. "Both of you, out of that door. Come on, move it.'' There

58

was the sound of feet hitting the road, then a slap. The trucker's cap Belial had been wearing spun onto the road.

"Well, well, well," boomed the voice. "Howler, cover them from the truck."

"O.K., Cat-back," came a cracked reply.

"Juicer, lay off that fucking wine—you can drink when we've cut these fuckers up some. Now, you two, where are the others?"

"What others?" came Belial's quiet voice. "We're truckers from the Fief, and you'll get. . . ."

There was the sound of a blow.

"Shut up," roared the voice. "You're that carrot-headed Angel bastard, Belial, aren't you, boy? And there's two more of you Angels hid up in the truck somewhere, or else you dropped them off earlier. Now you're going to tell me where they are, goddammit."

He must have shoved them along the truck, for two pairs of legs stamped and staggered in front of Long Range's face. Facing them were two others, four feet in heavy black riding-boots. Long Range could see three more riders in Gypsy colors and odd bits of Fief military clothing standing by the bikes, and guessed that there was a sixth man, Howler, on the truck. He lay in fear and uncertainty, feeling practically defenseless with only the long knife in his hand, as out in the sunlight the booming voice of the hunchback went on.

"Wait till Bad Hand and the rest of the boys get here. He couldn't slip through those posts like we did, dressed up like soldier-boys, not the way he looks. He's gone round, so he's an hour or two behind, but when he gets here he'll cut you up so bad your mother wouldn't know you—if a guy like you had a mother, that is. You must be gamma-happy, redhead, getting caught so far from home. Wait till Bad Hand gets here. . . ."

"Who's Bad Hand?" said Belial. There was the sound of another blow and a hideous yell as Howler, the Gypsy on the truck, threw back his head and howled in delight.

Then his howl changed to a scream, as with a dull chunk a bolt hit him square in the chest and knocked him back-

59

wards over the side of the truck, crashing out of sight on to the road. The Gypsies froze, staring up at the roof of the trailer, where Milt crouched with his bolt-gun, empty now, in his hands.

At that moment, from under the truck Long Range swung out with his knife, slicing Cat-back behind the knee. Cat-back screamed and dropped his gun; Belial shoved him over, and, ducking behind the Barrel, slipped sideways toward the cabin of the truck.

One of the Gypsies standing by the bikes swung his bolt-gun up to shoot at Milt, who leaped forward over the gap between the truck and trailer. But not fast enough; his enemy fired, and the bolt caught Milt in the buttock. With a scream of pain and rage he lost his footing and fell off the top of the truck, landing squarely on top of Cat-back and the Barrel, the whole group tumbling to the ground in confusion. Long Range saw his opportunity and rolled out from under the truck, slashing up at Cat-back as he came. The latter's gun fired wildly; the bolt thudded into the struggling form of the Barrel, who died instantly.

Belial had reached the front of the truck. A Gypsy took aim at him and fired but he had flung the cabin door open and was diving inside as the bolt slammed into the tanker's metal door. Two Gypsies ran forward to deal with him, but before they were on him he slipped back out from the cabin door with bolt-guns in both hands, and holding both arms straight out in front of him, shot the two of them at once at point-blank range, the force of the metal bolts as they passed through their bodies spinning them backwards into the dust. Belial leapt forward and, crouching, scooped up the knife that one had dropped.

Milt and Long Range were grappling wildly with Cat-back and the other Gypsy. The last of their enemies, Juicer, hovered on the edge of the heap of struggling bodies, tugging at his bolt-gun. Belial moved in quickly toward him, but Juicer looked up, and, dropping the empty bolt-gun, drew a long knife, curved like a sickle, from behind his back.

Belial and his opponent faced one another for a long

moment, each stepping sideways toward the tanker, trying to get their backs to its bulk. The point of Belial's blade was weaving backwards and forwards and the Gypsy found his attention unwillingly fixed on it. Then with a jerk he swung two-handed at Belial, who leaped away from the stroke effortlessly as a cat, his right hand flickering in as his hips snaked away. The enemy screamed and held his arms to his chest, one hand dangling by ligaments brilliant white in a rush of bright blood. Belial lunged forward again and drove his blade underhand upwards into the wounded man's stomach. Juicer fell to his knees, then toppled over and lay writhing on the road, curled up around the great slash in his belly, his heels kicking in the dust so that his hunched body was forced round and round in agonized jerks until the final convulsion came.

Long Range was wrestling frantically with Cat-back, the hunchback's swarthy face pressed close to his as the Gypsy tried to use his weight to pin the young Angel and bring his knife in. Long Range smelt the fetid breath, turned his head just in time as the Gypsy tried to butt him and smash his nose; he could not pull away far enough and the greasy head smashed painfully into his ear. He felt his strength begin to go, and in desperation tried a schoolyard trick, spitting in the Gypsy's face, but the hate-filled face never wavered, the corded neck stiff with the exertion of trying to crush him, saliva dribbling over his hardened scars. Fighting down panic, Long Range thought quickly and hacked backwards hard with his heel on to the slash where he had cut behind the Gypsy's knee from under the truck.

He connected, and with a howl of agony, the Gypsy's grip jerked loose, and Long Range fell on him. In an instant his razor-edged blade slashed in at Cat-back's head, and again and again, chopping to keep the screaming, flailing body beneath him at arm's length. The knife skidded off bone, then bit deep into flesh at the neck. Long Range jerked back instinctively as a gout of hot blood splashed up over his face; he recovered and went to cut again, but saw suddenly from the lolling bloody head that it was over.

On all fours he flung himself away from the heap of

bloody flesh. Looking around wildly he registered that all was still, Belial and Milt standing looking at the bodies of their enemies. He staggered to his feet and, stumbling to the edge of the road knelt with his back to the scene, rocking slightly on his heels, staring out at the mountains.

After a while Milt came over to him with a water sack. They looked at one another. Then Long Range took the water with trembling hands, drank some and spat, then drank again. Pulling out his handkerchief he soaked it and wiped the blood off his face and hands, then cleaned his knife and sheathed it. Then he got up. They walked back to the truck to find Belial dragging the Gypsy bodies into a rough line.

He grunted as they approached.

"Going to take their heads."

They stopped. He straightened, taking their uncertainty for criticism.

"You did well," he said, "but I killed half of them. I killed him, and him, and him. Going to take their heads, put them in a row across the road. They can say hello to their friends." He smiled dazzlingly. Long Range noticed that he looked relaxed, like a well-fed cat.

Long Range and Milt had seen it done, the taking of the trophies. But on the empty road it seemed senseless. Long Range went to speak, but Milt cut in.

"Your fight will make a fine song, Belial," he said earnestly. "Perhaps they will even sing of how Milt got half his ass shot off and fell off the top of the tanker." They smiled involuntarily as Milt went on. "But no one will sing if they catch up with us."

"The heads will slow them down," said Belial, "make them frightened."

"But it would slow them better if they thought we were dead," said Milt. "If we had been burnt in the truck in a fight, the same way they burnt the soldiers."

Belial thought for a moment, then nodded once and, stooping, began dragging one of the bodies feet-first toward the front of the tanker. Long Range and Milt took the Gypsies they had killed and dragged them to the cabin. They sweated and strained to pass the dead weight of the blood-stained bodies, like big sacks of water, up to Belial in the cab, who arranged them along the seat, then jumped down to help them haul the Barrel's lifeless bulk up to the cabin and, panting hard, lift him up and wedge him behind the wheel. Long Range felt a surge of helpless hilarity at the sight of the Barrel, his fat face placid like a baby asleep behind the wheel.

"Pork meat and pickles," said Milt beside him.

"Cream cheese and walnuts," said Long Range. They jumped down. The sun was getting up and flies rose from the shot bodies.

Ten minutes later they had covered their tracks, arranged the enemy bikes and bodies, stowed the extra gas they would need for the run to Harmony and fired up their own machines.

Belial, standing by the tankers, produced a metal box of matches from his pocket, struck one and, lighting the soaked rags he had stuffed in the tanker's gas tank, ran lightly off the road and through the scrub toward them. He was halfway when, above the roar of their engines, they felt the gas tank ignite with a dull thump. Flames and thick black smoke licked around the cabin as Belial reached his bike, jumped on and kicked it into life. As Long Range looked back for the last time at the flames in the sunshine and the ropes and gobbets of fire burning on the road, the window of the cabin, blackened inside, now cracked and shattered in a thousand shards, and as flames leapt around the cab and wreathed the whole front of the truck, Long Range thought he saw a blackened figure writhe and straighten, its arm waving up in ghastly farewell.

Then he turned to the road ahead and they shot off, Belial pulling his front wheel up in exuberance, each of them going up through the gears, winding their twist-grips up to eighty and more, the wind tearing at them, whipping their hair, their sweat chilled dry, hauling away from the pillar of black smoke in the desert as fast as they could run.

* * *

BESEECH. SEARCH. BEAST. CRÈCHE. SHE.

When Long Range awoke it was evening, and he lay on the bed in the twilight, staring at the ceiling of logs with split cedar sticks laid in a herringbone pattern between them. Some strings hung down from the cracks, and he idly wondered what they were for; then he remembered where he was. Harmony.

The evening before, they had turned off the road a few miles to the west and circled below the town, finally bumping in on a cattle trail from the south. At a stable on the outskirts they had left the bikes; the place had a courtyard with thick walls of adobe, two gates, meaning two ways out, and sheds and stables all around the yard. They had left Belial there too.

"They know me," he had said. "That Gypsy Cat-back knew my name. We may fool them with that bonfire back on the road, but even if we do they'll most likely come on anyhow to try to meet with our contact. You go to town, let whoever it is we're waiting for know you're here. But look out for anyone who could be Gypsies."

"Especially big strange men with bad hands," lisped Milt, and drew a flat silent stare from Belial. When it was dark they left him curled up in the straw by their bikes, eating a bowl of refried beans he had bought from the Mexicans around the stable. With their saddlebags they trudged warily up the darkened street and entered the biggest cantina. They had a brief impression of the lamplit bar with a few men sitting around before they were shown the rooms they had asked for, on the landing above. Alone in his room, Long Range had stared about him, feeling strange and tense with tiredness. Stiffly he shed his boots and clothes and with a bowl and jug washed the grime and blood from his hands and face, then jammed a chair against the door and slid between the soft coarse linen sheets. He listened vaguely to the babble from the bar for a while, before sliding into oblivion.

I must have slept the day around, he thought. He got up, gingerly feeling the bruises on his head, and walked, stiff, naked to the window, and looked out onto the main street. The town stood at the foot of the mountains, the scene soft and dusty in the evening light. He saw the houses of gray adobe—all of them seemed to be only half-finished—and the washing strung across the flat roofs, stirring slightly in the warm breeze. He looked down into the street and watched the way the tall Indians in thin cotton clothes held themselves and walked; saw ox carts trundle by, and burros moving patiently, invisible beneath mountainous loads of brushwood; saw the men in straw hats and heard the women shouting at the children playing in the dust; heard a guitar somewhere too.

He stood there watching, fascinated and excited by the strangeness of the place; anything seemed possible in this warmth, this soft light and warm air. Then he smelt charcoal and wood smoke, warm bread and coffee, meat grilling and pots bubbling, and was suddenly aware of a ravenous hunger. He began pulling on his clothes when there was a knock on the door. He let in Milt, who beamed and handed him a bottle. Long Range groaned and said, "You ain't loaded already, are you? And what is this shit?" gesturing at Milt's scrubbed face, clean shirt and scraggly hair unsuccessfully plastered down with water. "What are we, Citizens or something?"

Patting his bandaged buttock, Milt replied, "When you sleep on your stomach you don't sleep so long, see, so I been up for an hour or two. So I know what's downstairs, see?"

"What's that?" said Long Range, taking the bottle and half choking at the first fiery swallow of colorless liquid.

"Go ahead and choke, son," said Milt loftily, "that tequila takes some getting used to—but I guess you'll learn to handle it after a while. What's downstairs? Why, nothing but good-looking women, which if you can't get for love I believe you might get for money."

He suddenly let out a whoop and cut a caper, shouting, "Beautiful! Young! Black-haired! Women! I *knew* they must have built that goddam road to get to something besides goddam juice. Come on," he pleaded, "get your pants on and let's get down there. How do you feel anyway?"

"Oh, rested up. How's your backside? Want me to have a look at the dressing?"

Milt slapped his hand away. "Anything just to get at my gorgeous body, eh? No, I'm all right, I did it myself. Come on, let's go."

Long Range pulled on his boots and stood up. "You know," he said, "this town seems like a pretty nice place."

"And you ain't seen the half of it yet," chortled Milt.

They walked along the landing, looking down at the smoky lamplit scene below. For a moment Long Range felt a twinge of uncomfortable familiarity with the big room full of tables and chairs. It was early in the evening and a quiet murmur of voices rose, the only real noise being shouts from a tableful of players as they slammed down their cards at the bragging game of truco. A mariachi band sat talking quietly on chairs at the far end of the room, their brass instruments gleaming.

As they descended the stairs Milt nudged Long Range and nodded across at a line of chairs by the side of the dark wooden bar. Four ladies sat there with considerable dignity. Two were extremely large, and one skinny to the point of stringiness, but the fourth was a good-looking Mexican girl in a purple dress, her plump honey skin brushed with darkness, her eyes laughing as they approached.

"The one in the purple's not bad," grunted Long Range.

"Ah ah, ol' buddy, she's spoken for. That there's Lizzy Gomez, and I saw her first." He raised his voice as they walked across to the bar.

"Olá Lizzy, qué tal? Quieres tomar una copa con nosotros? Tienes una amiga par este feo aquí?"

"Oh hell," said Long Range, "if you're going to show off your languages all evening I'm going back upstairs." He called the barman and said, "Let me have another bottle of that and three glasses."

The barman, a large white man with a glistening bald head, thick black whiskers and immaculate linen, said, "If you want to drink with Lizzy it will cost you, friends."

"Drinking ain't all I had in mind," said Milt.

66

"That'll cost you too," said the barman. "Five coins and you can drink with her all evening, and do whatever you like upstairs after."

Milt threw the money on the counter.

"Usually they pay me," he tried to grumble, concealing his excitement with difficulty as Lizzy snuggled up to him.

"How about you, son?" said the barman to Long Range. "You see anything that tickles your fancy?"

Long Range shook his head. "And even if I did I'm too damn hungry to do much about it. Where can we get a meal?"

"Why right here," said the barman. "How about half a dozen eggs, a beefsteak, refried beans, gravy, corn bread and all the coffee you can drink? Cost you a coin."

"Sounds all right to go along with," said Long Range, flipping him a coin. The barman caught it and glanced at it.

"Fief coin, huh? You boys from out that way?"

"Nah, our trail-boss did some deal with them here, so we got paid off in it. It's good money, ain't it?"

"Sure, sure," said the barman. "It's just that there were some guys in here earlier, asking if anyone had come in that might be from the west, you know, from the Fief."

"Oh yeah," said Milt casually, "four or five guys?"

"That's right, there was four of them. You know them?"

"Yeah, they might be some friends of ours," said Long Range.

"Or maybe some friends of friends," said Milt, nodding. "Now listen, we'd really like to surprise them, so if they should come in again, if you was to tip us the wink, well, we'd really appreciate it," he concluded, flipping a coin to the barman, who caught it deftly.

"In case they were these friends of friends which we wouldn't recognize, that is," said Long Range, flipping another coin at him.

The barman smiled slightly.

"*Inquiring friends*, huh? Well, tonight you can relax, they said they'd call in again tomorrow. I'll let you know who they are, boys; but whatever it is—not in here, eh? Or *my* friend might have something to say."

"Your friend?" said Milt, and then they both noticed that the barman was holding, so that it was just visible above the counter, a shotgun with double barrels cut off short.

"Oh, that friend," said Milt, "well we surely wouldn't want to get that little lady upset. We'll just take our bottle and Lizzy here and sit over there by the wall until the food comes, eh? And thanks."

"No problem, boys," said the barmen expansively, his hands on the counter again. "It's a pleasure to do business with reasonable men."

As they walked to their table Long Range said quietly, "We'll have that piece off him before we split."

Milt nodded emphatically.

They took their places at a quiet table to the right of the door and opposite the bar. Milt poured drinks in silence, and Lizzy sipped demurely.

"Four was a good guess," said Long Range after a while.

"Ycah," said Milt, "and if Bad Hand had been one of them I reckon the barkeeper would have said something— you know, about a big ugly guy or something. He must be hid up somewhere, same as Belial."

"Well right now we seem to have the drop on them," said Long Range. "Tomorrow early we'll go get Belial and stake this place out, and they come in and Baldy there lets us know, we'll just destroy their asses."

"Naturally," said Milt ironically.

"Naturally," said Long Range expansively, pouring another drink and tossing it down. Shuddering, he added, "Of course we could just buy them a couple of bottles of that stuff, which would probably do the job for us twice as quick."

"Oh come on now, son, look at Lizzy here, she can handle it, can't you, dear?" said Milt, pouring another drink for the girl, who put her hand up to her mouth, burped once, and giggled. A man passing their table said,

68

"Evening, Lizzy." Milt glowered at his retreating back, and Long Range said, "Oh, she can handle it all right, but the question is, can you?" Milt turned to glower at him until they all collapsed in fits of laughter. At that moment the band struck up.

"Oh God," said Long Range, "well here's to whisky on a rainy day, anyhow."

"Here comes your grub," said Milt, and Long Range turned. An Indian girl in a loose blouse with a heavy silver chain about her neck and a long red skirt of velveteen wove her way gracefully through the tables with a tray. Long Range stared at the beautiful oval of her face as she stopped at their table and, keeping her eyes down, quietly placed plates and dishes of steaming food before him. Milt was talking Spanish to Lizzy, who giggled and said something in dialect to the girl. She was placing the last dish and a spoon and fork of horn on the table, and looked down at Long Range, gazing frankly at his face with clear black eyes; Long Range thought they were flecked with gold. Then she smiled, said something to Lizzy without taking her eyes off Long Range, and swirled away with the empty tray, moving lightly to the music; men shouted their appreciation, and then she vanished behind the bar.

"Now eat up your supper," crooned Milt.

"What you say?" said Long Range.

"I said eat up your supper—you remember, you were so hungry you could *die*, and all."

"I mean what'd you say to her, fuck-face," snarled Long Range.

"Well all I done was tell Lizzy to tell her that after you got through with the grub you were liable to be hungry for something else."

Long Range groaned. "And what'd she say?"

"She said you were to be a good boy and not drink too much, and—but no, you better eat your supper first, or you're liable to get too excited to get it down."

Long Range reached across the table and lifted Milt by his shirt-front half out of his chair.

"What did she say, motherfucker?" he hissed through clenched teeth.

"Aaah, I'll tell you, I'll tell you, I'm too young to die," chortled Milt. "She said she'd be seeing you upstairs in your room after midnight. Though what she can see in such an ill-favored and brutal person actually eludes me," he concluded prissily, winking at Lizzy.

"But who is she?" said Long Range. "What's her name?"

"Her name's Rita, but they call her *La Virgen de la Medianoche*."

"What's that mean?"

"The Midnight Virgin," said Milt, rolling his eyes. "Think you can handle that? Lizzy says she's not one of the girls, she just helps out in the kitchen. Just picks and chooses now and then. And Lizzy says look out; she's got quite a temper."

At that moment another man passed, saying, "Hi Lizzy, how's it going?" and walking away before Milt's scowl could take effect.

"Goddamn," laughed Long Range, "God double damn."

He fell on his food, Lizzy watching indulgently and then nudging Milt and mimicking Long Range's chomping jaws.

"How is it that he has such hunger?" she asked Milt in Spanish. "Has he always such a hunger?"

"No," said Milt seriously, "it is only in the past month that we have truly come to know hunger."

"And why?" said Lizzy.

"It was after we shot the cook. After we'd ate him, all we could do was take bites at the beef on the hoof—like this," he yelled, diving on Lizzy and sinking his teeth in her neck as she screamed and choked on her drink. So the night went swirling and whirling. The bar filled up with carousing cowmen and townspeople, and above the noise the band got lively. The next man to speak to Lizzy was a large drunken storekeeper who thrust his face close to hers, ignoring the Angels, and demanded a dance. They were well into the second bottle by now, and Lizzy's response

70

was to grind her shoe-heel into his toe; he yelled and went to hit her, but Milt brought a boot-heel crashing down on to his other toe; and as the man howled and his hand groped behind his back for his knife, Milt snaked out of his seat, reached round the man in a flash, jerked out the knife and tossed it out of the cantina door. In the same motion he wrapped both his arms about the drunk and began to whirl him round the floor in time to the music, stamping on his feet whenever he struggled; when they reached the door he whirled the hobbling fellow smartly about and booted him out through the curtain of bones hung on thongs, which jangled gaily as he fell into the street and Milt yelled after him, "And save the last dance for me, sweetheart." He walked back to the bar, trying not to breathe too hard, and said to the barkeeper and his friends:

"What was he, gamma-happy or something?"

"When he's drunk he's just a disaster looking for a place to happen," the barman said apologetically. His hand went below the counter and Milt tensed, but it came up with a bottle.

"Thirsty work, huh? This one's on the house."

"Why thank you kindly, cousin," said Milt. Long Range had jumped up and grabbed a guitar from one of the band; he was mockingly serenading Milt back to their table, when across the smoky room he saw that the noise had brought Rita from the kitchen to watch. On impulse Long Range played the opening bars of a tune he knew, looking across at her. She stood still in the kitchen doorway.

The band tentatively followed what Long Range played; he went through the verse tune once and then began to sing to the lilting tune, keeping his eyes down.

> "They call her the Midnight Virgin
> She smiles and the day's not the same
> They call her the Midnight Virgin
> For at midnight she'll whisper her name.
>
> She's seen hard times and misfortune
> And she's come through it all with a smile

71

I've seen hard times and misfortune
And I need to be near her a while.

They call her the Midnight Virgin
She smiles but she won't play their game
They call her the Midnight Virgin
But at midnight she'll whisper my name."

There was silence, then a few people clapped, led by
Lizzy, who stared at him from the table with shining eyes.
He handed the guitar to its owner and walked back to the
table as the band struck up a dance tune; he glanced across
at the bar, but Rita had disappeared again. As he sat down
Lizzy kissed her own hand and then touched it to his cheek.

"Oh no," groaned Milt, "not with you too."

"Ah, go comb your hair or something," said Long
Range, "can't you see it's just my soul she loves."

"Oh brother," said Milt and reached across the table for
the fresh bottle.

LONG RANGE SAT ALONE ON HIS BED AGAIN. IN AN
earthen bowl on a chair by the bed a candle flickered in a
slight draft from the shuttered windows; outside the wind
blew dust and tumbleweed in the street, and moved on
across the night land. No more than a murmur of voices
rose from the bar. It was well after midnight.

His previous mood of excitement with the town and high
spirits from the drinking and fooling downstairs had passed.
He had watched the dark-haired Rita serving other groups
of men with food, dodging their hands, joking with them,
and as Milt and Lizzy became more and more gay and
outrageous, gloomily concluded she had forgotten her previous intention, or that it had been a joke. At midnight he
had left the other two dancing fiercely on top of a small
table and gone up to his room, washed his face and drained
a cup. He felt neither tired nor particularly drunk.

Sitting on the edge of the bed, gazing idly at the strings
hanging from the ceiling, things seemed clear but discon-
nected. He had taken out the knife his mother had left him,

72

unscrewed the side plates and looked once more at the picture engraved on the handle, the moon and the sleeping figure beneath the hill. He thought about his mother and father; about the Gypsies somewhere in the town, asleep probably; about Lila and Belial. It seemed an age since the day of the fair. He could make no connection between the various strands of his life now, find no principle that combined all his thoughts. Finally he left it and put his knife away. A spot where he had cut himself shaving earlier itched on his jaw; he scratched at it slowly, thinking about Rita; her silver ornaments and shining dark hair, the way her breasts moved beneath her loose blouse as she bent to serve him, but most often her expression as she smiled at him. He had just realized that he felt somewhere between disappointed that she had not come and nervous that she still would, when there was a scratching on his door.

He hesitated for a moment, paralyzed, and the scratching came again. He forced himself to pick up his knife and with his left hand remove the chair blocking the door.

Rita slipped through noiselessly. He fixed the chair against the door again and turned. She was seated on the far side of the bed, and the light from the candle burnished her copper skin, was lost in her dark hair, lived again in her eyes as she glanced across at him.

Long Range stepped forward slowly, trembling, and sat down on the other side of the bed. Rita reached over and deftly took the knife from his hand, placing it on the bedside chair. Then she put both her hands on his shoulders and gently pulled him over so that he fell back on to the bed. He gazed up at her as she leaned over him, her breasts through the blouse brushing his chest, the dark hair cascading, framing her young face smiling down at him.

He cleared his throat and said, "I thought you weren't coming. I thought you were going with the others."

"Oh no. You are the one."

"You're beautiful."

"No, you beautiful. You, you."

She gazed at him a moment more, then let herself down on top of him, and they kissed.

They took off each other's clothes; Long Range couldn't believe it was happening.

There was no denial, no hesitation, but no hurry either. Where he might have been uncertain, she showed him. She was soft, all her movements quiet, gentle. When he was inside her at first he ran mad with despairing pleasure, tearing into her, cutting deep, not daring to believe that he would lose what he wanted so much; but that passed and she was still there, wiping perspiration from them with the edge of the sheet, and then their bodies began to talk to each other, she squeezing him with her inside, he moving slowly all the way in and out of her as she moved in patterns of her own beneath him, and they built each other's pleasure slowly, inexorably, locked in a kiss again, then groaning and sighing, rising and swelling with seething heavy-bodied pleasure until they tried to stop and were not able any more and went with it up over the lip and burst together, and pleasure flowed and exploded in their bellies and behind their eyes and out to their fingertips and toes; and when it was over they lay exhausted exchanging small kisses, lazy but insistent, caring.

The night was a river. After the candle was blown out, they lay together on the old bed in strips of silver moonlight filtered through the shutters, drifting lazily, cut loose from their past and future. The night took care of them.

ABOUT AN HOUR AFTER SUNUP, HE AWOKE TO FEEL HER stirring from the bed, slipping out from under his arm.

"Where you going?" he muttered. "Don't go."

"Work," she said, "I see you tonight."

"But I don't know—we might be gone tonight."

"Then I no see you."

"Don't you care?" said Long Range, feeling wrong as he said it.

Rita looked at him for a while and said, "You know I care. But for you, me, now—today, maybe tomorrow, all we can have." She looked at him intently for a while, then asked, "Why you sad?"

"Right now I'm not sad, except that you have to go."

"You sad," she said emphatically, "here, here," tapping on his chest with a small brown fist.

He thought, and struggled to express his feelings.

"All my life I've been pulled around, pushed about"—he gestured with his hands—"not by people so much as by—things in me. Now it happens again; this time I must go with my friends—but it happens again."

"Things be different."

"Easy to say that, here, now." He leaned across and kissed her.

"You must have hope. Man need hope."

Long Range spoke quickly. "I'm all out of hope. I hoped before, I trusted before. It's a trick, a trap, I don't get caught twice."

She smiled sadly and said, "I see that in you." And then, "Ah, there is a man I wish you meet."

"Here in town?"

"No—there," she gestured vaguely, in the direction of the mountains to the north.

A thought struck him. He said carefully, "If me and my friends wanted to ride that way, how would we go?"

"Leave town to northwest, go through canyon. Two hills, then one mountain. Valley. Hill. Two rivers. Then climb mountain pass, very hard. Down far side. Three suns' travel by mule."

"Not the mules me and my buddies are traveling on," laughed Long Range. "Is there a trail?"

"Yes. But rough."

"And what's on the other side of the mountains?" he asked.

"Maybe what you look for."

Long Range was suddenly alert. He glanced across at her and said, "How's that?"

"Hope," she said simply, slipping out of bed. He looked at her passing to and fro across the shafts of light from the shuttered windows, fascinated by her beautiful slim body as she stooped to collect her clothes with quiet, graceful movements; watching her firm breasts bobbing as she walked, his eyes drawn to the fuzz of dark hair between

75

her legs that he knew was so silky to the touch; gazing at her shapely back, and at her dark hair as she shook it outside the pale blouse and turned to find him staring at her. She raised her eyebrows, but he beckoned for her to come over to him; she frowned in mock-severity, but he mimed that he had something to whisper. Slowly she approached the bed. When she was close enough he caught her wrist and tugged gently until she consented, and let herself be tumbled softly onto the bed, spreading her legs beneath him, her eyes closing in the silence as his hands found her.

As she got ready to leave again Long Range said, "Tell me one thing, it's been crazing me ever since I got here. What the hell are those bits of string hanging from the ceiling for?"

"When it rain, water come through roof, down string, into bowl. I put one over bed. Cool you down."

She bent and picked up his shirt.

"I wash for you. Blood?"

"Yep. That cook Milt was telling you about."

She sniffed. "I do best. When you come down, food cooked too."

"I thank you," said Long Range, and their eyes locked. She smiled frankly at him once, as she had when they first met, and then slipped out of the door.

Long Range lazed in bed for a few more minutes, enjoying his feeling of physical well-being and complete content. If everything went well, he thought, he would come back for Rita when it was all over and take her home with him; he knew this wasn't very likely or serious, but enjoyed the thought nevertheless.

Finally he rolled out of bed, and, going to the window, opened the shutters and stood gazing across to the mountains. It was still only two hours after sun-up and the street was quiet; a few women were sweeping their steps and porches; a horseback rider loped away, but most travelers were already gone before first light to catch the cool of the day. Somewhere a cock crowed.

Long Range washed and shaved, dressed, pulled his boots on and stuck his knife in the right one. He thought of taking his bolt-gun but it seemed unlikely that the Gypsies would return this early. He deliberately avoided thinking of what would happen when they did. Going out on to the landing he stopped outside Milt's door, then thought better of knocking him up. The state of his head would probably be pitiful. Long Range thought he would eat before finding out. As he walked down the stairs he felt again the twinge of disquiet, stronger now, with the familiarity of the scene; the stale-smelling barroom, overturned chairs.

Chairs. A big room full of chairs.

He had reached the bottom of the stairs. There was a slight noise behind him. He turned to see a man emerge from beneath the staircase. He held a bolt-gun in his left hand, leveled at Long Range's stomach. Simultaneously four other men appeared, from the far corners of the room, from behind the bar, from outside the jangling curtain, and moved in toward him. A part of him flashed with the memory of dreaming this scene at the doctor's house. But then his whole attention was riveted on the man in front of him, very tall and broad-chested, his shoulders perpetually hunched forward, his black-bearded face weaving slightly from side to side, scowling, gesturing him forward with a hideously shrunken and contorted right hand.

THE BOLT-GUN NEVER WAVERED AS, WITHOUT ONCE TAKING his angry eyes off Long Range, Bad Hand raised his ruined hand to his lips in a horrid parody of the gesture for silence. He waved urgently to the other Gypsies who padded up the stairs and along the landing to Milt's door, and set themselves on either side of it. There was the sound of two or three heavy kicks and wood splintering, and then silence in which Long Range tried to stare back at the bearded face glaring into his. In contrast to his big head and thick black beard Bad Hand's eyes were small, set close together, and bloodshot. They never wavered.

Then the other men came trotting down the stairs, making negative signs with heads and hands. Long Range's heart skipped.

"The window was open. The bitch was gone too. Bed was still warm," said one of them, a thick-set dim-looking man wearing a black leather vest and trousers.

Bad Hand cursed in a rumbling monotone. "He must have heard us."

"Want us to go after them?" asked the leather-clad cretin.

"No, Clot. Cut-lips, you take the door with Happy. Weasel, you take the back. Clot, you and me will ask sonny here some questions."

He turned to Long Range, who had been scanning the room quickly. His head was still turning as Bad Hand swung his bolt-gun hard up into his stomach, winding him and bringing tears to his eyes.

"Now pay attention, sonny," rumbled the giant. His crippled hand went to Long Range's hair and settled in it; the sensation was repulsive, like a giant insect or carrion bird so close to his face, and Long Range found himself shaking his head wildly trying to free himself. Clot stepped in and hit him around the mouth.

"Listen, sonny," muttered Bad Hand, jerking his head up, "we know who you are, and we know about your friends, and we know you're meeting someone. Now where are your friends and who are you meeting?"

Stall, thought Long Range.

"Mister, I don't know what you're—"

It was as far as he got before Clot hit him again. His head rang and he felt sick, and panicked by the thought that he could not take much beating.

"Sonny, I told you that we *know*," growled Bad Hand. "Your friend the barkeeper who you paid to make us, well he figured there was more money in us making you." He laughed deep in his throat. "We paid him off all right."

He gestured to the bar; the body of the bartender was slumped over it, the immaculate white of his shirtfront splashed with dark blood.

Long Range took a deep breath. All he had to hang on to was the thought that Milt and Belial would come back for him. He straightened up, spat blood and said, "You must have got the wrong guy."

Bad Hand glared at him in silence. Then he nodded. "O.K., Angel, if that's the way you want it. Clot, get him over that chair, tie his hands to the front legs. If you try and get away I'll shoot you in the leg so you'll never walk right again, sonny."

"My name's Long Range, you son of a bitch, and I'll see you in hell."

Hand went on unperturbed. "Now I'm going to tickle your balls a little with this blade of mine. You must have heard I'm pretty good at that. Ever seen them do it to horses? That's how I'm going to do it to you. And you'll be there, boy, you'll feel it all. Unless you want to talk now." The Gypsies by the door were sniggering. Clot seized him by the scruff of his neck and forced him to bend forward over a high-backed chair. His wrists were lashed to the front legs. He felt sick and humiliated, didn't trust himself to speak. His head was upside down and his mouth filled with blood and saliva. He spat on the floor.

"All right, sonny, all right," muttered Bad Hand. "Clot, pull down his pants." Long Range heard the cretin's leather outfit creaking behind him, heard him say, "Can I . . . ?"

"Later," laughed Bad Hand, "that's when he'll need cheering up." Long Range felt the Gypsy's hands on his hips, fumbling with his clothes; his heart was thumping, his mind too outraged to think. Then Bad Hand said, "Hey, check his right wrist, the cord looks loose; when he kicks the fucker won't hold."

Clot came round to the front of the chair and fumbled with the thong at his right wrist. From the corner of his eye Long Range could see the idiot face, upside down, knotted in concentration. It left his field of vision again as the leather clothes creaked again and Clot began to straighten up. Then there was a thud and Clot's face, wobbling now, fell back into his field of vision, crashing forward to hit the floor. From the back of his head protruded five inches of metal bolt.

There was a moment of shocked stillness. Then Long

Range threw himself forward over the top of the chair, somersaulted clumsily and came up running, holding the chair ahead of him by the legs and crashing toward the bar. He was dimly aware that the bolt had come from the landing, but the bar was the nearest cover he could hope to make.

He was almost there when one of the Gypsies by the door raised himself from behind an overturned table and snapped a shot at him. He flailed desperately, trying to shield himself with the chair, but the bolt went wide and he heard it tumbling among the debris as he flung himself behind the bar, his impact dislodging most of the rickety shelves above him so that he lay cowering in a hail of falling glasses and shattering bottles. Then he was on his knees amid the broken glass and pools of liquor, smashing the chair on the floor again and again, his wrists in agony, until finally the chair came apart and he could reach his knife and cut away the pieces of wood still lashed to his wrists. He ducked instinctively as a bolt ploughed through the front of the bar and lodged in the woodwork behind him, then scrambled toward the end of the bar next to the door. As he passed the bartender's dangling feet a thought struck him, and he scrabbled above his head on the shelf below the bar until his fingers found what he was looking for, the walnut stock of the barman's sawn-off shotgun. He tugged it down, cocked both hammers and scrambled on toward the end of the bar. Curses, heavy breathing and the grim zip-thud of bolts came from the other side.

Peering cautiously around the end he could see the doorway virtually next to him, but not twelve feet away was the overturned table behind which the two Gypsies Happy and Cut-lips crouched. With only two shots in the double-barreled gun he could not risk one at random at the table. He scrambled to his feet and threw himself at the doorway, but was less than halfway when from behind the tables Happy's golliwog blond curls rose smoothly into sight less than ten feet from him, his bolt-gun coming up to center on Long Range.

Long Range instinctively swung the shotgun barrel at him and pulled the first trigger.

The noise inside the room was deafening, heart-stopping. Long Range had a brief impression of his enemy blown backwards in a haze, and then he was flailing through the jangling curtain and sprinting to his left down the dusty street. At the corner of the cantina he halted and turned, shotgun ready, but no one was following. He ran on; startled-looking Indians and women were scurrying for their houses. He rounded the next corner and saw his bike and Belial's leaning against the adobe wall beneath his window; he guessed that the other two must have wheeled them there, climbed in at the window and taken up position on the landing. He crouched for a moment, then stuck the shotgun in his saddlebag, and jumping on Belial's bike kicked it into life; it spluttered and roared as he got off and started his own machine, rubbing the dull black paint of the tank affectionately as it caught, reaching over to Belial's throttle with his left hand to keep both bikes running.

A minute later there were two thuds as Milt and Belial leaped from the window above and hit the dusty street.

Belial jumped on to his bike. Long Range grinned at Milt's excited face as holding his bolt-gun he scrambled on behind, Long Range letting out his clutch, and then both riders shot forward, rounded a last corner and roared down the main street toward the stable, dodging children, scattering chickens, raising dust. Long Range felt the wind in his face, kicked into a higher gear and glanced across at Belial; the Angel's face was pale and he looked grim; Long Range guessed that the fight with Bad Hand had not been pleasant for him. Long Range himself felt light-headed with relief and exhilaration and he whooped aloud above the snarl of the bikes as they turned fast in at the gates of the stable compound and skidded to a halt, Milt already off and running to his bike and the side-hack, switching on, tickling the gas and kicking over almost in one practiced motion, the other two revving impatiently until his engine caught and he skidded the bike and sidecar out from the stable in a plume of dust and out of the far gate of the

81

compound, turned left and drove north through the town again, bumping up a narrow street that ran parallel with the main one. A mule tethered to a hitching post kicked out at them, terrified by the noise. As they passed a gap in the buildings Long Range glanced through at the main street and caught a glimpse of three bikes flashing by in the opposite direction.

The houses began to thin out, then turn to cane and brushwood shanties, and finally they were clear of the town and bumping across stony waste ground toward the low mouth of the canyon.

Belial drew level with Long Range and yelled, "Slow down."

Long Range shouted back, "They're after us. I saw them back there."

Belial yelled, "I know. But I didn't get to change our tires, these are the road tires."

Long Range cursed and throttled back. On the chair they carried spare wheels and tires, knobbly $4.00 \times 18''$ and $5.00 \times 16''$ monsters with safety rims, right for cross-country riding but not able to stand up to the high speeds they had been clocking on the blacktop of the Route. For that they had set out with lighter tires; Belial was to have changed these, but they must have been jumped in the cantina before he had done it. And the road tires would not stand the punishment of high speeds over rough terrain for long.

Long Range swore again and yelled across to Belial, "Shall we change them?" Long practice, sometimes blindfolded or in the dark, had made them capable of changing a wheel in less than three minutes.

But Belial gestured behind them. Long Range looked back. Less than half a mile back three columns of dust were moving after them, slowly closing the distance between.

So they ran, pushing as fast as they dared through the rock-strewn canyon and following the trail weaving up and down the brush-covered slopes of the gray foothills. But they did no more than hold their lead on the Gypsies, who

82

had no decisions to make about the trail but could simply follow them, slowing only at possible ambush points. The chair held the Angels back too, and after an hour the Gypsies were close. Milt was driving demoniacally, using every ounce of the 1000cc motor's power, standing up continuously, hurling his weight to the left to help balance the bouncing machine, the sweat streaming off him as the sun beat down from the bright blue morning sky. They were still climbing, now reaching the early slopes of the first mountain. At the lower end of a sloping ravine they rode fast along the valley floor for a while before the trail began to ascend the right-hand side of the ravine. They racketed up the narrow path, sheer rock wall to their right, to the left the cliff falling away further and further below.

Long Range glanced back and saw their pursuers entering the far end of the valley. Ahead of them the path twisted and emerged into a shallow rocky pass that rose for over a mile toward its summit; it would be slow going. As they rounded the curve of rock up into the pass there came a sharp crack and Long Range jerked his hand up to see Belial wrestling his machine to a halt, the rear tire flat.

Long Range's mind raced; then as he entered the pass he wheeled his machine about, stopping for a moment to wipe his hand across his dusty face and red-rimmed eyes; Milt turned and gaped, but Long Range waved him on fiercely, jerked the shotgun from his saddlebag and, holding it in his left hand, nosed his bike back down the narrow trail. As he approached the bend he could hear the sound of motors laboring up the mountain toward him. He cocked the shotgun with his thumb, feeling completely cold but fiercely elated. His heart lifted as he reached the bend, the valley floor on his right a dizzy distance beneath, and roared round and down the hill as fast as he could.

He was closer to the oncoming machines than he had calculated, and closing with them fast. He had a second's glimpse of the incredulous expression on the face of the black-bearded leader, then he was concentrating on steering to the inside of him as Bad Hand braked. For a moment it looked as though they would collide. In desperation Long

Range swung the shotgun toward him; Bad Hand saw it, ducked, wobbled, stamped instinctively on the rear brake; his rear wheel locked and his bike slewed sideways, and suddenly machine and rider shot off the path and disappeared, plummeting screaming over the edge. Long Range just had time to swing the shotgun and then he was on the other two Gypsies, pulled close together into the inside wall, nearly stationary, one flinging up an arm as Long Range triggered the shotgun, hearing their cries above the blast and the rending noises as their bikes went down in a tangle.

He coasted, unbelieving, down to the bottom of the path and wheeled around on the valley floor. He could see the wreckage of Bad Hand's machine further down the valley at the foot of the cliff, a faint cloud of dust floating over it.

Jamming the empty weapon into his saddlebag he gunned his motor and rode up the path again. As he approached the fallen machines of his enemies he saw there was enough room for him to pass and then noticed with a shock that one of the Gypsies was moving, clutching a bolt-gun, crawling blindly on all fours up the path. He turned as he heard the sound of Long Range's motor and tried to bring his gun to bear. Coldly Long Range rode him down, hitting him as near center as he could with the front wheel, fighting to keep control of his machine under the crash-thump of impact as he skidded on up the trail, inches from the edge. When he could look back the Gypsy lay near the edge of the path, sprawled and motionless.

He coasted up the hill to the plateau where he found Belial and Milt dismounted on either side of the track, bolt-guns cocked and ready. Belial gave him a long look as he switched off his engine. "We thought we'd catch them if they got by you," he said slowly. "But they didn't get by you, did they?"

Long Range shook his head and told them what had happened.

"Do you want we should go back to make sure of them, and take trophies?" said Belial.

Long Range shook his head. "I saw two of them dead and Bad Hand go over the edge—he's probably in pieces all over the cliff."

"Or hung up in a bush, like the Oldest Angel," said Milt.

They were silent for a moment. There was a legend among them that, in pre-BLAM days, the founder of the Angels, the oldest of them all, had ridden his bike off a mountain road and been flung into a tree, where he had hung in agony all day. Miraculously he had survived and lived on for years, a pill-dispensing visionary and elder statesman. Milt's words reminded them that such things could happen.

"All right," said Long Range, "I need a bolt-gun. I lost mine in town." Wearily he kicked his machine into life and rode down the track to the scene of the fight. He dismounted by the crushed body of the Gypsy he had ridden down. He stared at it for a moment, then began searching for a gun among the wrecked bikes. One had been damaged by the shotgun blast and the other was nowhere to be seen, presumably knocked over the cliff-edge during his second charge. He peered carefully over the edge but could see no sign of Bad Hand's body. He watched for birds circling, but there were none.

When he reached the others again they were squatted in the shade of the bikes discussing their next move.

"We can't hardly go back to town," said Milt. "The citizens very likely might become inquiring about those three dead bodies, and probably a couple more died of shock the way we rode out."

"You think they'll come after us?" said Belial.

"I don't reckon so," said Milt. "We didn't see any local law, and the Cartel troopers on the Route won't care 'cause it wasn't any of their people got hurt. If we were still there they'd probably string us up just for something to do, but I don't see them coming after six armed riders."

"But if we can't go back," said Belial, "how the hell are we going to meet our contact?"

"Well I figure it this way," said Milt. "If he was in

town he'll surely know which way we headed out: if he weren't there he'll hear about it, 'cause the Citizens ain't going to talk about nothing else all summer long. So he'll know which way to look for us. If we make camp at the next good spot, he'll find us sure enough.''

"For a country boy," said Long Range, "you figure it out pretty good." Milt giggled. Belial looked blank.

"If we follow the trail north from here, the way I heard it there's a valley, then another hill, then two rivers. We could camp by the first river," Long Range said.

"Are we going to change those wheels?" said Milt.

"Better," said Belial.

They went to work in silence, sweating in the midday sun, and were done in a quarter of an hour.

"I hope that contact gets to us soon," sighed Milt, straightening up from the chair. "When we ran off from town I lost my bag with my spare clothes and most of the grub in it. I'm hungry as hell."

"Me too," said Long Range. "We can set some snares when we get to the river, though. Fish too, maybe."

They ate and drank sparingly, then rested by some big rocks in the heat of the day, Belial and then Milt standing watch.

In the afternoon glow they mounted and rode on up the pass, the hillside around covered with pine and gray rock, with streams jumping down the steep rock faces to disappear beneath great flat stones. They rode to the top of the pass and looked ahead in the fine golden light. On the right they could see the range of mountains climbing to a peak. Below them the trail wound down to a valley bare of trees, carpeted with bunch grass already turning brown, at the end of which the hills rose again, their slopes partially covered with groves of piñon. As they began the difficult descent, holding the heavy machines on brakes and low gear, their noise startled a black-tail deer with wide antlers and it clattered away through tree trunks, twisting among the shadows.

"There goes our fucking supper," shouted Milt. "If only you'd got some extra shells for that scatter gun."

"I know it," said Long Range gloomily.

When they reached the valley bottom it was already in shadow, and they rode fast across the crispy brown grass to the tree-line at the far end. They climbed a hill, descended, climbed another, and halfway down that slope could see, nestled beneath the next hillside, the river winking in the evening sunlight.

The descent became easier and soon they were picking their way along the river bank, thick-set with timber. They came to a pleasant grove of dead cottonwoods surrounded by long bottom grass, halted there, dismounted stiffly, and looked about them. On the banks of the river grew fresh spring willow and thorny plum with curling tendrils of grape and hop between them, the cottonwoods glossy-leaved, currant bushes cluttering close. Their ears rang in the silence; slowly they became aware of the gentle ripple of the clear stream. They went to it, knelt, and drank.

Soon the shadows of the peaks fell across the valley. Belial went off on foot to hunt. Long Range made up a fire with dead branches off the cottonwoods. Milt, whooping incredulously, hooked trout after trout from the river until seven fish lay shining on some leaves by the fire. Long Range gathered currants. As darkness fell he and Milt lined up the three bikes and slung canvases between them, creating two small tents. The wind, there at the foot of the hills, came from all directions; they fed the fire, their eyes weeping as the smoke veered about to blind and choke them. They gutted the fish and skewered them on pointed sticks to grill over the ashes. Darkness fell and Belial came back quietly, his bolt-gun over his shoulder and a duck dangling from his left hand.

"It's no deer, but it'll hold us for tomorrow," he murmured, scooping clay from the river bank to bake the bird in beneath the embers. "I lost the goddam bolt, though. I'm down to maybe seven or eight now."

"You can have mine," said Long Range sourly. "I've no bolt-gun and no way to get one out here."

"Hey, these are just about done," said Milt, brandishing a trout on a stick. Long Range put the coffee pot in the embers and filled their mugs with the last of the wine. They gorged on the trout, the crisp skin and tender meat, eating straight off the sticks with salt and a little hard bread, washing the food down with gulps of wine. When it was done they lay back on their blankets and Long Range passed them each a handful of hard little currants and filled their empty mugs with steaming sweet coffee. Their backs were cold, their eyes intermittently filled with smoke, but a mood of great content came to them at the end of the bloody and uncertain day. Gazing at the fire, Milt hummed and then sang quietly: "Dancing in the meadow. . . ."

"Angels on the hill," completed Long Range. "But right now I feel more like a Citizen. You know, fat and lazy."

"I found a ford," said Belial. "Down there about half a mile. Some young timber and weeds. The bottom looked all right. Some of the trees were gnawed up. Beaver I guess."

"Could be bear claws," said Long Range.

"Didn't look that way, no tracks. But you can bet this is bear country all right."

. He paused, thinking, then said:

"One other thing. With the wind shifting about and all I couldn't be sure. But I thought I heard a bike. Back there," he said, gesturing in the direction from which they had come.

They lay in silence for a while.

"Maybe it's our contact," said Milt. "It would figure, from the gas caches, if what we're meeting is outlaw riders."

They were silent again.

Then Belial said, "Are the bikes ready to go?"

Milt nodded. "We checked them over and gassed up."

"How is the gas?" asked Belial.

"We're looking good," said Milt, cautiously optimistic. "We only did about a gallon and a half each today. About forty miles, with all that climbing. I topped up, so that's four and a half gallons each in the tanks, and ten and a half in the cans on the chair."

A gallon weighed seven pounds. With the spares and

equipment they could carry no more than fifteen gallons extra on the chair. With what was in their tanks, nine and a half gallons for each machine altogether. On level ground their machines would do about forty miles to the gallon. And each bike could thus travel about 350 miles. They had been told the gas caches were about 200 miles apart. It was vital arithmetic for them.

"The first cache is close," Milt continued; "twenty, maybe thirty miles away, on the next river. Plenty in hand."

"And if we ever have trouble locating the caches, we can spin out the gas that's left by just sending one of us out to look." Cautiously optimistic. Pushing back the thought of the faint noise behind them, the body missing on the trail, the weird songs and stories they had heard about Bad Hand.

"When our contact gets to us, finding the caches will be no problem," said Milt. They were quiet again, listening to the river gurgle and ripple, resenting it now for the way it deadened the sounds around.

"I think we should push on to the first cache tomorrow," said Belial. "The contact'll know we have to get there. And it's further from—" he gestured back the way they had come.

"Bless the night," muttered Milt, an old saying with them; none of the bikes had lights, and pursuit ceased with nightfall.

"I'll take first watch," said Belial, rising. "How about the fire?"

"I figure it'll be all right," said Milt. "No one much out here. Some guys run sheep in the valleys like the one we come through. Trappers. Anyway, if we kill the fire, what about your damn duck?"

"Rather have raw duck than us cold on open slice," said Belial. He began stamping the fire out. Milt, grumbling, took his blanket to the tent and crawled between two of the bikes. Long Range crawled in next door. They had cut branches to spread the blankets on, and they wore their leather coats and all their clothes. Even so the chill from the earth and the water nearby soon worked through them.

Lying on his front in the shadows of cottonwoods, facing the river with his chin on his hands, through the willows by the water Long Range could see the moon, one night from full, rising above them. With a sudden pang he remembered other willows, and the crescent moon shining. From the other side of the bike, Milt spoke.

"I never told you how I came to get out of that saloon this morning, did I?"

"No," said Long Range; "I figured you heard them moving around downstairs."

"Nah," said Milt, "me and Lizzy was too busy to hear anything. Then somebody heaved a rock at the shutters. Real hard, they nearly smashed. I figured it might be Belial so I climbed off and opened up. And you know who it was?"

"No," said Long Range.

"It was your girlfriend. Rita. She whispered up that our enemies were downstairs. I get my pants on, shove Lizzy out the window and go to get you. But when I peeked through the door they'd already got you and they were coming up for me. Whew! Bam—I was out the window. Like shit off a shovel, you better believe."

"What happened to Rita?"

"I don't know. She and Lizzy must have took off somewhere. I guess we'll never see them again.

"It's funny, you know," he went on, "that was my first time alone with a girl. It entirely beats doing some poor captive wench with all the brothers standing around giving advice. Lizzy was, I don't know, she was. . . ."

"Yeah," said Long Range, "I know."

They lay in silence, thinking. Long Range discovered that when he thought of Rita his mind filled with peace, and happiness. He found that he just had to think of her face and peace came to him, so that he smiled in the dark. Through the rustling leaves he could sometimes see the stars. He recalled her again and again, and doing so, fell asleep.

90

HE DREAMED. SHADOWY FIGURES WRITHED AND BECK-
oned beneath as three birds, wide-winged, beat their way
into the vapors of the upper air, striving higher and higher.
One fell away; the two remaining beat their way onwards,
up and up into the thin atmosphere, until one faltered, wing
beat weakened, and it too fell away, for the last bird could
not slacken its effort. Ahead lay a shining disc of silver
white, the sun, and the last bird flew to its brilliance, flew
into it, for the sun was a tunnel and now he was riding;
the canyon walls opened out and they rode into the light
again, he and the familiar, unfamiliar faces, rejoicing and
laughing, and in the distance across the plain he could see
that the feast had already begun, and he kicked his pony
ahead of the others for he could make out the form of the
Old One, and he knew the Old One was aware of him
already, and he hurried on to the circle of the fires; flung
himself from his mount and ran to fall on his knees at the
Old One's feet, overcome by the familiar joy, lacking so
long: home.

Milt was shaking him awake to stand the last watch, the
dawn watch. He took the gun and bolts and moved to his
position, away from the trees, with clear ground around
except for the bushes which would cover him if he had to
fall back on the camp. The curve of the river secured him
from behind.

Settled squatting on his blanket he began to quarter the
area carefully with his eyes. The moon was still up, and
soon his sight adjusted to take in every detail of the damp
silvery clearing and probe the shadows beneath the trees.
His ears struggled to sort out the noises of the wild creatures, the wind in the trees and anything that might be an
enemy approaching. His limbs grew painfully stiff but he
maintained his position, as he learned to do while hunting.
He was nervous and it kept him awake. In the background
the river gurgled and chuckled invisibly. Time passed and
one by one, then quickly overlapping, the birds began to
sing, and the shape of things began to stand out from the
darkness. Mist hung among the trees as dawn came, slowly

and undramatically. Long Range rubbed his stubble and yawned, chilled through and tired but forcing himself to listen for the sound of the machines as the light returned. Nothing came.

When it was full light he went and shook the other two awake, gave Milt back his gun and began to make up the fire. The mist lay all about; the small noises they made as they moved about seemed contained, unnaturally clear and loud.

Belial said he had set some snares the night before and padded off to check them. Milt went off behind the bushes. The wood was dew-damp and difficult, but Long Range gathered some dry twigs off the dead trees, shaved three of them and piled the rest around them. When the fire had caught and the coffeepot was on he sliced the last of the bread and knelt over the fire to toast it on his knife.

He glanced up at the sound of running steps close by. He saw Milt running desperately through the cottonwoods; as he got near the fire he shouted once.

"He got Belial. . . ."

Then Long Range's eyes were drawn to the figure behind him, running in a shambling light-footed shuffle, so that for a moment in confusion he thought that it was a bear attacking them, and in his surprise the knife with the toast still on it slipped from his fingers and tumbled into the fire. At the same moment he realized the horrible familiarity of the dark shape, and Bad Hand raised the bolt-gun in his left hand and shot Milt in the back.

Milt cried out once and went down, and lay still and silent on the other side of the fire before Long Range fully realized what had happened. When he moved to help his friend Bad Hand had already unslung and cocked a second bolt-gun, and now motioned for him to stay where he was. He advanced to about fifteen yards away, keeping the fire between himself and Long Range, who stared mesmerized at the black hole of the bolt-gun barrel pointed at his head.

Bad Hand stopped.

"Well, sonny," he rumbled finally, "we've got some settling to do." He paused. "That was a pretty neat trick on the mountain there. Trouble for you is, I'm lucky, see? And you left me. That's kind of the Angel way, isn't it, sonny?'' he snarled, suddenly furious.

Long Range was trying desperately to think, to prolong this inexplicable reprieve until he could see a way to take advantage of it. ''What do you mean?'' he asked.

''What I mean is I've been left by you bloody bastards before,'' said Bad Hand, his face livid, the gun trembling in his good hand.

''But we never got close to you before,'' said Long Range, helplessly trying to prolong the talking.

''Oh, the Angels and me used to be close all right,'' rumbled Bad Hand, grimly amused.

''What do you mean?''

''I mean I used to be an Angel,'' shouted Bad Hand. ''And I was left for dead out in the west one time and not one brother came back to see if I lived or fetch away my body. And I lay knocked cold under my bike and the acid from the battery did this''—he waved his hideous right hand in the air—''and I wandered for a week, and came out of the forest naked and stone crazy at the Gypsies' camp, and they took me in because all I could think of and say was how I hated the fucking Angels. And that's why I drink Angels' blood. And that's why I had the strength to crawl off that mountainside yesterday and put together a whole bike from the two wrecks you left me so kindly, and trail you to the valley back there, and keep coming on foot all through the night''—He's boasting, thought Long Range, and, Use it—''and lay for the redhead by his snares, and catch your friend here with his pants down and kill him with his own gun, and that, sonny, is why I'm going to breakfast on your balls.''

When Bad Hand had mentioned Milt Long Range glanced across at the still form of his friend and rage kindled in him at the exact moment that he realized what he must try to do.

''You may have been an Angel once, but you've forgotten how we die,'' he shouted back, his voice taunting, staring the black-bearded giant straight in the eye. ''You

93

just want to cut me so I'll be like you, no hand, no brains and no balls either, you gutless cripple. Is it because you've only got one hand you can't make it except with a weapon against an unarmed man? Put down the gun and show us what a great fighter Bad Hand is on his own, you bragging, treacherous, ugly piece of pigshit, you bloody bearded woman, you.''

He stopped, breathless. Bad Hand was nodding slowly.

''Why not?'' he muttered and, stooping, gently placed the gun on the grass, sliding a long knife from his boot as he straightened and moved in toward Long Range.

And Long Range never hesitated.

Jumping to the fire he plunged his hand in, scooped out his own knife, and with a scream of pain and rage leapt over the fire, swinging the burning blade in a great over-hand arc and plunging it full into the giant's chest, just as Bad Hand's thrust caught him in the ribs.

The two men fell apart: Long Range gasped and tumbled to his knees, looking desperately behind him for the final attack. But none came; Bad Hand lay writhing and choking on his back in the grass, the steaming knife still sticking from his chest. Long Range crawled; as the drew closer to the giant his eyes fell on the other blade lying in the damp grass nearby, covered with his own blood.

As he knelt by the huge prostrate form, Bad Hand's convulsions eased. His eyes were open, casting about, and they seem to focus on the knife handle protruding from his chest; the wooden panels had burnt away and the design on the handle stood out clearly. Bad Hand's eyes widened and then a feeble smile played across his features. He whispered something. Long Range knelt forward, mesmerized, awed by the death agony of the giant.

''Sonny,'' whispered Bad Hand, his smile wonderful, ''sonny, sonny, sonny, son, son, son,'' until his voice faded away to the faintest sibilance.

Long Range looked away, up at the trees with the mist burned away by the sun now, across to the river, down at the knife in his hands. He realized already that it was identical to his own, and he knew who he had killed. His eyes blinded with tears, and he took his father's scarred head in his hands and held it in his lap and cradled it, rocking back and forth and weeping, crooning incoherently. But it was too late for the giant to hear.

And then he felt himself going; his grief and the wound in his side welled up and he slid over and lay curled up beside the giant, their bodies mingled, live and dead on the wet grass, listening to the river run for a moment before oblivion moved in.

III   THE LOST TRAVELER

"The wisdom of the teaching was from vision and the
vision was from Wakan Tanka."

— Black Elk: *The Sacred Pipe*

For a period he had no way to measure, made up of
fragments he did not wish to connect, Long Range wandered between dream and waking.

Again and again, he was in a tent. Often he imagined
Rita was there, caring for him; but she seemed different,
dressed in buckskin, and her hair braided. Across from
him, always there, it seemed, there lay an old Indian who
never spoke; sometimes he communicated with Rita in sign
but always his dark eyes were fixed unwaveringly on Long
Range. This must be a dream, the Old One he had dreamed
of before. He would slip into other dreams of chasms, steel
and pain; then deeper reaches still, from which he would
float back to the tent dream; why so often?

In it—it seemed to him not for the first time—he was
mildly surprised to see Milt; his friend's left shoulder was
in a sling, his features drawn but animated and hair unruly
as ever as he bent by Long Range and talked, reciting, as
far as Long Range could make out, again and again, an
unlikely tale, a wish-tale of what might have been.

Milt would be telling the way they had got to the Indian

96

encampment where they now lay; how Belial had recovered from his clubbing by Bad Hand and ridden on to get help for the two of them as they lay wounded; how at the gas cache he had come on the camp of these Indians, who called themselves Lakota, and how Belial's life had been saved only by the presence there of Rita, who was herself one of the Lakota; how Rita all along had been their contact in Harmony, and how it was the Lakota whom Professor Sangria had contacted, who had passed his message along and set up the chain of caches across the plain along the route east to Iron Mountain where the Professor was working. Milt would finish the story, describing how the Indians had come for them both as they lay wounded, and borne them on litters over the last mountain pass, down to their camp here under the cottonwoods on the river; while Belial ferried their bikes to the camp, riding back between on an Indian pony.

Long Range absorbed this story in fragments at first, but as Milt repeated it tirelessly, tiresomely, day after day— could it be day after day? could it be real?—as somewhere in him he partially accepted that it might be, his reaction was to withdraw; he would turn away from his friend's words as he did from the old Indian's eyes, direct, and, he knew, concerned to help him; for to accept the story and the help would mean to accept something that he had done which he only half-remembered, a dream of horror that he knew he could never face.

So he turned his face to the tepee wall and lay not speaking a word.

As Milt ducked from the tepee one evening, sighing at yet another failure to communicate with his sick friend, Belial stepped up and grabbed his arm.

"They're doing it again," he snarled. "Only this time they're calling me something else. Now it's 'Datakan,' 'Datakan,' all the fucking time, even the kids follow me around and call me that. Whyn't they call me by my fucking name? You tell them, Milt, if this keeps up, I kick red ass. You tell them."

Milt sighed. Belial hated the Lakota, and he could not

understand that for them it would have been impolite to call Belial by his proper name. They had dubbed him Wa Gi'Om, which, when he objected, Milt had explained meant Thunderbird, since he had come out of the west on a roaring machine, recalling the Thunderbird of their myths, the winged power of the west. Milt had reluctantly passed on Belial's objections to his given name to the Lakota.

"I tried to tell them you didn't go for your new name, but now they're calling you Da Te Kan?" said Milt. "Let's see." Then he laughed, till his wounded shoulder made him gasp with pain. "Yeah, it figures."

"What the hell does it mean?" shouted Belial.

"It means 'Keeps-His-Name,' " chuckled Milt, and went on, "but listen, you know what they're calling Long? Because of where the knife burned him? They're calling him Bad Hand." When Belial walked off Milt chuckled to himself. Maybe that would throw some kind of scare into the bastard.

He stood thinking, filling his lungs with the pure air. He had learned a smattering of the Lakota tongue during his schooldays at the Fief, and this together with his knowledge of sign language allowed him to communicate with the Indians, though a few, like Rita, spoke English. The Fief had acknowledged the existence of the bands of wild "savages" on the plains beyond Harmony in only the vaguest terms, and learning the rudiments of their tongue had been presented to the class almost as a linguistic exercise; though it was now evident that the Fief had known more than they had allowed.

He wandered down to the river. It was dusk; he stood by a tree, savoring the silence—how quiet the Lakota camp was by comparison with the Angel home and even Harmony—and tried to calm his worry at Long Range's withdrawn condition, and his own solitude in the absence of his friend's company.

He turned to watch the women at work outside the tepees, laying strips of meat to dry on pale rocks or the berries on sheets of bark, slicing the wild artichokes and onions and mushrooms, pounding nuts to a paste or wild cherries into the meat. Above the camp the evening star rose. Cooking smells wafted to him, and the people called from the tepee where he was lodging. He had found out that this band was known among their fellows as "the Greedies."

"Well," he thought, "there'd be worse ones to fall in with."

After supper it was dark, and above him as he stepped outside the tepee for a moment the stars had begun to glitter. He heard ponies whinny and stamp outside the circle of tipis. He approached dark shapes beside his host's lodge. Stripping away covers of rawhide he revealed his bike, touched the cold metal of the tank and the leather of the seat, then straddled it and sat with his hands at rest lightly on the familiar grips, alone in the dark.

ONE DAY WHEN THE WOUND IN HIS SIDE WAS HEALING well, Long Range awoke to find that Rita was gone and her place taken by a tall brave of about forty. His nose was sharply hooked, the set of his lips almost contemptuous in its self-sufficiency; but his face was softened by dark eyes which, though fiercely bright, were full of joy, far-seeing and compassionate. Long Range felt an instinctive awe and respect for him.

"You are awake, brother," said the brave in English. "I am called Black Horse Rider. Sky here," he gestured at the silent old brave, "is a wise man, and he wishes me to speak of the way we Lakota see the world; to put our vision like a seed in your center, which will grow in your heart.

"Brother, will you hear us?" The glowing eyes fixed on his, and Long Range found himself nodding.

Black Horse Rider sat by the old man in silence. Long Range's own silence had been unbroken, but the Indian's stillness was something he could not resist. After a while Long Range found himself looking at him in awe and admiration. And when at last Black Horse Rider rose without a word and fetched down the pipe, the time seemed right, the simple action curiously significant. The fragrance of sweet grass filled the air of the tepee as a pinch was burnt

99

on a glowing coal to purify the pipe. And Long Range knew from the talk the day before that as the pipe moved from left to right, sun-wise, around the circle they formed, it represented the motion of life itself from its source in the south until its return to where it began; and that when it was raised in the air and touched the ground, the two great powers of sky and earth were invoked.

"When you pray with this pipe you pray with and for everything," said Black Horse Rider once again when they had smoked. "Yesterday I told you that you did not understand, as yet, and I think one thing you do not fully know is why you have come here. I think that the other young men, your friends, have come for the glory, and that you have all come eastward because you were told it was necessary.

"But there is a power, something very clear and powerful, that can direct our acts. Our grandfather, Sky, feels it could flow in you. That is why you have come; the other things are not the real reasons."

Long Range felt a queer tenseness in the enclosed space of the tepee, felt the atmosphere building as Black Horse Rider was silent for a while, then went on speaking.

He began by outlining the way in which the Lakota, together with other groups of Indians, had reacted to the cataclysm of BLAM; they had understood it as the time prophesied for so long by their wise men, the end of a cycle, when the Wasichu, the white man, and his ways were swept away.

The few Indians living at that time felt the coming of a new age. They freed the few buffalo that had survived, like themselves, as captives of the whites, and together they journeyed to the plains; and there they lived, men and animals, and grew in numbers and in spirit. The old ways returned, and there were mighty warriors, for they felt they were living the birth of a new first age, an age of great spirit power.

And they remembered how their people had been deceived before by the Wasichu into surrendering their hunting and their lands, and being shut away from the earth.

So they killed, ruthlessly, any who wandered into their lands; and their very existence was a matter of conjecture, of frightened half-tales, to the people in the lands around the plains, who usually considered most of the prairie to be dead lands—which indeed some of it was.

But, said Black Horse Rider, now he considered that this first fine age had drawn to a close. Things were changing. To the west and north the tribes were safe from attack. To the south they had held the white men who had begun to come on to the plains; they fought them, and rubbed them out. Also the chiefs had hit upon a plan; they sent members of the Indian tribes there into the towns, in the same way Rita had been sent, to keep the tribes informed of the Was-ichu's numbers and intentions; and to work to continue the fiction that the plains were dead lands, which had, in the south, mostly succeeded up till now.

"But to the east . . ." and here Black Horse Rider paused, and looked at Long Range in silence. Eventually he said:

"I do not know what you have heard of the people to the east. We have to understand them, to know them as the hunter knows the ways of the buffalo; for they are our enemy, they are many, and if we cannot out-think them they will destroy us.

"We know that after the sky fell, the people of the east knew hard times; terrible days of sickness and hunger. It was then that those who survived there began to say that if they lived, it was their God who willed it. That only they serve Wakan Tanka, Great Spirit, truly. That they must cover the face of the land, taking those who will hear their words and destroying those who will not.

"Lakota know, all the Indian peoples know, that Wakan Tanka, Great Spirit, made all; all things and all people are places where he stopped. But the men of the east think that they and they only have the truth, that their way is the only sacred way, that all people who will not say this is so must be destroyed.

"We think that this madness comes to them in the lonely nights. For they are lonely—they cut themselves off from

101

each other, from other peoples, and from the earth itself. Alone at night they must think of themselves as great wise men and conquerors; for if they are not that, they are no more than lost frightened children. Now we know that this is so, all are only children of Father Sky and Mother Earth; but it is the fear in them that makes them destroy, not create.''

Long Range listened hard; Black Horse Rider's words were expressing his own discontent with the Angels.

The Lakota went on. He said that the Indians had soon realized the power of the East, and knew that once before they had been overrun by crazy men from the East. They knew that to hold them back they needed weapons, and to whip them, they needed friends.

At about that time, some of the Indian spies in the southern towns had made contact with agents from the Fief, and others with similar men from the Peregrine Fief. These countries to the west seemed to offer less of a direct threat to the Indian nations than the South did; so they had spoken freely to them of their position.

Both the Fief and the Peregrines had heard of the East's growing power and their predatory intentions; and were not slow to realize the benefit of the buffer between east and west that Indians in arms would provide. So, hidden in the same way the Angels had been, they sent to the Indians guns and ammunition, the means to make their own bullets, explosives, grenades, and everything necessary to wage a guerrilla struggle. This allowed the tribes to harry the Easterners, and hold them to the Dead Lands to the east that separated their country from the plains.

But there were problems. The flow of manufactured goods from the west began to alter the tribes' way of life. And each year the peoples of the East grew stronger; as hard and as cunningly as the Lakota and the others fought, they could no longer challenge the East directly, but had to content themselves with keeping the Eastern forces pinned down, and picking off stragglers. The chiefs and wise men could see that it was only a matter of time before the East broke out of the Dead Lands and swept them away.

102

"There was a Lakota, Yellow Bull, whom the Easterners had captured and put to work for them. Last year Yellow Bull escaped and told us of the Professor, the one they call Sangria, the one you have come for. It seems he was born in the South and is no true friend to the Easterners, but only with them could he pursue his work. And this is work we Lakota can understand; for he strives to renew the earth.

"But it is cruel work. You see Sky here; he is sick and dumb because when we fought around Iron Mountain and he was wounded, his pony wandered into the lands where Sangria was testing. You see how he is now; maimed, dumb. Tunka Shila; our grandfather.

"Yellow Bull had talked with Sangria of ourselves and of the words of those who sent you, the Fief; and the Professor said that he would go with them, or with the others, the Peregrines, so long as they would help him complete his work; for he is nearly done now, and he does not wish the Easterners to gain from the earth that he renews."

Black Horse Rider paused, turned his dark eyes penetratingly on Long Range and continued.

"So you will see that there is more to this than we Lakota, or your masters the Fief, or the Professor himself, serving our own ends.

"That is why we Lakota have provided caches of fuel across the plains for you, and why a party of our warriors will accompany you east to the Iron Mountain, to help you reach the Professor and to cover your flight with him.

"It seems to me that we all share an idea. All Indian peoples know that the earth must be renewed; by our prayers and dances; by our blood if need be. I have said things have changed with us after the first time when the buffalo fell. Even if we whip the Easterners, it is not enough. For Lakota ways to live we must be in a world that understands their wisdom. Before we were innocent, and it was good; now it must be organized, deliberate. We cannot stand alone.

"So we need you. Sky needs you: I need you: all Lakota need you to help with this work. To fetch the Professor, to explain Lakota people to the Fief. We need a friend, one who knows our hearts.''

He stopped, and Long Range felt a ringing silence in the enclosed space; he was aware of every detail of the scene, every wrinkle on Sky's intent face, every little drawing of man and horse on the tepee cover, the shadows under carbines stacked in the corner, the smoke curling up from the fire pit, the lingering aroma of the smoke mixture and sweet grass. At the same time his mind was full of the Indian's last words. ''We need you.''

This old man, Sky, needs me.

It came as a complete shock: it changed everything. He tried to speak, cleared his throat and said in a hoarse voice, ''I am not fit. I killed my father.''

AT DAWN MILT WATCHED THEM BUILD A SWEAT LODGE, bending the peeled willows into two hoops that crossed each other, covering them with skins, digging the fire pit for the hot stones at the end of a trench a little way off to the east.

It was the morning following the day of Black Horse Rider's visit to Long Range. The previous evening Milt had seen a medicine man and his helper join them in the tepee, and the sound of low chanting to a drum and rattle began soon after. He guessed it was an attempt to cure his friend but hated not to be there. All through the night as he awoke from fitful dozing the wind carried to him the sounds of chanting, shake of the rattle and throb of the drum.

This bright morning people had gathered to watch the building of the sweat lodge, and now a gasp arose from them as the medicine man and his helper emerged, backwards, from Sky's tepee, still chanting and shaking the rattle; and then Milt stepped forward, as Long Range staggered out into the sunlight. He was clearly very weak, his head drooped, but his glazed eyes kept raising to the rattle and his footsteps stumbled forward as the medicine man danced backward to the sweat lodge.

''Looks like they've slipped him something,'' thought

Milt after his first relief at seeing his friend on his feet again. By then Long Range had disappeared through the low entry to the sweat lodge, Black Horse Rider following holding the bag with the pipe, and another brave carrying Sky in his arms. They all ducked inside the lodge, and after a while the helpers began to take in the heated stones.

LONG RANGE FELT AS IF HE WERE FLOATING.

The day before, after he had got out his first words, he went on to tell the two Indians how it had been. Black Horse Rider listened gravely and put his tale into sign language for Sky's benefit. When he had finished they sat in silence for a long while; then exchanged one phrase of sign language, and Black Horse Rider rose and left. Long Range felt taken aback; unconsciously he had supposed that once he had told someone he would be reassured; the small part of his mind that had not recoiled from the horror had still understood that the killing could be seen as an accident of circumstances. But his silence and mindlessness had been keeping at bay the conviction that the circumstances were unimportant, that he had been doomed to participate in that scene and the key to his life was that curse, not the explanations.

After a long while Black Horse Rider came back with the medicine man. Long Range's eyes ranged over his finery, his fringes and dyed porcupine quills, and the big shadow his horned headdress cast on the tepee wall as he bent over the sickbed of skins, chanting prayer after prayer interspersed with shakes of his rattle. Sometimes Black Horse Rider would mutter a translation of the prayers like a response, but never looking at Long Range as he did it. Long Range gazed at the eagle feathers shaking on the rattle; he had heard Milt say that to the Lakota they represented the rays of the sun, up where the eagle flew. The soft, high chanting began, and the young brave who had slipped in with the medicine man, his helper, began to drum, the chanting voices twisting up through the thick sound of the drumming like birds spiraling, like a cloud thickening, like smoke.

After a while he began to feel slightly oppressed by the noise and the monotonous syllables of the chanting. Physically, ever since he regained consciousness he had been experiencing a queer suspended feeling. The pounding of the drum continued. Boom, boom boom boom. Boom, boom boom boom, and he felt a further shift to weightlessness; something within his body seemed to be moving, sliding backwards and sideways as he lay. As soon as he became aware of this it was very unpleasant. He tried to concentrate on something, details of the scene around, but each time his attention wandered he experienced this involuntary movement, and at the same time a hypersensitivity within his frame, a seething, tingling feeling.

He shut his eyes, and in an instant was struggling with the Gypsy Cat-back on the hard road; his knife bit home again and blood splashed over his face. He snapped his eyes open wide, his heart pounding and his breathing quick.

It happened again: he closed his eyes and this time the road unwound ahead of him as he tore down it—only, disturbingly, the highway seemed to continue right back through the caverns of his eye sockets and into the tunnel of his skull.

Twice more as the oppression in the tepee grew his eyes closed and each time scenes of horror from his journey flashed on him.

He lay sweating after reliving the plunge of the knife into Bad Hand's chest, and stared hard at the medicine man; he found himself hanging on to the weird shape of the dancing figure; for the leader was now raising and lowering his fringed arms like a great bird as he turned on the spot where he stood, stamping to the drum's thump. Long Range peered, trying to make out the man's eyes beneath the shadows of the horned headdress. Against the amber half-light of the illuminated skin walls, as Long Range gazed, the dancing figure became stranger and stranger: and then for an instant there seemed to be a great bird, pale like an owl in the dusk, hovering and swooping within the tepee. Long Range gasped. The horror was driven from his mind. Sometimes he would be seeing the medicine man

106

dancing again, but the vision of the great shining bird stayed more and more, and finally Long Range slid into it completely. He too was flying, round and round the enclosed space for a moment, then following the great bird up to the smoke hole at the top of the tepee and through, out into the night sky. He felt terrific, staying aloft by a combination of thought and movement, following the pale shape of his guide as they rose on the breeze, leaving the tepee circle behind. Then they swooped round and beat their way eastwards across the starlit plains, the flat lands and wide rivers sliding beneath them. After a long while the country turned to tree-covered ridges once more, and below them Long Range made out clusters of buildings which he knew to be the camps of the enemy. On the slopes of one hill lights burned, and he guessed it was Iron Mountain. Swooping around the fences and buildings there, they flew off to the south, following a ridge which they crested where a stream fell to reveal a secluded valley. He followed his guide spiraling down the side of the ridge to the valley floor, winging along the shallow brook there until the valley forked and they swung down the right-hand canyon until it widened to become plains once more and they were flying back the way they had come.

At last as they reached the tepee circle again the vague gray light of predawn showed the shapes of the country without shadows. His guide cried once and fluttered round to face the east. He followed suit and they hovered.

With a fanfare of light the sun rose above the eastern horizon. Long Range gazed into the orange ball and finally seemed to discern, within its orb, three spokes spiraling slowly out from the center. The silence of dawn began to be broken up by a regular thumping, a hissing rattle and crying voices. The three-legged wheel was moving faster, and as he looked it spun out smoking from the center of the sun and as his eyes followed the shape became the trunk and two dancing legs of the figure of the medicine man stamping to the drum, and the power that had kept him aloft waned so that he fluttered downwards to the camp and before he knew it found that he was on his feet, stumbling forward in the dusty sunlight after the dancing medicine man, surrounded by people crying excitedly, heading for a low hide-covered tent. He felt weak and confused as he ducked into the sweat lodge, but Black Horse Rider came in after him and sat down easily beside him, gazing into his eyes and smiling warmly. Long Range smiled back.

In the darkened sweat lodge they had smoked and prayed, the aromatic steam rising about them from the hot stones dumped in scented water, their bodies glistening in the half-light in a slick film of perspiration.

Long Range, feeling light-headed from hunger and disoriented by his experience of the night before, had asked Black Horse Rider what it could have meant.

The Indian answered gravely:

"As you must know, we Lakota are great thieves. When you lay sick and silent, your father's ghost had stolen your soul. Then the medicine man caught your eye—and stole it back again.

"But to go forward you need a vision, a gift from Wakan Tanka, for strength and understanding. Our young men at your age go to cry for one. So shall you, when we leave this place."

Long Range watched the rituals and listened, noting again the emphasis on the four directions and their qualities. He remembered his awareness of the cardinal points during his dream flight; and felt an obscure knowledge within himself of the powers of the world, powers that a man could touch by ways of living which acknowledged them; the same powers that had come and taken him out of himself and carried him across the night land.

Then Black Horse Rider passed a water-pot and they drank, Long Range parched and drinking deep through dry lips. It was time to go.

EVEN BEFORE IT HAD BEGUN, AND LONG RANGE WAS standing on the edge of the clearing at the foot of the final hill, exhausted beyond exhaustion by the effort of matching Black Horse Rider's tireless pace on the long walk from the camp up into the mountains; even as he squatted panting and looking around him, he felt the place to be especially strange and beautiful. The pine-clad hills lay all around in fine clear light, the forest floor carpeted with soft needles, sweet smelling, and fallen trunks at angles in the still and dusty shadows. Across the folds of the mountainsides he heard birds singing; but in the clearing where he sat the stillness was absolute, and uncanny.

Helpers had been before them and at the top of the hill above them had dug a shallow pit and sheltered it beneath a covering of bison hide slung between stakes. In the ground about it stood a circle of four posts, one at each direction, with offering bundles and feathers fluttering from their tops.

Long Range was to pray and dance to one post, return to the center, then continue round to the next, sun-wise, and return again to the center, and so on round and round in a circle about his shelter. The song was a chant that had been drummed into him when he was sick; the dance, a simple back-and-forwards step which the medicine man had shown him, and which he still felt foolish doing on his own.

He looked up to find Black Horse Rider standing over him, and rose to face him. The older man handed him a waterskin and kept his hand extended.

"You must give me your knife. Weapons are no part of the sacred way."

Long Range was unprepared for this. He stammered something about bears and wolves, but Black Horse Rider just shook his head, and Long Range shut up, knowing that was not his real reason for wishing to keep his knife, and knowing that the Lakota knew it too.

Then a wave of incredible anger toward the Indian took him and he thrust his face forward, his right hand moving behind him toward the knife hilt, inwardly cursing the Lakota for interfering with him.

Fucker thinks he'll take away my knife—skin son of a bitch. . . .

He was pure Hell's Angel again. It was more than temper or irritation; he was possessed; he could kill, the fight-

109

ing moves were plotted and ready, the power of his previous kills welling up in him; he was a pulse away from going for the man across from him. A part of him felt his eyes were mad, distended; that part had to fight to keep control. And he suddenly knew that his ferocity, which he had thought of as outside himself, caused by the bloody events of their journey, was in fact deeply a part of himself, his own temperament and the armor of ruthlessness that had been forged for him as far back as he could remember, the business of becoming an Angel. When he had gone silent, that had been part of the armor too. Knowing this made it not easier but harder to stop acting that way.

But in a fraction of a second the mood shifted, for the eyes of Black Horse Rider, who had remained relaxed but rooted to the spot, began to speak to him; the impassive face was like a sponge soaking up his waves of violent feeling. But far from seeking to pacify him in any way, all Long Range got back from the Indian's eyes at first was the unmistakable shock that here was a man who had killed often, could kill effortlessly, in his own way as ruthless as any Angel.

Yet with this difference: the Indian's body told that he had nothing to prove or to protect. Long Range could feel it almost tangibly as they stood face to face; he realized, as if he had known it all along, the difference was that the Lakota could not only kill, he knew how to die. As the seconds passed Long Range read the message in the tiny changes of expression around the brave's eyes and in the mood about them, as the wind sighed once through the pines and then fell silent again; the Indian's power was not force, it had no end in mind, of subjugation or victory; it simply was, no more personal than the wind itself, or the tallness of the trees, the soaring of a hawk. And Long Range was overwhelmed, knowing through and through he could not think of defeating this power; he only wanted to live beside it, long enough perhaps to learn some of its wisdom.

He looked again, and Black Horse Rider had gone before
110

him once more; the black eyes were kind and smiling; Long Range felt they knew what he had been thinking.

He reached behind him, slipped the knife from its case and handed it to Black Horse Rider, who took it without a word. Suddenly Long Range was close to tears; but the Lakota's strength gave him courage, and all he did was say quietly:

"I don't want to be well again. Ever."

The Indian nodded as if he understood that too, but all he said was:

"Do not neglect your prayers and your dance."

And turning on his heel, he walked firmly away down the hill, leaving Long Range alone in the stillness of the clearing.

After a while he turned toward the top of the hill and walked up, remembering to cry out as he did so:

"Wakan Tanka be merciful to me
And let my people live."

Once he reached the top he stripped off his breech-cloth and moccasins and stood naked by the cover. The first thing he thought of was how hungry he was, but he soon found that thinking about it only made the pain in his belly worse.

Tentatively at first he faced the west, the home of the thunder-beings, and began to jig about and chant his prayer, his voice sounding thin and absurd in the empty silence around. He hated it. He went back to the center and drank some water, and then, principally because he could think of nothing else to do, he walked heavily to the northern post and danced and chanted there, painfully conscious of his penis jiggling about as he did so.

Things failed to improve as the afternoon wore on. He felt tired and dispirited, and no power came as he sang and stamped on his own and cried to the powers to help him and the shadows lengthened from the trees. Coolness came with the evening and hunger struck him again. Several times he thought of returning to the camp, and only the thought of Black Horse Rider prevented him. As darkness fell he walked back to the pit at the center and huddled down on his robe spread on the bed of sage left by the helpers, exhausted and miserable, but remembering laconically to place his head to the center post and his feet to the east.

Close to sleep his only consolation was remembering the dream flight east to the Iron Mountain, and sensing once again how his dreams and this vision seemed to form a pattern, though he couldn't yet see what it might be. Black Horse Rider's words, "a power that can direct our acts," came and went in his head. If. . . .

Then he was asleep.

HE SLEPT DREAMLESSLY AND AWOKE TO THE BREEZES THAT whispered just before dawn. He came awake immediately, sprang up naked, and without thinking he strode to the western post and sang his song in a clear voice, dancing the stiffness out of his lean body. He did the same at the north post, returned to the center and, crouching, swallowed some water, trotted to the eastern post, danced, sang his song. . . .

And the sun sprang up over the rim of the plains, and waves of power began to flow through the landscape which, he realized with detachment as his feet continued their step and his voice its song, was composed of a cellular texture through which the power waves could insinuate themselves without disturbing the ordinary world with their energy dance. But now he could feel them, be them! It was as if the entire earth was undulating, breathing, in the same strange and delicate way that he realized his stomach was—his breathing that bore the same relationship to "normal" breathing as the pulsating organism all about him, and above and beneath, did to the "normal" country and earth and sky.

He was aware!

He danced on as the sun rose, feeling a little numb, his chest tingling, his teeth indistinct; but although every atom of his being was concentrated on the dance it was no more to him than moving a wrist or nodding would have been before, so perfect was his coordination, for his self was away, feeling with amazed and joyous disbelief the passage of the waves of power through him and about him. He found he was crying hard and it was difficult to sing, but that was beautiful too.

Then later he was chortling his song, roaring with laughter at the idea of his previous self solemnly learning the qualities of the four directions—how could he have failed to feel them?—and then holding them all in his head and trying to coordinate them! To put them together! A harmony which nothing could touch anyway! It is, it is! he roared. Thank you, thank you!

The sun's warmth was a smile on him, but an Indian smile, after nothing for itself, inscrutable—a mystery which was echoed in the mauve and violet shadows beneath the trees, the shifting blackness in the seas of evergreens, the cobalt of the sky above like a single abrupt syllable, a clapped hand.

The sun had gone out of sight above his head when he found himself lying in the shadow of the pit, waves of energy pulsating gently from his stomach to ooze out throbbing from his fingers and toes. He knew it was as well he was back in the pit; the last time he had faced the east to sing, something (the sky?) had reminded him of the terrible war between the east and the west. Only the power of the western energy had held him from falling as he realized, like remembering; felt, through and through, the old war, the ancient power of the east, sinuous and malign, submarine, as wise as age itself, locked inextricably forever in combat with the bright sky-borne rays of the west.

Down in the pit, brooding, he drifted into sleep.

THE SCUFFLING BROUGHT HIM FULLY AWAKE; HE FELT confused and giddy, but alert. It was night, and he peered over the edge of the pit into the purplish darkness.

The scuffling continued, and Long Range made out a dark, hulking shape, wrapped in a kind of spectral phosphorescence, moving about in the darkness. A raw animal

113

odor came to his nostrils, musky and overpowering. He became aware that he was crouching down in the pit, and with an effort of will, half raised himself. The creature seemed to notice him then, and started forward, lumbering toward him.

Something rose in Long Range and without thinking he leapt out of the pit and tore at the charging beast, hitting it full tilt with his whole body, his naked chest full of joyful strength as he felt the wind driven out of it, flung his arms around its hairy bulk, and, wrestling it to the ground, began to squeeze with all his might, as its arms closed around him and began to squeeze in their turn, grinding and crushing his ribs. Yet there was no thought in him to use the schoolyard tricks; it was a pure contest of strength, and though the pain was sharp, anger like joy rose and rose in him, and power came to his arms, as clasping his right wrist in his left hand he crushed the beast. The more his grip increased the more the power came and he wrestled his way on top of his opponent and crushed and crushed, and the animal, strange, began to shrink, until he looked down, teeth gritted, and gasped and leapt back; for he had caught a glimpse of what he was crushing beneath him, and it was himself.

A cry ripped from his lips:

"My son! My son!"

And he saw that he was alone again, but feeling a new power in his chest and forearms. He saw his shadow in the glimmering light, and it was animal but like no animal he had ever seen—as he had leapt at the beast he had thought it a bear, or the man-bear by the water; but now he saw that it—he—was something else, loose-limbed and hairy, upright but crouched, forehead sloping, dangling arms that he raised and beat on his chest, uttering a yell, half speech, half wild cry that he sent out over the hills, telling his triumph. He knew that he had his father's power, yet he felt infinite tenderness towards his "son," his unborn self.

He had a strong instinct to lope over to the eastern post; once there he squatted down, arms folded up around his chest, mouth open in expectation. He sensed shapes similar

114

to himself squatted down around him on the hillside in the luminous darkness, dreamily facing the east, waiting.

And the dawn came, light spilling up like a tide over the hill; but even as he felt the joy and warmth of it on his chest, a part of him was aware that it was a false dawn, the colors tinged with unreality. And the dawn came again, and again, and again, and around him the hills writhed and rippled in colors like the light before a storm, and Long Range trembled as the ages passed and the war continued.

Finally he got up, exhausted, and wandered back to the pit.

Down in the dark earth, he rested. He lay with eyes closed but his vision was spangled with crosses; a forest of winking, interlocked crosses set between the boughs of an actual forest that he was moving in before he knew it, moving towards one tree with an irresistible curiosity, for as he approached he could see a man hanging in it, spread out high up in its boughs, a man wearing Angel colors who he guessed to be the Oldest Angel in the story, until he approached close enough to see the man's features.

And it was himself, hung in agony, the powers ripping his chest and shoulders apart, his whole being torn like tearing meat, a scream that echoed through the universe frozen in his throat, and it never ended as he hung, for he and only he was the focal point in the war between east and west, good and evil, his existence agony without end, his vision a blurred scarlet whirl, a nebula of blood.

Through it he saw a woman walking toward him and his heart sprang with hope, but she could come no closer, must remain beyond the veil; though the blood veil itself was turned by her presence to a crystal sheet shot with bright but gentle colors, blues and greens, aqua and turquoise. She gazed at him with an expression of deep tenderness and complexity, love, pity, laughter and sorrow—and something more, some further mystery so profound that he was lost in it even as he sobbed bitterly from the knowledge that she would always remain beyond the veil for him.

The agony was gone, and he sank into a deep sleep to dream unfathomable dreams like children's songs.

He dreamed he was the tree he hung in, and that the tree was singing and that the world, east and west, north and south, birds and animals, trees, plants and people, were all circling the tree, above and below and all about, all dancing in time to the music the tree made. He grew and sang from the still center where he existed, unmoved, unchanging, and knew all, and was all.

The dew fell on him like his own tears, and in the thousand tiny particles of moistness he came together, came to himself again.

He got up, and in the cool of the morning walked to the eastern post. Without thinking he began slowly, through parched lips, to chant the song and stamp out his dance again. The sun had just come up; it was a new morning and he thanked the sky and the earth with his whole being that he was alive to see it.

In about an hour they found him there, Black Horse Rider and the helpers who came with horses, and they brought him back to the others.

"Ho, son!" said Black Horse Rider to Long Range. "I am to be your father. On this day which belongs to Wakan Tanka, he has seen our faces; the dawn of the day has seen us, and our Grandmother, the Earth, has listened to us. We are here at the center, and the four powers of the universe join in us. This meat I shall put in your mouth, and from this day forth you shall never fear my home, for my home is your home, and you are my son."

And he placed a piece of tender meat, purified with sweet grass, in Long Range's mouth.

It was the climax of the ceremony of Hunkapi, making a relative, which Black Horse Rider had proposed that he should carry out as soon as Long Range had returned to the camp and rested; with them both present as individuals, and also as representatives of his people and the west.

The Lakota thronged around with friendly faces, for news of Long Range's vision had gone through the camp and he was considered especially fortunate. Now with the rite completed a great shout went up from all the people.

After that, the feasted all night, lolling, stuffing with meat, on skins beside the roaring fire at the center of the tepee circle, the Angels passing round the last bottle of whisky from their saddlebags among themselves; the Lakota would have none. Long Range, his face still painted from the rite, and wearing a fine red shirt of buckskin, one of many presents the Angels had received from their new "relatives," sat by Black Horse Rider watching the magical figures of the Indians dancing, feeling the drums in his chest; painted faces in the firelight were weird with animal markings, possum faces, bear faces, horned buffalo masks and feathers, quills, buckskin figures shaking and swaying to the power of the beating of the drum as high yells, sparks, rifle shots, crackled out from the circle of fire into the night sky. Long Range felt that there was no sense of trying to keep the night at bay; the power of the night was in the drums and the dancers.

Black Horse Rider watched him watching and then nodded to him, and Long Range got up and moved forward to lose himself in the circle of dancers.

When he returned there was a lull as the drummers refreshed themselves, and the idea occurred to Milt and Belial to treat their hosts to a proper Angel drinking song. They hit upon "The Citizen's Daughter," and launched into the first verse.

But almost immediately their voices were inaudible as the normally impassive Lakota were convulsed by their performance. Women clapped their hands across their mouths, children pointed, the camp dogs threw back their heads and howled, and the braves fell about clutching their ribs, rolling close, even into the fire, or lay on their backs, kicking their heels in the air in agony. The two Angels felt put down, and sulked, but in its way their song was a great success; from time to time during the rest of the night, a brave would come up, look them seriously in the eyes, clasp them by the shoulders and attempt an un-

117

recognizable imitation of their singing before running off, overcome by the memory of it.

Late in the night Long Range wandered drowsily back to the tepee where he was lodging. He was hopping about, pulling off his buckskin leggings, when he realized that someone was in his bed. Ducking down to kneel on the coarse fur of the robe he peered at the dark shape, smelled a familiar fragrance and felt smooth dark hair brush his face as Rita raised her face to meet him. After a while he knelt, and scooping her up in his arms still wrapped in the robe, carried her from the tepee and out of the camp, down to a place by the river where they spread the robe in the shadow of a cottonwood tree and lay down under the stars.

In the morning they swam in the sparkling river, splashing and laughing; Long Range was careful not to let her catch him gazing at her when she was not aware of it.

Then he noticed Black Horse Rider standing under the tree by their robe, and swam over, smiling hello. But the older man only smiled gravely and gestured to him to get out and get dressed. Long Range was puzzled but did it, and waving goodbye to Rita, followed the brave back to the camp in silence. It was still early morning and the circle of tepees was quiet after the big feast; smoke curled up slowly from the ashes of the big fire. They came to Black Horse Rider's tepee and he gestured Long Range to go in.

When his eyes had adjusted to the gloom, Long Range saw that the tepee was empty save for Sky, who lay on his robes with his hands folded on his chest. Long Range knelt beside him. As soon as he had entered the circle of the tepee he had known the old man was dead.

He gazed at the strong impassive face, at the change; he thought there seemed to be a hint of amusement in the curve of the thin lips; but that would be the muscles contracting, the rictus. He knelt there, his mind a blank, his attention finally fixing on the frail long-fingered beautiful old hands, their backs lightly freckled, resting curved and still on the unmoving chest. The hands had a message for him.

118

After he had knelt for a while he got up and went outside.

Black Horse Rider said quietly:

"He passed on during the feast. Soon I will tell the people and all will lament. We will keep his soul among us for a time and gain knowledge from it; it is another rite we have which you will learn. But I wished you to see him first, for the last thing he told me was that he was at peace now that you had come, and how he was glad when the holy man told him of your vision, for it made him sure of you. He said he knew you were strong, but he hoped the vision would help you to be kind. It is my hope also."

Long Range nodded and then walked away, back toward the river. He thought, who could ever feel worthy of that? He thought he would have to try to be. Behind him the sharp cries rose in the morning air as the women began their lament. Long Range walked on. He was thanking Sky for his gift; for showing him a death he need not fear.

That evening two riders came from the east and the whole camp soon knew that the time had come for the war party to move across the plains against Iron Mountain. They left five days later; the women stayed at the camp by the river, Rita with them.

A WEEK LATER THEY WERE FAR ACROSS THE PLAINS, AND Belial killed a turkey.

The country and the weather had changed dramatically. The plain rolled out on all sides, the mountains a mere memory in the haze at their backs. Each day at dawn they faced the rising sun, and three hours later the heat was like the heat from an oven as you open the door, and haze shivered the rolling plains where parched grasses, tall and white, quaked in the hot blast.

Each day the three Angels stayed behind as, rising well before dawn, the Lakota war party noiselessly broke camp and pushed their ponies off at the mile-eating trot that put sixty and seventy miles behind them daily. During the day the Angels lay low under shelters rigged over their bikes, bored, dozing, suffering constantly from the bugs like white ears of corn in their blankets, the big grasshoppers that bit, the voracious mosquitoes; themselves only eating a little dried food, eking out the water until evening when, dizzy and weary, they fired up and rode across the plains in the dusk to rendezvous with the main band. Often as night was falling they edged carefully on, having failed to locate the camp; but the Lakota would send out horsemen, homing on the sound of their motors, and lead them in as the darkness gathered.

Twice they met other bands, pulling back after fighting the Eastern troops, silent and exhausted men with tattered clothes, emaciated ponies and badly wounded braves strapped to litters. Both bands confirmed the growing strength of the Eastern forces; a motorized spring offensive had caught them unawares and inflicted heavy losses. When they saw the Angels' bikes they scowled and muttered. The Easterners had companies of motorcycle troops which were a bad memory for them.

The Angels also often had reason to curse their bikes. There was constant trouble; punctures, snapped clutch cables, wheels regularly needing rebuilding after the day's punishment; once one had the braided steel oil lines snagged on a sage bush and split, and all the time the rear cylinders of the big V-twin engines, since they were air-cooled, suffered from overheating. The size of the big engines, which when they were running at speed had saved them, was now nothing but a burden. One evening at the fire Long Range burned his fingers on some meat and said, "Glitch!" Black Horse Rider asked what he meant, and Belial, whose push-rods had needed adjustment every day, muttered that if the Indian knew anything about bikes he'd know all about Glitch. The other two nodded wearily. Long Range never forgot the incident, because it was the nearest to a joke he ever heard coming from Belial.

And the present discomforts and difficulties were not their only worry. As they approached Iron Mountain, the nature of what they had to do there became increasingly apparent, and it was fearful. They pored over their maps, which showed, on the highest of several exposed plateaux halfway up the western slope of the mountain, the barbed wire perimeter and deep ditch encircling a complex of barracks and a vehicle park; and outside this, but behind a fence of its own, the building housing Professor Sangria's laboratories and living quarters. They questioned endlessly the braves who had been in direct contact with Yellow Bull, their informant from inside the camp; and every night they discussed possible plans of attack with Black Horse Rider.

They soon realized that the camp was the base for at least a battalion of Eastern troops, protecting the Professor and assisting him with his fieldwork, and also guarding the hundreds of men, women and children who were brought in, ostensibly for their own protection, from the surrounding areas, and then held as prisoners in brick-built cellars beneath the camp compound before redistribution to government labor camps elsewhere. The Professor's person was also under constant guard, so there was no possibility of his escaping, and with that number of troops deployed, no chance of even a surprise direct attack succeeding. Some radical form of diversion was going to be necessary.

It was Milt who came up with the idea. If the war party alone would not be able to pin down the Eastern garrison long enough for the Professor to get away, what about the three or four hundred men held prisoner? If they could be freed, whatever happened to them afterwards, their escape would surely create a major diversion; during which they hoped the Professor could be snatched, and he and the Angels ride on Lakota ponies, with the Indians covering them, to the canyon, twenty-five miles south in the same range of hills, where they could pick up the bikes; then race back over the plains, fording the rivers on rafts that the Lakota would leave buried, together with submerged guide lines, as they crossed each one on their way east; and if all went well cover in just three days the distance that, at the pace of the Lakota ponies, had taken weeks.

But going back over the plan they could only think of one way to be certain of organizing a breakout by the prisoners exactly when it was needed; and that was from the inside. As the implications of this sank in, the Angels looked at one another in silence. They were the only possible candidates, and they were going to have to let themselves be taken by Eastern troops. Even if, as they later decided, they were to pose as local dirt-farmers running from the Indians, the prospect was not a bright one, for by that stage the Eastern army was making little distinction between their actual enemies and the homesteaders already living on the frontier. The Angels could look forward to a rough time.

It was the day after this plan had been finalized that Belial shot the turkey. It happened in the evening; they had arrived early at the night's encampment, a grove of seared oak trees by the thin trickle of a fast-drying stream. Belial had padded off with his bolt-gun after game. Long Range noticed that now he used any excuse to get away from them all; his speech was curter and his temper shorter than ever.

Half an hour later he returned, a large prairie turkey dangling from his left hand. A brave was passing as he reached the bushes at the edge of the camp, and walking up to Belial with his bowlegged horseman's gait, stopped him and began to make signs, pointing at the turkey.

Belial looked down at him.

"Yeah, well," he muttered, "you'll likely get a piece too." He made to move on to the fire, but the brave blocked his way, continuing his signs and shaking his head vigorously.

Milt and Long Range had noticed the disturbance and walked over quickly. As they arrived Belial tried to push past the brave, who waved his arms as he might to turn a horse. Milt said, "Hold it, Belial, he's trying to tell you we can't eat the bird."

"You dudes don't have to," said Belial shortly; "I'll eat the fucking thing myself."

"No, hold on there, you don't get me, Belial," said Milt calmly. "They're not allowed to eat them when they're out fighting. The turkey's a cowardly bird, see, and their religion says if they eat it now they might get cowardly too. So no one in a war party gets to eat turkey."

122

"I'm not in their fucking war party, they're riding with me," flared Belial.

"Look, take it easy, man," said Milt. "Put it this way. We're with them, we should do things their way."

"Bullshit," hissed Belial. "I killed the fucking thing, I can eat it or wipe my ass with it or any damn thing, and I don't need your or no one else's say-so to do it."

He stood there glaring, and at that moment the young Lakota brave did a foolish thing. Tiring of the discussion he could not understand, he plucked the turkey deftly from Belial's hand, lobbed it far into the bushes and, turning on his heel, walked away, thinking he had settled the matter.

Belial stood in the dust uncomprehendingly for a moment, then before anyone could move, exploded in a silent rush at the Indian's back. Both his hands came crashing down on the brave's neck, and as his knees buckled Belial kicked his leg out from under him. He drew back a booted foot to smash into the fallen man's ribs, but Milt flung himself on the redheaded Angel and knocked him away, yelling, "Cool it, cool it, Belial!" But Belial, fighting like a machine, held Milt off with one hand and, swinging the elbow of his free arm into his jaw, knocked him cold. He was moving in on the groaning Indian again when he heard Long Range's voice say, "Hold it, Belial, or I'll blow your fucking head off."

Belial turned to find the barrels of Long Range's shotgun pointed unwaveringly at his chest, heard the hammers click back.

"Well now," he said, after a pause, "I know you got no shells for that thing."

Long Range reached in his pocket and threw something at Belial's feet. Belial, peering in the gathering dusk, made out the brass rim of a shotgun cartridge.

"Our friends gave me them," said Long Range, shifting the gun to his left hand and helping Milt to his feet.

"Our friends," sneered Belial, "that's about right, ain't it? You're really one of the family here, ain't you? Prancing about with them, getting your rocks off with that skinny

123

little red-assed bitch, I'm beginning to think you've forgotten what you are, boy.''

"And what's that?" said Long Range quickly, helping the young Indian up and gently pushing him off toward the fire, smiling reassuringly.

"A bastard and an orphan," snarled Belial, "but first and last an Angel, you dig? You got your colors, that's forever, you're a brother now; but both of you side with that fucking skin against me, another Angel. When we get back they're going to hear about that, we'll see what Frank has to say to that.''

Long Range stooped and laid the shotgun carefully on the ground at his feet.

"Listen," he said, walking toward Belial, "you could have hurt that guy badly, or even killed him, and if that had happened how much more help do you think we'd get from his band? You talk about Angels, well Frank gave us a job to do and the best way to do it now is get along with these people whether you like them or not. Understand?" he concluded, shaking his right hand in Belial's face, so that the scars from his wound showed clearly in the flickering light from the fire.

Belial stared at it for a while, then said, "Yeah, but that ain't it. You really like these skins, don't you? When they made you get better and you went up the mountain that time, since then you've acted like you're something special, you got something going with them that we're too dumb to understand. You really believe all that magic bullshit, and it makes me sick to see it. I never did like you much, but now all this shit has got to you and I think you're no good. I don't think I'd feel good with you at my back in a brawl. I think if you get a chance you'll stay with these scum. Well if you do, I tell you this; I'll be the leader of the party that comes for you. And you know what we do to renegades," he grinned.

"I'll be happy to oblige you, Belial," said Long Range, "but if that time ever comes it'll be a long way from now; we're far from home and we got a job to do first. But no, I'm not denying that I found something here that I never

124

found with our people; and I guess I have thought of staying, if they'd have me."

"You hear that," shouted Belial, swinging on Milt, "you hear him say that? I want you to remember that for when we get back."

Milt rubbed his jaw and said delicately, "Go fuck yourself."

Long Range went on to both of them, "I'm sorry if I've seemed conceited in any way. I'm sorry . . ." he faltered, "it's been a difficult time; since I went up the mountain."

He turned away, but Belial grabbed his shoulder and spun him round.

"What kind of Angel are you, girl?" he sneered. "You're nothing."

Long Range knocked his hand away and said, "I've broken no Angel law. Can you say the same, Belial? Would Lila if we asked her?"

Belial went very still. After a while he licked his lips and said, "You're shooting blind."

"We could always check it out with Half-Lugs and Rexit," said Long Range.

Belial stood looking at him; Long Range had time to take in his red-rimmed eyes and the tautness of fatigue that gave his features a pinched look, like a tired child.

Then Belial walked away without a word.

"Whew," said Milt finally. "Whew and double-whew. We was on the edge there all right. What the hell was it all about?"

Long Range sighed and told him quickly what he had seen on the night of the spring fair.

"Oh hell," breathed Milt, "and you've had to travel with the bastard all this while, feeling the way you did about Lila. And what the fuck are we going to do now? Now he knows you know he's not going to let you get back alive, because if you do and the story gets out, he's finished. How come you didn't tell Frank straight off, anyway?"

"Lila, I guess," said Long Range. "And Belial and the boys were Hawks. But mostly I reckon I couldn't be sure

125

I wasn't telling out of spite, because I was mad that Belial and Lila and the others had made me look a fool to myself.''

"Yeah," said Milt, "but our laws, and the chapters make a lot more sense to me since we seen those Gypsies. You remember that Cat-back? And Howler? And the idiot, what did they call him, Clot, the one I put a bolt in at the cantina. Cripples, imbeciles—a pitiful bunch. That's what you get where everybody gets to hump everybody else and there ain't many of you. Anyway," he went on, "we're in trouble. Belial will try to get you, and me too, most likely. Maybe we should snuff him now."

"I don't think he'll do anything just yet," said Long Range. "He needs us to get the job done. He'll leave settling till closer to home."

"The job? What does he care about the job?"

"Well the way I see it, he cares about his song. More than anything. What other people think of him. That's why he doesn't like it now, because no one much is thinking about him at all."

Milt laughed bitterly. "And will screwing an Angel's daughter go in his song? Or killing you and me, two of his brothers?"

"No," said Long Range, "that's just it. He can make his life just the way he wants it, afterwards, in his song."

"Yeah, what we're all after," said Milt, "doing it over again, a fresh start. I reckon you've found one; and a little more honestly than rewriting it all in a song."

"That's it," said Long Range. "It's just that I can't tell you about it. I mean I could tell you stuff that went down, stuff I saw, but I don't have the words to tell you how it felt. It turned my head around, all right; I mean the world hasn't seemed the same since."

"From what you've said about it," Milt said cautiously, "it sounds kind of like what happened to us when we smoked so much that summer. Or when they gave us that stuff to drink, when we got our colors; I'm pretty sure it was made from the magic mushrooms, you know? I mean,

126

you were tired and strung out and you hadn't eaten for days—"

"But that was just how you get there, it didn't make it happen," Long Range burst out. "Dope, tiredness, hunger, they don't make different worlds, they show us what's there all the time. I feel that we go around like blinkered mules—missing it. I've often felt so sad in the last few weeks . . . seeing you. . . ."

He stopped. It was dark and his features were indistinguishable. After a while Milt murmured, "Don't worry, man, it'll all grow back, you'll see."

He could feel Long Range smiling as he said, "No, man, no."

"Well I tell you," said Milt, "if you did ever feel like telling me what went down up there on the mountain, I'd surely like to hear it. Maybe I could write it down."

"Write it down?" said Long Range.

"Yeah," said Milt, "you know when I was up at the Fief learning languages and all, they asked us to write down stuff like prayers and dances and related stuff that we might see or hear about."

Long Range was silent.

"Religious studies, they called it," said Milt rather lamely.

"Educated Angel, eh?" said Long Range with a slight smile, and shook his head.

Stooping to pick up the shotgun, he walked away toward the fires.

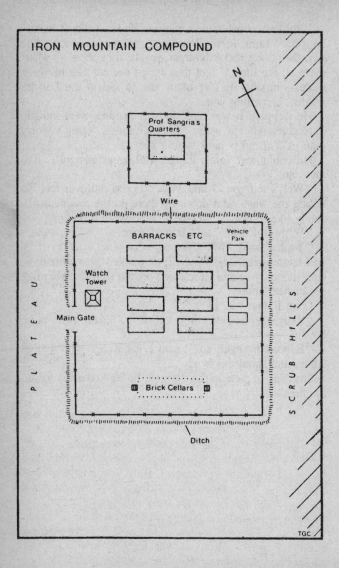

IRON MOUNTAIN COMPOUND

N

Prof Sangrias
Quarters

Wire

BARRACKS   ETC   Vehicle
Park

Watch
Tower

Main Gate

P L A T E A U

S C R U B   H I L L S

Brick Cellars

Ditch

TGC

IV   THE RETURN

Optimism is another way of saying space.
　　　　　　　　　　　　　　— Jerry Garcia

Ten days later Long Range was chained and underground. The cellars were of vaulted brick, arch giving on to brick arch in the dim light and rank air. They were all naked; lines of men sat opposite one another, their backs to the curving walls, their pale shapes like a line of ghosts tapering into the gloom, the chains' umbilicus connecting them to each other and the wall. Somewhere a man moaned, over and over. The stench rose; they sat in their own droppings, the floor a slop of fetid mud. Once a day they were mucked out like cattle, disinfected water flung over them and the guttered floor swept down.

There were a few Indians, captured in battle or after, but most of the prisoners were white settlers from the lands around. Long Range's neighbor, Billy, a farmer aged about fifty with a grizzled beard, a stringy body and work-calloused hands, had hissed his story to Long Range after the guards had passed—no talking was the cellar rule; how the troops had come to his farm and cleared it, separating him from his family, saying it was for their own protection against the Indians; but Billy knew better, he had heard of

129

the same thing happening further east: when the government troops consolidated an area, they cleared out the existing population and resettled the farms and villages with their own people, usually ex-soldiers. Meanwhile the men from the area were placed in S.D.E.s, Self Defense Encampments, which was a euphemism for mobile labor camps, where they worked till they dropped on the new roads which the government used to carry the fight to the Indians and trade to the frontier.

Long Range was cheered by Billy's anger. He guessed that part of the purpose of the cellars and their humiliations was to break the spirit of men like him. Long Range thought they could use that anger when they made their break.

A guard strolled by, his high boots echoing on the brick ramp between the two lines of men.

When the patrol had picked them up, as they had intended, in a valley close to the Iron Mountain camp, the Angels' first reaction had been amazement at the Eastern troops' appearance—great insect shapes, the hard shell of large rounded helmets merging with tinted visors and the lower half of the face covered with gridded stone-guards; the upper bodies of the men bulked out grotesquely with armored vests, the legs skinny in high boots. None of it was strictly necessary, and the men sweated under the heavy gear in the heat; but as Long Range never saw a soldier dressed differently he guessed they must be under orders to wear the full equipment all the time. He remembered Black Horse Rider's words about the Easterners' way of separating themselves from their surroundings.

The Lakota had spotted the patrol the day before, and a small band moved up on foot with the bikers and left them on a track in the valley where the patrol's truck was bound to pass. The Indians would watch as they were picked up, and send word back west immediately.

Long Range remembered standing by the track in the dusty morning light, listening to the whine of the truck's motor approaching, his stomach tightening. This was the first of many moments of maximum danger; all it needed was a trigger-happy or sadistic soldier at this point and they would be dead before they started.

But the troopers, visored and impersonal, were indifferent, shoving them up into the back of the truck and not even bothering with their carefully worked story establishing themselves as farmhands running from the Indians. They were in the net, and whoever they were made no difference to the soldiers. Even their accents weren't noticed.

As the truck had rolled into the compound at Iron Mountain, three pairs of eyes checked the white two-story building beyond the wire; the Indians had been told by Yellow Bull, their contact with the Professor, that this was Sangria's laboratory and living quarters. They had only a glimpse of it before being herded into a hut with other prisoners, to strip, be showered and shoved naked down into the cellars.

Long Range looked at the light filtering dimly down the ventilation shaft half a hundred yards further down the cellar. In the tepee where he had spent the last days with Rita, often he had lain with her head on his chest, staring up at the rays of first light and the bundles and shapes hanging in the shadows, among them the curve of a bow hung to season.

It had been different from how he had always imagined; the time had been strange, fugitive, and it had passed before he knew it. He fingered over it gently in his memory, images of their closeness coming and going too quickly.

There was a sudden commotion in the cellar as the guards sprang to attention, foul mud flying, and a tall figure with an officer's crest painted on his helmet strode down the brick ramp.

"As you were, sergeant. Four o'clock sharp, so I suppose I'd better have a look at these beggars."

Long Range listened incredulously to the man's peculiar nasal accent and bizarre way of talking; he had noticed these things with the other officers he had seen, and guessed correctly that they affected them as a mark of superior

131

caste—though he could not know of their origin in the East's infatuation with the memory of the British.

The racking cough of the man who had been moaning all day cut across the officer's words.

"What's this, sergeant, one of the chaps not feeling too hot? Let's have a look at you, old man," said the tall officer, raising his visor to reveal a fair complexion and red-rimmed pale blue eyes, as he knelt down to peer at the shivering sick man.

"I say," he went on, "we can't have this sort of thing. Sergeant," he said in an aggrieved tone, "this man's *sick*. He's not well. Have two of your men take him upstairs and have him seen to at once."

The sergeant bent and unchained the sick man and two troops slung their carbines and dragged him to his feet, supporting him along the brick ramp and up the stairs.

"There," said the officer, "that's better." Raising his voice he said, "He's a lucky fellow you know," to the prisoners in general. There was a pause and then suddenly the muffled crack of two carbines rang out from above.

"That's right," nodded the officer in his exaggerated, almost pantomime manner, "a lucky chap. He thought his troubles were over, and now," the officer chuckled, "well now they jolly well are."

He strode to the middle of the main tunnel and raised his voice again.

"Now I want you chaps to pay attention," he said in ringing tones. "You've just seen what happens to people who are slack, and I can tell you right away that we will also tolerate no insolence from you, either. The sergeant here and the other fellows look after you, they feed you"—here he touched a dinner plate with his toe—"and it's up to you to show them the respect they deserve.

"Now things may seem a bit bloody for you just at present," he said, looking around at the naked forms, some visibly shocked by the sudden shooting and the final realization that a ruthless power had complete control of them, that they were helpless.

"But I want to assure you that we're not, basically, a

bloody-minded lot, though we can be jolly hard if we're pushed. You won't be here much longer; when the transport is assembled, you'll be off to your S.D.E.s where you'll have the privilege of working for the Eastern Seaboard Federation; of becoming a part, however humble, in our great drive westward, our civilizing mission.

"My teacher at the university, who was a very wise man, was talking to me once and he compared the Federation to a body, and a young, growing body at that; the capital with the government is like the head, and the various provinces are the limbs; growing, stretching, grasping out until the continent has been spanned and we achieve our destiny, our fullest potential for growth, the sovereignty of the country as a whole.

"Isn't that an exciting idea? And you'll be a part of it."

"What about our families?" shouted a voice.

"That man!" shrieked the sergeant, and two of the troopers ran to the prisoner who had shouted and clubbed at him with their rifle-butts until the officer's cries of "I say, steady on" restrained them.

"No, it's a fair question, although," he chuckled, "you know you really must learn not to interrupt when one of us is speaking. Your families have been lucky enough to be taken east already"—here some of the men groaned involuntarily, but the officer pretended not to notice, and raising his voice went on—"where homes and jobs will be found for them in our factories and in the military bases; if all goes well you may be able to join them there one day, though of course I can't make any promises. At any rate they will be safe from the Redskins there. That's one reason you're down here; sometimes before, chaps have got a bit homesick and wandered off from here, and of course Johnny Redman made mincemeat of them. So it's really all for your own good, and I know you'll appreciate it later when you can look back and see what an important part you've had in the history of a great nation." He chuckled wryly again. "You may even look back on this old cellar with a certain amount of affection, as the place where your new life began.

133

"Oh yes, and you white men needn't worry; the red men here go to separate camps; we've found they can't seem to get used to a proper job of work in the same way we do and they don't usually last very long, poor devils.

"All right, any questions?" He paused briefly. "No? Well, the best of luck. Carry on." And clapping his visor down into place, he stalked from the cellar.

There was a silence among the men for a while, as what he had said sank in; many had had no idea what was to happen to them. Long Range sat enraged at the obscene hypocrisy. At length he waited for the guards to pass and then muttered to Billy, loud enough for others to hear, "Well, if the Federation is one big body I reckon we just had a few choice words direct from the asshole."

Some of them grunted and passed it on. Long Range kept on joking and talking behind the guards' backs; he could see the men cheered by someone doing this, and ready to pay attention to what he said. He and the other two had known what they were in for and planned accordingly; knowing what they would have to try to do gave them an assurance which the other naked men sensed.

There was food—bread, water and thin gruel—morning and evening only; some of the men who had known what to expect when the troopers came had secreted coins and valuables about their bodies, and as the second day wore on, one after another would wait until guards were passing singly, catch their attention and trade coin for candy bars and rations. The guards seemed to be used to it. The only other incident during the day came when two or three of the prisoners were unshackled and taken up to fetch the food for the rest. Long Range noticed how time-conscious the Easterners were; everything happened as near as he could judge at the same time every day. They would use that.

They shivered through the next night, and as Long Range watched the light filter down the shafts, he knew this was the day they made their move, and that there was a good chance it was also the last day he would ever see. For no reason he could think of he felt excited, had to restrain

134

himself from chuckling. There would be some changes made today, O.K.! He looked at Billy as the stringy rancher peevishly caught and cracked a flea crawling on his chest.

"Wild and woolly and full of fleas, eh?" he said, and they snorted with laughter. Then Long Range told him straight out that he was going to try a break that evening. Billy listened expressionlessly, then nodded.

"With my wife and the kids and my place gone I got nothing much to try except kill a few of these bastards and make some sort of run before they get me," he said. "But you reckon this is the place?"

"The way I see it," said Long Range, "they won't expect it. Once we get out of the cellar there's only the wire. Further east, no way—they'd be all around; here it's frontier and most of us know the land, once we get clear we got a good chance to hide up and start over. And shit, down here there's more of us than there's fiddlers in hell. The S.D.E.s are small, I hear."

"That's only the truth," said Billy, and set about spreading the word. By the time the food came the combined efforts of Long Range and the two Angels further down the cellar had persuaded most of the prisoners; and the rest were impressed enough to know what sort of chain-strangling trouble they would be in if they tried to stop the attempt.

The hot hours of midday came. The stench rose but nobody dozed. Some of the guards caught the tension and walked carefully, gripping their weapons tightly, through the silent lines of men.

In the afternoon Long Range finally dozed, but snapped out of his reverie as from the corner of his eye he saw Belial holding out his hand to a guard and the trooper bending to take something from him. Long Range's heart raced with shock—it was far too early to begin their bid. But the guard merely took whatever it was from Belial's hand, straightened and walked on. Long Range's mind seethed—what was going on? In a minute or two word came down the line; the redheaded Angel had bribed the guard to get him on the evening work detail, saying he was desperate

135

for fresh air. Long Range nodded, slowly relaxing; it wasn't part of the plan but it could be useful to have a man outside the cellar when they made their break. They had drawn straws before their capture and Long Range was to be the one to make the actual move—the other two could be elsewhere. He settled again; across the way Milt caught his glance, rolled his eyes and whistled silently in relief. Belial was unpredictable.

Slowly the shafts of sunlight moved across the cellar, and the stillness grew more and more pronounced. Intervals between the troopers' routines seemed to grow longer and longer. Long Range tried to keep his mind off the hundred things that could go wrong, but the hours and minutes dragged painfully, as motes of dust floated in the golden shaft light, and slowly the cellar became dimmer.

Finally with a clatter of boots the evening relief of two troopers came down the stairs, presented arms to the afternoon guard and received the keys from them, with that characteristic stiffness and formality which the squalid surroundings made absurd. They exchanged a few words and then the afternoon guard climbed the stairs; two of the relief troopers unshackled three prisoners, one of them was Belial, and marched them up the narrow steps to fetch the food and water for the prisoners' evening meal. Their steps receded. Stillness hung in the dusk, but the two guards remaining failed to feel the tension. Long Range watched one of the guards pass him; the soldier looked lightly built, but it was hard to tell with the armored vest. It was time, time to make his move. But the guard passed again, and his stomach was too numb; his mind raced with the thought that he couldn't go through with it, wouldn't. He barely got himself under control as the guard approached along the brick ramp for the third time; he swallowed hard and fumbled under his left armpit, and as the guard drew level held up the gold coin he had taped there, and hissed.

"Soldier!"

The guard stopped, looked around and then leaned toward him, bayoneted rifle at port arms.

"What do you want?" he muttered.

"Food," murmured Long Range.

"Can't wait for the slop pail, eh?" came the soldier's voice from behind the visor and stone-guard. He sounded young. As Long Range watched intently he shifted his carbine to his left hand and fumbled in a pocket in the bullet-proof vest, fished out a candy bar and leaned down to exchange it for the coin. Long Range had time for one last look sideways—there was no sign of the guard—and then he had grabbed the hand with the candy bar tightly, and as he pulled the unbalanced soldier over on top of him, lashed up with his right foot, toes stiffened, and caught the falling soldier a kick in the throat below his stone-guard. With a gurgle the trooper collapsed on to him, carbine thudding into the muck as Long Range dropped a loop of chain about the helmeted head and twisted and tightened it with all his strength around the exposed neck until the trooper's feet ceased thrashing and he lay quite still.

In the absolute silence, from the far end of the dimly lit cellar, Long Range finally made out a regular slapping sound, the undisturbed pacing of the second guard. Feverishly, with intense revulsion, he plunged his bare arm into the dead soldier's pocket. The boy's body was still warm. There were no keys in the left-hand pocket; chains rattling, he and Billy heaved the body over to get at the right-hand side. The sound of pacing at the other end of the cellar was getting louder. There were no keys.

Long Range closed his eyes for a second, thought, then desperately tried the flak jacket pocket where the soldier had kept the candy bar. His fingers closed on a ring and then two keys. He was so excited that as he pulled them free they skipped from his trembling fingers and fell into the foul mud. His fingers scrabbled for them, found them, and the first key fitted his manacled hands. He staggered up, hopelessly stiff after the enforced sitting position of the past day, and grabbed the soldier's carbine. The ring of the second guard's boots on the brick ramp drew nearer. A shot would be fatal for them all. Fingers shaking, he detached the bayonet from the carbine's muzzle, and, followed in slow motion by the turning faces of the two rows of prisoners like pale ghosts in the dim light, he hobbled on bare feet along the brick ramp toward the curve in the cellar, the rifle in his left hand, bayonet in his right. He was twenty yards away from the corner when the second guard strolled into sight, carbine at port arms, and stopped dead in his tracks.

Long Range acted instinctively from schoolyard days. Flipping the bayonet around in his hand so that the blade lay between his finger and thumb, he drew back his arm and hurled it as hard as he could at the soldier who was fumbling to jack a round into the carbine's chamber. The bayonet struck him; Long Range had forgotten the bullet-proof vest; the weapon bounced off the trooper's chest, but the force of the blow was enough to knock him backwards off the ramp, and as he staggered among the chained men, legs thrashed to trip him and chained hands clawed to bring him down. Gasping and flailing he stumbled and fell, and the chains beat at him until the bayonet appeared and one of the prisoners bent and used it.

Long Range dragged himself back to where Milt was and fumbled to unchain him, then ran to the body of the trooper he had killed and began stripping his uniform. He tossed the keys to Billy, who unchained himself and, passing the keys to his neighbor, bent to help Long Range, who was tugging helplessly at the soldier's trousers. Billy had to show him how a zipper worked. He struggled into the uniform trousers and shirt and the bulky flak jacket, broke his fingernails on the boots which were too small, and finally squeezed into the helmet. Billy had appropriated the guard's pistol; now he checked Long Range's appearance and slapped his shoulder, and the Angel trotted down the corridor to join Milt, who was straightening up from dressing in the other guard's clothes. They smiled at each other's appearance involuntarily, and then Long Range hissed, "Where's fucking Belial?"

"I dunno," said Milt. "Do we wait?"

"Maybe he's laid for the other two outside."

He glanced round at the silent crowd of men whom Billy

138

and the other two prisoners with the guards' automatics and bayonets were marshaling at each stairway; the last were unchaining themselves.

"We can't wait," he said. "Let's go." They picked up the carbines and trotted to the stairs where Billy stood.

"We're going up," Long Range said. "If it's clear, we'll whistle. If you don't hear nothing for a minute, come out fast, spread out and go for the wire."

Billy gripped his shoulder and squeezed, and then they lowered their visors and trotted up the brick stairs, emerging quickly into the warm dusk. They stopped for a moment, breathing the clear air and looking around them.

The cellar lay on the southern perimeter of the camp square, which was bounded by a ditch and then a barbed-wire fence to the height of twelve feet. To their left were the main gates with a lookout tower beside them; and straight ahead across the square, beyond the perimeter, in its own boundary fence, stood the Professor's house. Separating them from it at a distance of fifty yards was a cluster of wooden buildings, barracks, kitchen, headquarters, armory and radio hut, all connected by neat paths lined with whitewashed stones; and beyond them, rows of meticulously spaced vehicles. They could make out some soldiers moving about there, but no one seemed to pay any attention to them.

Long Range turned back to the cellar steps and whistled, then, taking a deep breath, nodded to Milt, and they loped off in step across the parade ground in front of the buildings, toward the gate in the northern fence that led to the Professor's compound.

They were drawing level with the perimeter's main gate when from their right a familiar voice rang out, "Halt!" and round the side of one of the buildings doubled the officer who had spoken to them the day before, at the head of a squad of armed troopers. He stopped at about twenty yards' distance and shouted at them.

"Where the devil do you think you're going? And where are your bayonets? We've heard there's going to be trouble in the cellars; you're supposed to be the bloody guard and

139

you're wandering about at will. Sergeant, arrest these men and. . . ."

But they never discovered his plans for them, for at that moment his mouth fell open in disbelief and after a fractional pause the guns of the squad swung in the direction of the pale torrent of naked men silently flooding from both entrances of the cellar. One of the fleeing men paused; it was Billy, and taking in the situation he raised his pistol hand above his head, brought it down to sight and snapped off the three spaced shots with the captured automatic; despite the range, dust kicked up close around the feet of the officer, who flung himself flat. Milt and Long Range had time to drop and bring up their carbines, but at that moment from the northern fence behind the soldiers something came sailing through the dusk, and a grenade exploded in the air and knocked them down in different directions like ninepins. There was an ear-ripping whoop and then a volley of shattering fire from the northern ditch, as Long Range and Milt bellied sideways to the ditch on their left and flung themselves in. Tearing off their helmets they crawled toward the northern end, Milt shouting above the firing, "I thought they'd never get here."

A burst of automatic fire rang out close behind them. Turning on his back Long Range looked up to see the gunner in the tower by the gate raking the northern perimeter. He took aim but Milt was quicker, and one shot blew the man backwards off his platform, crashing down into the dust.

They turned again and crawled awkwardly on elbows and knees, trembling with exhaustion, until they rounded the corner of the ditch and Long Range found himself looking down the barrel of a carbine. He shrieked. "No!"

There was a reassuring chuckle. A Lakota brave crouched before them in a headband of dark cloth and ghost shirt of fringed pale buckskin, crisscrossed with cloth bandoliers.

"Do not worry, brother," said Black Horse Rider, "you smell like Hell's Angels."

140

"Yeah, we been sitting in a heap of shit for three days," gasped Milt.

"Where is Keeps-His-Name?"

"We don't know, he went out ahead of us."

"We have no time to wait. If he is alive he knows where our camp is. Let us get the Professor, quick. Already the dogs try to flank us." He popped his head up and snapped four rapid shots at a group of troopers working their way round outside the wire to their right. Ducking back he ran along the ditch a little way, Long Range and Milt following clumsily, and stopping, pumped his hand up and down in a signal to the other braves. Their firing grew more intense, an ear-splitting uninterrupted crash, and then Black Horse Rider was sliding over the rear lip of the ditch and sprinting in a crouching run through a small garden toward the white house not fifty yards behind them. Long Range and Milt followed, feeling helplessly exposed as they threw themselves from the ditch and stumbled forward, their backs unprotected as rifles cracked and bullets whirred around them in the dusk.

They were about halfway across when Milt cried out and fell forward into a flowerbed. Long Range made a weaving run back to him, yelled desperately, "Are you all right?" and when Milt groaned grabbed his collar and began to drag him toward the doorway of the house, but Milt's groaning turned to cursing and he stumbled to his feet, Long Range got an arm round him and they ran and half-fell into the door of the house.

"What was all that?" cried Long Range, as Milt knelt, cursing steadily. "You all right? I thought you were hit."

"I was hit, you asshole," groaned Milt. "I thought I was dead, I forgot about this, that's all," he snarled, slapping the bulletproof vest; the cloth was punctured at the back. "I'm all right, but my shoulder feels like a fucking mule kicked me. Shit!"

Long Range turned to Black Horse Rider who crouched with two other braves in the doorway, dead Eastern troopers sprawled around them. Bullets smacked into the outside wall of the house.

"Where's the Professor?" he shouted.

Black Horse Rider pointed upward.

"First floor. We did not go to him for fear of alarming him."

Long Range sprinted up the stairs, Milt at his heels, and stopped on the landing at the top. He knocked on the door facing them. There was movement inside, and the Angels flattened against the walls to each side of the door. Then a loud voice said, "Who's there?"

"We're from the west," shouted Long Range, gripping his carbine and listening intently above the noise of the firing outside. Was the Professor alone?

The door opened and a very tall figure stepped out. He had an almost swarthily dark face, with dark hair, and unruly moustache, and quick dark eyes. He wore a suit of clothes, dark gray or black over a white shirt, with a top-coat of dark green whipcord and in one hand carried a leather bag which his great height made to seem like a toy.

He stood dead still at the sight of them.

"Don't worry," said Long Range, "we borrowed the uniforms. We're Hell's Angels from the west, and we've come a long way to get you."

"Then we should go," said Professor Sangria, and started down the stairs two at a time. The Angels followed, Milt still wondering why the Professor carried no weapon.

FIVE HOURS LATER THEY WERE BACK AT THE LAKOTA CAMP from which they had set out three days before to be captured. In the darkness ponies nickered and stamped, and shapes moved about them. There were no fires; although the valley was inaccessible and had been a safe area for the Indians for years, tonight they were taking no chances.

They huddled in the center of a circle of activity, ravenously munching the dried meat that Black Horse Rider had brought them. Sangria was silent. Finally Milt struck up cheerfully.

"You feel all right now, Professor? How did you come to fall off the pony, anyway?"

142

"It's been some years since I sat a horse," the tall man replied, "and when I did it had a saddle. Tonight my animal took fright at one of the fugitives."

"By God, the poor buggers were thick as flies back there all right," said Milt. They all remembered the scene as they had fallen back from the camp to the arroyo where the Lakota had left their ponies, with groups of naked prisoners in the dusk sprinting through the bush in every direction. The confusion had helped them escape.

Long Range was silent. The night's ride had been uncanny for him, for he could sense the familiarity of the direction they took, and kept remembering snatches of the flight he had experienced during his illness, the silent soaring above the ridges and valleys which they had painfully traversed by pony that night, dropping men off at first to hold off their pursuers, trotting on exhausted along the narrow trails and switchback hills under a starry sky. Sitting now with the dark bulk of the hills rising behind them he knew he could point to the direction they must take to leave the valley, the trail that crossed the stream and then forked, left up a box canyon, right taking them northwest out of the valley, and heading straight for the river crossing and the first gasoline cache on the long road home.

"If Belial doesn't make it by sun-up, I reckon we should ditch the sidecar."

"I ain't taking his bike," said Milt quickly. "No way am I taking his machine."

"No, we just turn yours loose from the chair, you brought a sprocket so we can gear it for solo."

"Yeah," said Milt, "but what about the spares and juice?"

"We'll take as little as we can—change the front tires now, you know they last three times as long as the back ones—then load our carriers at the back with a rear wheel each, five gallons of juice and a bag of spares and food and water."

"And one of us double up with the Professor? It'll be heavy as hell," said Milt dubiously.

"We'll take turns. And did you catch a look at the sol-

143

dier-boys' bikes there? They're small, 250 most likely. On the plains we can outrun them however loaded up the bikes are.''

The Professor spoke up. ''Those machines you saw, you know that they're two-strokes.''

''Oh yeah,'' said Milt, ''we heard about them, but the Fief can't make much alloy. So we stay with the big old iron lunkers. They can be a bitch, but they're quick.''

''And you are not disadvantaged by their weight?'' the Professor inquired.

''Well I'll tell you, speed will get you out of most things,'' said Milt.

''If you can just hang on,'' Long Range added.

''I'll bear that in mind,'' said the Professor.

''I wonder if you won't be disappointed with the Fief,'' said Milt. ''When I look at these carbines—and the truck we rode in—and two-stroke engines—I don't know, things at the Fief are a lot simpler, more—'' he groped for a word.

''Old-fashioned?'' said the Professor. ''That won't be a consideration. Technological progress can always be matched, given basic resources. No, the fault I found with the East was not their achievements, but their direction.''

''Is that a fancy way of saying they're a bunch of cock-suckers?'' said Milt.

''You spent some time in the cellars, I believe,'' replied the Professor; ''you know what their power is based on at the bottom end. I have higher hopes for the land which my process will reclaim than that it should be distributed among ex-troopers and worked by captive serfs. But distasteful as that is, it would not have been sufficient reason for me to change allegiance. The truly disturbing thing for me is the way in which the Federation is duplicating rapidly the mistakes of former times, the times before the great war. Principally, a central government which concentrates power and wealth in itself, serves its own preoccupation with control and growth and ignores the real needs of the communities it subjects. The growth preoccupation automatically leads to abuse of the land

144

and of human resources, and to the creation of phantom enemies—projections of itself.

"Don't misunderstand me—I am no friend of the simple life for its own sake. I probably will find much that seems willfully backward in the western states; what I hear of their religious ideas sounds ominous. I am interested in making as many as possible of the benefits of technology and science available to as many human beings as possible; and not to do so in the interests of an idea of nature or a religious belief seems to me to be willful. As an example of how technology can help in all kinds of ways, take your machines. I would guess that those rear ends make for a rough ride—a little design work there could make a lot of difference."

Long Range nodded slowly but Milt said, "We don't mind, see, we're used to it. They work real good as they are; we leave them alone."

"But you suffer unnecessary fatigue; that could give the edge to your opponents."

"No one gets the edge on us," said Milt flatly, in spite of himself.

The Professor paused. "My mistake," he said finally. "I should not be one to underestimate the caution with which technology should be applied to long-established societies; it was one of my special areas of study. Your group's ethos would seem to be stoical. But also unexpectedly conservative."

"Well up till now we've had no cause to change," said Milt. "We seemed to get everything we wanted from things as they were. But you're right, we can't fight these things"—he slapped the carbine—"with our old bolt-guns. So I guess we'll have to change our ways. But for me, it's just one more reason to hate the East."

"The contradiction I have to live with," said Sangria, "is that if it were not for the East's ambition I would never have had the resources to bring my research to fruition. But I am determined that the benefits of it should not be used to further ideas I despise."

145

"Don't get me wrong," said Milt, "but don't you feel bad about leaving your own people?"

"I might do if they were my people," smiled Sangria. "But no, I come from the south; I went up east because only there could I pursue my work. I have no family, and only two or three close friends, all scientists. Now I move again. Only the work is important to me.

"I am obsessed by something that I can seem to see and others cannot; that this time, this age of history, is a sleep, a retrogression, a second dark age; that man could be so much more than anything we will ever see, if he would only organize to help himself with the resources of an enlightened science."

"I'll bet," said Milt, "they talked just like that before BLAM."

"I know what you mean about seeing something and not being able to make other people see it," said Long Range. "But I can't go along with what you said against nature. All the rest doesn't make any sense if it can't be a part of nature."

"But what is that?" said Sangria. "You'll find there are as many ideas of what constitutes 'nature' as there are human societies. If a government wants to forbid something, the first thing that they do is declare that it's 'against nature': if it wants to promote something, it has only to say it is 'natural,' 'a part of human nature.' In fact the word denotes a convention; there is no such thing in itself."

"I know what I mean by it," said Long Range, "because I've felt it."

"But that's no argument," said the Professor; "someone else could say equally well that they've felt something completely the opposite."

"I don't think so," said Long Range. "I get the feeling that people who feel what I'm talking about would feel much the same all over. The Lakota do."

"But can't you see," said Sangria, "that with them it's a social convention also? I talked a good deal with Yellow Bull, the brave I first contacted, and it rapidly became apparent to me that the core of their religious experience, the

146

vision, is induced by physical deprivation, and that its structure and contents are dictated by tribal myths and the suggestions of the wise men. If you took all that away, what would be left?''

"Yeah,'' said Long Range, "but I thought we were talking about *not* taking away, about what's best for human beings. Well, I say that we, human beings, we're more the same than we're different—that the Indian myths and beliefs are just one way of saying one same thing—that we all come from the same place and are part of the same thing: that's what I mean by nature. If people lose sight of that, they're truly lost.''

"Yes,'' said the Professor, "but I'm interested primarily in what you can *do* for people.''

"Yeah, Long,'' put in Milt, "what you know, what's the *use* of it?''

Long Range shrugged his shoulders helplessly. "That's a tough one. It has no use that I can show right away. All I can do is figure what happens if you ignore it, ignore spirit; what have you got left? I could point to the Easterners and say, that's what you got; but really, we're not so different. I mean, Professor, my friend and me, we're men of blood. Most of us don't think very much because it doesn't help us do what we do. But in our first week out this time I killed five men, and one of them happened to be my own father. Well, why not? What's the reason not to? Like I said, we're men of blood, it's what we're trained up to do and enjoy doing. But I had to think why; think about what we are and what things we can't help doing, and if we can help it, the things that we should and shouldn't do. And one of the things that came over very clear to me is that there's a limit to how much we should interfere with the world, because there's much more to it than we normally think and see.

"Now five men is nothing to the harm your work can do. We know an old brave who'd wandered into one of your test areas; he was crippled and his speech was gone, and he's dead now. You could do that many times over. And then there's what you said about changing societies;

all the good that would go out with the bad things. But the way you talk I get the feeling that in the end you think it will take care of itself, what's right; I mean the limits of what you will do, things you shouldn't do with your science even if you can. . . ."

There was silence, and then the Professor said, "Well, yes, that is part of the reason for my being here." He stood up and said, "You're remarkable young men; anyone who can persuade me to engage in debate in the early hours of the morning after a five-hour horseback ride will repay study. I hope we have a chance to talk again under more leisurely circumstances, but now I really must get some rest."

"Right," said Milt, "there are blankets for you over there. There's only a couple of hours till dawn, but it's better than nothing, I guess."

"Good night," said the Professor.

The Angels said good night, then walked wearily to the sidecar and bent to work on it.

After a while Milt said, "You were talking like a Professor yourself in there, Long. Classy shit."

Long Range did not reply for a minute, then, still bent over his front wheel, said, "If you've thought about something, the words seem to come more natural. Easier anyhow. Here, pass me that second tire iron."

"Right," said Milt. "Listen, what do you think of him? The big cheese?"

"The Professor? He seems O.K. Citizen-minded, mostly; but O.K."

"Yeah, it seems weird, doesn't it?—we go through all this shit to get him and at the far end there's just another citizen, nothing special. Still," he went on, straightening and groaning, "he's all right by me. So long as he doesn't fall off my fucking bike like he did that pony."

Long Range grunted and went on working. He was sufficiently impressed with Sangria as an individual; but somehow disappointed that this man, this agent for the regeneration of the Dead Lands, should not share the feeling of communion with the earth that he had learned from the

Lakota. In the midst of his practical worries and fears for the action ahead, he felt a more complicated anxiety; at the direction of thought which the Professor's work had indicated, and what it meant for the probable future of his adopted people.

LONG RANGE AWOKE TO NIGHTMARE. SOMETHING plopped, whistled, shrieked, and the first bombs exploded in patterns of four all about him, deafening, the ground he lay on rocking and rippling. He half rose and then flung himself down as another wave exploded, and another. On all fours he crawled in the half light to where the Professor crouched.

"Mortars," shouted the Professor.

Hideous shrieks rent the air. "Oh hell," screamed Long Range, "they've hit the ponies."

The crackle and whine of rifle fire added to the din from the mortar barrage. A figure came in a weaving run toward them and Long Range raised his carbine, but it was Milt, who flung himself down beside them in the scant cover of the knee-high thorn bushes. They peered around; from the hills to their east smoke drifted and they caught the prick of muzzle flashes from the dark bulk of the slopes. Single rifles banged nearby as the Lakota fired back, but their position on the valley floor firing up at the dark hills with the sun behind them was hopeless.

Long Range flinched as shrapnel whirred close by, looked at the other two and shouted, "Let's go before they get the bikes."

"Which the fuck way out?" said Milt shakily, hugging the earth as more bombs burst.

"Don't worry, they're hitting around the edges," put in the Professor. "They don't want me dead, yet," he chuckled grimly.

"Right," said Long Range. "Cross the stream low down and fork up the right-hand canyon. I'll take the Professor; stay close and they maybe won't fire at us."

Milt hesitated. Another round of bombs exploded and a

149

pony lunged by, its bright guts dragging. Long Range shouted, "Do it!"

They flung themselves through the clouds of swirling dust and smoke toward the dark shapes of their covered machines.

Long Range was nearly there when twenty yards away he caught sight of a brave, his groin ripped open, propped against a bush, laboriously lifting his rifle and firing toward the hills. Long Range stopped. It was Black Horse Rider.

The Indian fired again, then sensing Long Range's presence, turned toward him. As he met Long Range's eyes, through the tautness of pain on his features the beginnings of a smile came. Then a burst of automatic fire from the hills, searching for his muzzle flash, kicked up dust around him and Long Range saw the bullets smacking home, shaking the brave's body until suddenly it was lying flat, dislocated and still, the limbs at odd angles and all around dark blood soaking into the earth.

Milt was shouting at him and pulling his arm, and he went on to his bike, kicking it over mechanically as the ricochets whirred about them and a shouting line of Eastern troopers emerged from the smoke less than a hundred yards away at the base of the hills, running and firing at the remaining Indians as they came. With the soldiers less than fifty yards off his motor caught, the Professor scrambled on behind and they tore off, spitting dirt and dust behind them, Long Range oblivious to everything but speed, his mind a blank, his body zigzagging the heavy machine effortlessly through the scrub and into the glittering stream, blasting through water in second, heading for the right-hand valley so fast that a part of his mind almost idly registered, behind him, the Professor screaming with fear. The valley raced by in an eye-watering blur. He was suddenly aware of the presence of troopers to their left, running frantically to cut them off. One was close; through slitted eyes Long Range saw him raise a weapon, then he was no longer there, ridden down and knocked spinning by the deep purple blur of Milt's machine as it shot in beside him, Milt white-faced, his hands on the raised and spread handlebars more hanging than steering, his body pushed back by the wind of their speed as Long Range coldly shifted into top and the big machines lunged forward again, faster still, the valley widening out around them; they missed holes by inches, dodged bushes, jumped banks, racing on.

Further on Milt caught his attention and, jerking his thumb back, clenched and unclenched his fist twice. Long Range shot a glance behind; there were columns of dust in the distance, probably as many as the ten Milt had indicated. It was nothing to Long Range. Muscles rigid, eyes never blinking, he was his machine. He was riding as fast as he had ever ridden over country, and he knew he could push it even further; but as he calmed down his mind was occupied solely with the problems of a successful getaway, and he knew he could not risk overheating or a burst tire, with two up. He had the lead he wanted; the river would stop their pursuers cold. He motioned Milt to ease off and they roared on westward.

At the river the Professor stood ashen-faced, recovering, as they wordlessly hauled up the cable slung from one bank to the other and dug up the raft the Lakota had built and concealed for them when they crossed going east. Sangria helped them with the tricky business of loading the bikes on to the raft and stood holding one of them as Long Range heaved them hand over hand along the cable, Milt covering the bank behind them with a carbine. As they neared the other side, above the ripple of the wide river came the whir of motors in the distance; Long Range pulled desperately and as they reached the far bank the raft wobbled wildly as Milt kicked his engine into life and, the moment the raft grounded on the sandy bottom, rode straight off and up the bank. The Professor scrambled off and clambered on behind Long Range as he did the same, then ran back to unhook the wire from the tree to which it was attached and cut the raft loose. As it drifted slowly away down the winking water, motorcycles, sand-colored, appeared on the opposite bank, and in an instant bullets were splashing and whining about them.

Milt yelled, "Adios amigos!" and followed as Long Range pulled away, but his laughter turned into cursing as his bike skidded and nearly fell over. He screamed at Long Range who wheeled about, rode close and shouted, "Your back's flat."

Long Range roared his machine up over a bank and into the cover of a dip behind it, jumped off and, bracing himself at the crest, sprinted down the exposed slope where Milt was revving his engine, his deflated rear wheel spinning in the sand as a rain of bullets smacked close around him.

"Glitch bugger them," Milt was shouting, "the bastards are shooting at my bike!"

Long Range ran behind him and together they laboriously began to push and strain the heavy machine up the slope. There was a patter of feet and before they could stop him the Professor was with them, standing behind them, his tall figure seeming painfully conspicuous in the hail of bullets whirring about them and kicking up sand around his feet.

Then the firing slackened and stopped, and the Professor turned and leaned his body to pushing the bike, and together they heaved it up and over the slope into the cover behind.

Milt dived for the tool kit and began to loosen the rear wheel. Long Range looked across at the Professor who smiled back and said, "I told you, they don't want me dead yet."

"Yeah, but they seemed to take a little time making their minds up," said Long Range, and gripping his carbine he crawled to the ridge and looked back over the river. The Professor was holding the back of Milt's machine up so that he could slip the wheel out when Long Range called back, "Hey, there's some sort of truck come to the edge of the water and they're loading the bikes on to it. Hey Professor, come and have a look. What is it?"

Milt checked the pressure of the spare back wheel and slid it home. The Professor, bent double, ran to the ridge and looked back. The last of the dun-colored machines was being lifted on to the back of the curiously wide, bulky truck.

"Oh dear," said the Professor, "it's an amphibian."

"What's that?" said Long Range, but at that moment the strange truck drove into the river and began to churn through the brown water toward them. Long Range shouted to Milt, "They're coming across, get your ass in gear," and as the scraggy Angel's fingers flew over the wheel-nuts, snapped a shot at the cab of the waterborne truck. The round splashed short, and he adjusted the sights and fired again, an armored metal shield with small eye-slits was cranked down to protect the driver, and his shot *spang*ed off it. The truck was less than seventy yards away and closing fast and they had to run crouching low back to the hollow where Milt was frantically stowing the last of the tools and securing the punctured wheel to the back of his bike. Their engines caught as the amphibian ground ashore, and ducking low they shot away through the scrub grass, heading west.

All that morning they ran before the pack of Eastern bikes and the amphibious truck lumbering along behind them.

They could not see how they would have looked from the sky above, crawling insectlike ahead of plumes of dust across the vastness of the undulating plains. All they knew was the deafening roar of their engines, the whack and sting of insects smashing on their chests and faces, and the blurred scrub ahead and all around them, the constant alert necessary for obstacles, hidden holes, jagged rocks that rushed at them through the blur, and the nagging anxiety that never left them; whether they were on course for the next cache of juice, whether they were holding their lead on their pursuers, and how the over-laden bikes were sounding and feeling. Their hands became stiffened claws clenched around the grips, their bodies numb with the constant thudding and vibration, their cracked lips bright scarlet areas in the dust-covered masks of their faces; in the midday heat fatigue dogged them and with clenched teeth they fought drooping eyelids. There was none of the exhilaration which the picture of their machines swooping across the huge emptiness of the rolling land would have suggested; it was a battle to survive.

Milt was cursing and gritting his teeth as each jar to the machine sent pain shooting through the big bruise on his shoulder where the bullet had hit his armored vest the day before. For the last hour they had increased their lead over the plains, where the big machines' power could be brought into play; but now they were threading their way along a dried-out arroyo, bouncing over rocks, picking their line in country where the lighter bikes on their tails would have the advantage. He figured them to have come about fifty miles since the last river; that would put them ten miles from the next one, and the gas cache.

Milt was ahead. For a hundred yards the terrain cleared and he gunned his motor, rushing over the clear ground in relief.

Then all his senses shocked to full awareness as he suddenly saw the rocky ground in front of him fall away abruptly. In the instants left to him he slammed on both brakes and kicked into lower gear; as he let the clutch out all at once and stamped on the rear brake, the back of his bike skidded round in a skein of dust and gravel and he found himself broadside on to the edge of a deep irregular pit that blocked their way. Long Range with the Professor skidded to a halt alongside.

"That was nearly it," shouted Milt shakily. "How the hell are we going to get round this one?" He gestured at the walls of the arroyo rising sheer on either side, and then looked back the way they had come. "They can't be too far behind."

Long Range was studying the pit ahead of them. Its right-hand side was steep, but the angle on the left hand seemed less severe.

"Professor," he said, "get off and get yourself across to the far side of that. Milt, I think we can do it. Up the right hand for go, then along the left."

"O.K.," said Milt, dubiously.

"Speed will get you out of most things, right?" shouted

Long Range, gunning his motor and roaring back down the arroyo; then hauling the heavy bike round and pointing at the pit, he revved up once again, dumped the clutch and shot forward. As the hole loomed he ran the bike at the arroyo's right-hand wall, went up it a little way, then at the very mouth of the pit reversed his turn and snaked his machine across the arroyo once more, using the momentum to run it smoothly on to the steep slope of the left-hand side of the pit. The Professor, watching from below, held his breath as for a long instant the heavy machine seemed suspended on the rocky face above him; but the tires bit firmly on the scree, and the big bike moved steadily across the edge of the hole and straightened out to halt in the arroyo on the far side.

Giving himself no time to think, Milt followed. As far as he could he took Long Range's line, barely resisting the impulse to brake as the pit was almost beneath his wheels; then he was hurling his hog up the left-hand side, stopping himself from holding the bike at an angle close to the slope, which though it might feel safer would send his wheels spinning out from beneath him. The bike rode the scree; Milt was holding his breath when suddenly it lurched beneath him, dropping over. Milt had no time to do anything or even scream before as suddenly as it had begun the lurch stopped, and hanging out over the drop the bike's momentum carried them forwards and out of danger.

The Professor scrambled up from the hole, and as he climbed on, behind Milt this time, shouted in his ear. "Why did you drop your machine over like that, in the middle of the slope? Does it give the wheels more purchase?"

Milt was incapable of answering. Long Range shouted across, "No, it's just he shows off a lot."

They bumped on up the arroyo, heading for the river.

But when they reached the thin line of trees that marked the water on the parched plain, there was no sign that they recognized, and they had no way of knowing if the cache lay north or south. They tore north on instinct, but the further they went the less familiar the river bank seemed.

Finally after five or six miles they gave up and rode back the way they had come—feeling hopeless, checking the east continually for their pursuers. About a mile after they reached the point where they had first hit the river, sure enough the first telltale plumes of dust were seen moving to their left.

Long Range pulled his machine out of sight below the river bank and eased to a halt. Milt pulled up beside him and said, "What's up?"

"If we move now and they spot us we're done for. Sit tight and they'll maybe follow our tracks north."

They crouched over their tanks in the shade of the trees by the river. The dots drew together, clustered by the bank. Milt said quietly, "I only count eight."

They looked around carefully.

"Looks like the hole took care of a couple," said Long Range. "The truck must have had to back up too."

The dots began to move again; for a long moment they could not make out which direction the enemy bikes were taking, then they breathed again as the plumes of dust showed, heading north, away from them.

"Let's go," said Long Range; then, "Oh shit, look." A single column of dust was moving their way. "They sent one to check this way. What do we do?"

"Is it one or two? It's one, isn't it?" said Milt.

"Yeah."

"Waste him."

"They'll hear a shot."

"Not this, they won't," said Milt, producing his bolt-gun barrel from a saddlebag and fastening on the stock. "Get right down."

They laid the bikes down and hugged the dry grassy bank, Milt checking through his bolts until he found one that suited him. Long Range lay trembling with tiredness. It was near to midday, and even in the shade by the muddy river they felt the relentless heat. It had been easier, when they were riding, just to keep going. Milt cocked his weapon and scrambled to the top of the bank. In the silence they could hear insects, the rasp of dry

156

leaves stirring one against the other in the faint hot breeze, the occasional gurgling of the river. The Professor's eyes were closed; he was licking his lips. Faintly a high whirring noise came to their ears. Long Range saw Milt tense at the top of the rise, listened to the whirring clatter of the engine cruising closer and closer. Then Milt jumped up and shouted, "Hey!" Long Range started to move forward as Milt leaned into his weapon and loosed the bolt; next moment he had disappeared, lunging over the top of the bank. Long Range ran up after him but by the time he reached the top there was nothing to be seen but dust and threshing figures beside a fallen bike that howled, throttle jammed wide.

Finally Milt came out from the mêlée, ran to the dun-colored bike and ripped the lead out, silencing it, punched a hole in the bottom of its gas tank with his knife and slashed the tires before trotting back to the other two, wiping his blade. He stowed the bolt-gun once again and they mounted in silence; as they pulled away Milt spat and cursed once, pointing. From the hills to their left the bug-like shape of the amphibious truck was emerging.

They tore south along the river. Brilliant orange flares burst, trailing powdery white smoke in the bright blue sky as the truck signaled to the bike pack that it had sighted the fugitives. The Angels ran as fast as they dared but the river bank was uneven and difficult going; they blasted through tributary streams and leapt the machines over ditches, worrying all the while about the juice sloshing low in their tanks.

Then at the same moment Milt and Long Range turned to each other and whooped in recognition at the familiar grove ahead. Skidding to a halt beneath the trees they scrabbled frantically until they hit the sod-covered wooden lid to the cache, lifted it clear and uncovered the drab five-gallon cans, and a jar full of dried food. In the distance the dark shape of the truck lumbered across the plain toward them. Milt splashed gas into their tanks and topped up the oil as Long Range and the Professor launched the raft and hauled up the cable. Stoving in the extra cans of gas with

157

his knife he jumped on the loaded raft and shoved off, and once again they were hauling desperately on the cable as the faint buzz of the truck's motor came to their ears. The Professor nevertheless stooped and refilled their big water-skins from the flood. The truck drew nearer but the trees shielded them; as they hit bottom again, automatic fire shattered the stillness, but the truck's gunner was firing blind and they rode free.

Glancing back through a dip in the bank Long Range saw the dun-colored bikes clustered around the truck, re-fueling.

The Professor tapped his shoulder and handed him a waterskin. Drinking gratefully he sluiced the dust from his throat and tongue and trickled a little liquid on to his bandanna and down his neck. Off to the left Milt was singing:

> "On my way to nowhere
> I'm on my way to nowhere."

They rode on into the blazing sun.

One part of him wanted to stop. He could almost hear himself yelling, "We got to stop! Oil the chain! Overheating!" and hauling to a halt, and lying spread out on the thin grasses. But maddeningly, nothing was wrong. His limbs and backside were in agony, his eyes strained and burning, his tongue scabrous and swollen, but the bike had never run better; he sensed all was well with it as it pounded beneath him unfalteringly. And the Professor behind never complained, fuck him. Maybe he could just fall off. Just fall off and lie there till they came for him. The cellar wasn't so bad—it was cool—water dripping somewhere, he could almost hear it. . . .

But another part of him wanted only to keep going. If you keep going it's all right, it's better. You never know what might happen if you stop.

So even when the country let them pull ahead and they could have stopped for a few minutes, they eased back on

158

the throttle but kept moving. Sometimes Long Range knew Milt was feeling what he was feeling.

He frightened himself when fatigue overcame him and he had to swerve jerkily to avoid holes he hadn't seen; and then he treated his body like a part of the machine—reached for a swallow of water or a chew of dried meat, and, careful for a few minutes, rode on.

Above the parched plain in the sky ahead of them it seemed the sun would never descend.

BUT AT THE END OF THE DAY THEY HAD LUCK; AS THE light went they stopped on some high ground above long gentle slopes of broken rocky country stretching in all directions. It was nearly dark, and as they listened no sound came from behind.

Still there was no rest for a time; while the Professor kept watch and listened from above, the Angels squatted by their machines in the shelter of a boulder, out of sight and out of the keen wind that began to chill the dusk. They had been in the saddle since dawn, nearly sixteen hours. Working mostly by touch, again they found their training paid as with numbed hands they checked over their machines, cleaning filters, draining warm oil and refilling them with fresh from the caches, tightening chains and bolts, replacing a frayed clutch cable, noting gratefully that the fresh one had been worked in. Miraculously nothing serious seemed to need attention, no gaskets blown or wheels to rebuild; no twisted forks visible.

"I don't get it," said Milt hoarsely. "Today we've done better than three hundred miles which is twice what we know we can hope to get away with, and nothing bad has gone wrong. But those little runs we did between camps, fifty miles and something fucked up every time. I don't get it."

"Maybe we weren't going fast enough before. Maybe the bikes know this is important," said Long Range. They squatted in exhausted silence for a while.

"You think they'll come tonight?" said Milt.

"I don't think so—remember they've done everything

159

we have today, and taken losses. They know we could pick some of them off by sound; in this ground they can't over-run us. How many are there now?''

"Six. One fell out in the afternoon, must have been about seventy miles back.''

"I don't think they'll come; they might try to get round and ahead, but then they risk losing us if we sit tight. I think they'll wait till first light and move when they see us.''

"I got an idea,'' said Milt. "Back there, rig a silent sentry.''

Long Range nodded. Picking up a carbine and the tool-bag they trudged back about fifty yards to a spot where the rocks formed a small defile. Milt took the carbine and cocked the weapon, checked the safety catch was on and the setting was automatic, then laid it down among some rocks off to the right, its barrel wedged between two stones; next he took two of their wire snares, unlooped them and wrapped one round the barrel and the other around the stock. Crouching, he set the sights to point-blank and lined them up to a point about three feet high in the defile. Long Range had cut forked sticks and hammered them into the stony ground, pegging the wires at each end until the car-bine was staked firmly in place. Next he fixed a running wire around the trigger and fastened the loose end to a considerable length of tough cord, which he ran quickly back across the defile, exactly in line with the carbine, then looped around the tall rock they had selected opposite, about a foot above the ground.

"That's enough,'' called Milt quietly when he felt the tension beginning to tauten the wire around the trigger. Long Range secured the cord around the rock and came stumbling back.

"What about coyotes tonight? Wandering into it?'' he mumbled.

Milt thought and then said, "Spikes. Might slow them others in the morning too.''

He rummaged in the bag and came up with a small cloth sack full of four-ended pieces of metal, sharpened and
160

welded together so that a point was uppermost whichever way they fell. These they scattered carefully on both sides of the rope, and Milt as an afterthought took what were left and walked away back down the trail. When he came back he saw Long Range propped against a rock, motionless.

"Come on, man, there's no way you can sleep here," said Milt. "I put the rest of them where they're likely to cut off once the firing starts."

"The catch," mumbled Long Range drowsily.

"What?"

"The safety catch. It's still on."

Milt giggled embarrassedly. "Oh yeah." Then cursed as he stepped on one of the spikes. He hobbled to the carbine, squatted, and very gently eased the safety catch forward. Then they went swaying back up the hill and flopped down below the rock where the Professor crouched.

"You can come down now," said Milt, "we rigged a warning on the trail, and we'll all hear them if they try and ride round."

The Professor slid down beside them. Wordlessly Long Range handed round the waterskin and the last of the dried meat.

"Sorry, that's it," said Milt apologetically to the Professor. "We didn't expect a pursuit—we were going to load the grub this morning. There should be some cached with the next lot of juice."

"That's quite all right," said Sangria. "Tell me, where are we?"

"I make us about twenty miles from the next cache," said Milt. "We cross that river, head down west by southwest, and it's about two hundred miles to the Lakota camp where we started out. Tomorrow does it one way or the other, all right."

"If we wake up in time for tomorrow," muttered Long Range.

Later he found himself sitting dully by Sangria. Weary as he was, relaxation was impossible; his eyes were staring and his whole aching body tense. The Professor, by contrast, though his dark clothes were blotched and creased with dust, seemed to possess unusual reserves of stamina; once he became aware that Long Range was tense still and unable to sleep, he began to talk quietly, drawing him out about his experiences journeying to the east. When Long Range had got to the point where Belial disappeared, Sangria remarked that it must be hard to lose him after they had gone through so much together.

Long Range grunted. "Yeah, I guess I should—squeeze out a tear for him. Glitch knows I owe him; he saved my life two or three times. You couldn't like him; he saw to that; but he was a power, all right. That's why I can't believe he's dead. Besides, there was something wrong— just when we got out"—he thought for a minute then shook his head—"it's gone. Anyway, turn Belial out in the hills naked and he'll roll in a month later on someone else's wheels, wearing someone else's fancy clothes, with a blade and a bottle and two or three women, in chains most likely. That's him."

He was silent for a long while, his eyes staring. Sangria watched him and saw him decide at length to speak.

"But I did see a friend die today, when they attacked this morning. It was one of the Lakota."

He was quiet again for a long while, then went on, "I say a friend, but now he's dead I feel I hardly knew him. He was a man who couldn't help but have an effect on you; but what did I know about him, really? It's so hard— even to remember how he looked, now; I try and try and there's only glimpses—blurred. That's what hurts. All that—time—wasted—for all that's left of him.

"He once said to me, 'Vision returns.' But memory? People that you loved that are dead? Do they return?" He shook his head wearily.

After a while Sangria said, "Believe me, they do."

"I wish I could believe it," Long Range muttered, huddling close to the rock.

Later this voice came again hoarsely, "You know we had a lot of luck today."

"I know," said Sangria. "But I suppose past a certain point, you have to believe in it."

"That's it," said Long Range.

He folded his arms, pulling his leather coat tighter about him. He seemed to fall asleep right away; but as Sangria watched his voice came again. "Did Milt fix the tire that blew this morning?"

"Yes, I saw him do it."

Long Range was silent for good. Sangria eased his stiff, weary body down into the shelter of the rocks, stretching out on the chill uneven ground. Yet he felt more alert and excited than he had for years. He looked at the exhausted sleeping forms of the young outlaw riders and felt a surge of affection and wonder that their physical strength and skill which had saved him today, and which was so foreign to his own nature, did nothing to diminish their humanity for him; Long Range in particular seemed curiously vulnerable, young, earnest and likable.

He thought of the day, the Lakota falling and screaming in the dawn. And at least one of their pursuers dead. He had known and worked with the Eastern troopers for years; bored, homesick, brutalized, within their limits they were not a bad bunch. At least one dead, more hurt, probably more still before it was over. He thought about that; it was all on his account. But if he was honest with himself he knew that he considered his work was worth it.

Accustomed to sleeping inside, now he looked up in awe at the glittering sky; suddenly felt the terror of its vastness, lying unprotected in the starlight. As the wind hissed through the rocks and scrub grasses, he pulled his coat closer about him and found himself touching his own genitals for the comfort it gave.

THE FIRST THING LONG RANGE KNEW WAS THE SOUND, the faint whir of motors in the distance.

He had been dreaming of Rita, reliving their last night together. For warriors about to go out there should have been no sex, but she had come to his bed, silently. In his dream he had said smiling, "You make your own rules to

163

the end,'' and she had nodded and begun to speak, when the sound woke him abruptly.

He sprang up before he was aware that Sangria was shaking him awake. He felt exhausted, sick and dizzy, as though he had only slept for five minutes; yet around him he could see the largest rocks in the gray half light before dawn. Sangria was shaking Milt as he stumbled to his machine and kicked it over, adjusting the choke and cursing as the cold engine failed; by the time it caught he was sweating in the morning chill, and the last thing he heard before its roar was the high distinct whir of their enemies approaching. Sangria clambered on behind and together the two bikes picked their way down the rocky slope.

They heard nothing behind, above the rumble and splutter of their motors. The broken ground gave way to rolling plains of quivering white grasses again and they ran on, cautious in the awkward light, until they felt warmth on their backs as the sun came over the horizon behind and flung shadows forward for them to follow. Long Range fell into the rhythm of riding once more; he felt fairly good. They carried their compasses slung on thongs round their necks, but when they approached the river these were mercifully unnecessary, as they both recognized the place and rode straight to the buried raft, crossed, and dug up the third cache while the Professor watched the far bank. He shouted back to them as two riders appeared there. They concentrated on filling and loading, and were stuffing their pockets with food as the Professor announced a third rider. They rode off as the buglike truck appeared, Milt waving three fingers joyously in the air as they peeled off southwest at right angles to the river.

"They must have caught the full clip," he shouted.

It was a bright and beautiful day and, in the cool of the morning, a pleasure to ride with everything running right. Long Range felt a curious weightlessness; the bike jolted and bumped as usual but he was off somewhere, floating free.

One more river.

164

They really had a chance.

He glanced across at Milt; his friend's lean and stooping body was transformed as he rode, one with the big machine, arms spread and long hair whipping in the wind. As if invisibly connected the two bikes sailed across the rolling land together. Off in the distance ahead, through a veil of haze the snow-capped mountains rose, painted on the bright sky. Long Range sang out:

> "Running home
> Home home home home home."

He turned to grin over his shoulder at the Professor, who winced at a bump and then smiled back.

ABOUT HALF AN HOUR PASSED, THEN SOMETHING CHANGED. He turned to look around. Milt's bike was falling back fast, running jerkily, and, as he looked, rolling to a halt in the thin white grass.

Long Range, his stomach turned to ice, swung his bike round and pulled up next to his friend's silent machine, and switched off to listen. No sound came to them from behind. They had at least four or five minutes.

"Juice?" said Long Range tensely.

"It's O.K. The way it went so quick it's the valves, I think. Didn't seize. Didn't lose power. Just choked up."

Long Range was spreading the tool roll and quickly unbolted Milt's purple tank, laying it awkward and heavy with slopping gas carefully on the ground, saying to the Professor, "Get the carbine."

Milt took over on the engine, sweat dropping on his hands as they deftly removed the chrome cover. Sangria looked around them nervously. The plain seemed totally different from the way it had when they had been moving across it. It was bigger now, emptier, quieter, stretching away endlessly on all sides. The lack of form menaced him; his back felt constantly exposed. He realized the ground rose ahead of them, but it was so gentle a gradation as to be virtually imperceptible. The only feature of the landscape was a single knoll rising off to the left, an insignificant bump of parched yellow earth.

He stared back in the direction they had come, expecting to sight the enemy riders at any moment. Long Range came up and took the carbine from him, checked the breech and looked around calmly.

"It's the exhaust valve in front," cried Milt.

"Check the spring," said Long Range, still looking around coolly. There were long minutes of silence. Sangria thought he heard a buzz in the distance, looked at Long Range's machine, started to speak and then fell silent. Long Range slapped at a fly on his hand.

"That's it," said Milt flatly. "Spring's broken clean through the middle."

"Spares?" said Long Range.

"We left them," said Milt, then, "time for you to go. Get going now."

"Bullshit," said Long Range. "How about the springs from the seat-post tube?"

"No time," said Milt.

"O.K. Reverse that broken spring so the ends meet in the middle," said Long Range. "It'll get you to that rise yonder. We'll hole up there; Lakota'll be here before long. Come on, man, I think I can hear something."

Sangria almost jumped. Far in the distance came the faint whir. Milt was hunched in concentration over the engine. Long Range waited for a moment then walked to his black machine, slung the carbine and, kicking the bike over, roared off the way they had come. Sangria watched as machine and rider dwindled to a dot on the furthest horizon of a swelling slope. There was silence broken only by the chink of Milt's tools and the rising whir in the distance. Sangria felt dizzy, almost intoxicated. The plain seemed to writhe about him in the heat.

He said to Milt, "I'll start for the knoll," and set off without receiving a reply. The scale of the plain seemed to mock his effort but it was the better than standing still. He went a little way and looked back. Milt was lifting the tank on. He strode on, sweat trickling off him. He heard a chugging mechanical sound behind him; Milt kicking his motor over. It came again and again. He seemed no nearer the knoll when a shot shattered the still morning, shocking, and followed by two more close together. He began to jog, soon wheezing and blowing painfully, feeling both scared and ridiculous. The roar of an engine behind him made him turn. Milt rode slowly forward across the plain toward him, his face a mask of concentration as he eased the bike up through the gears. Sangria could only watch as the machine approached, swishing toward him through the tall dead grass and roaring past falteringly without stopping. Sangria, cursing, jogged on. Then there was the sound of a second motor and Sangria turned to see Long Range tear toward him, trailing dust, and pull up beside him just long enough for the Professor to scramble on behind, before Long Range shot off again, front wheel lifting, back end snaking as they tore up to Milt, who shot a glance across at them.

Long Range shouted, "Got one."

Milt shrugged and gently increased power. They approached the knoll and on the last slope, though it was not steep, Milt's engine failed again and he skipped off and, using the last of the momentum, ran the heavy machine on to the bare top of the rise. Without stopping they ran the bikes to the center of the little hill, switched off, tightened the gas caps and laid them down. Unstrapping the bags and spare wheel they carried them to the edge where they could see the plains behind. Long Range handed Sangria a tire iron and pointed to the other side of the knoll, about twenty yards distant.

"Dig as much of a hole as you can there, Professor, shape it to your body, and pile the earth up in front."

"Why don't we use the machines for a barricade?" said Sangria.

"They'd get shot up," said Long Range, "like I just did to the joker's bike I just wasted. And I never fancied hiding my head behind a tank full of gas."

Then he turned, and with his knife and a tire iron began to scrabble away at the dry earth in front of him.

"Lucky again," he panted to Milt. "For round here this is a pretty good spot."

"It's a pretty good graveyard," said Milt, digging hard off to his left. "You should have got out. There's got to be three men, probably four or five, in that bloody bug that's trucking after us back there. Plus two more of them sorry bikers. How do we stop the bug if it takes a notion to come up here?"

"I've been pondering that," said Long Range, and ceased scooping earth forward with his hands long enough to toss an empty waterskin back to Sangria and say, "Professor, when you're happy with your hole would you put a little earth in the bottom of that sack and then fill it up with gas from one of those cans?"

Milt shook his head silently.

"Now listen, man," Long Range went on, "what have we got? The carbine, four clips, my scatter-gun, a dozen shells, your bolt-gun, what, half a dozen bolts? Food—two or three days. A sack and a half of water. We're looking good. Do you feel lucky?"

"After what just happened to my bike? You got to be kidding."

"Then I'll keep the carbine, because I don't feel bad at all. If anything happens to either of us, the other one takes my bike and runs like hell. Right?"

Milt nodded reluctantly, then said, "Uh-oh. Here they come." They squinted in the dazzling sunlight. About a mile away the unmistakable column of dust was moving forward.

"Man, we were so close," muttered Milt.

"I know," said Long Range quietly. "The camp, Rita, can't be a hundred miles away. Still. . . ."

"Why did it have to fucking happen this way," said Milt bitterly.

"It has to be Glitch," said Long Range, "don't you know he's got more twists than a fucking earhole?"

He noticed Milt was looking pale, and once again fervently thanked the wave of elation that was carrying him

168

through this time. How could he make Milt feel O.K. till the shooting started? Keep him busy.

"Listen, we have to think," he said, still digging, glancing up at the column of dust trickling toward them beyond the horizon. "Their bikes are just harassment, it's the bug we have to watch out for now. The cab is armored; the gas tanks must be—how about the back where the soldiers are?"

"It's armored," said the Professor. "With firing slits."

"But there's one thing," said Long Range. "They figure to fuel the bikes, and themselves, this far, and back again I guess. There has to be about another hundred gallons stashed somewhere inside. If we can stop it, then. . . ."

"A fire-bolt," said Milt.

"A fire-bolt, fucking ay!" said Long Range. "Nice."

"There it is," said Milt tautly. For a long moment under the parching sun they all looked at the black dot on the horizon moving toward them steadily, inexorably.

Even Long Range felt something flutter inside himself, felt his knees loose for a moment.

Then in the distance the truck stopped and two small columns of dust converged on it.

"Come to mama," gritted Milt, and reached in his sack for a bolt, from which he unscrewed the barbed head and began to fasten on something that looked to Sangria, glancing over his shoulder from the work in the dusty earth, like the tip of a bullrush.

They went on digging, glancing up continually at the motionless dots away across the plains. For what seemed like a long time, nothing happened. It got hotter, and Milt found that he was drowsing, eyelids drooping then jerking awake to the fear.

"What's keeping them?" he said, half to himself.

"Perhaps they're radioing back for help," said the Professor.

"Maybe," said Long Range, "but I don't think so. They come too far too fast for anyone to find them. My guess is they're trying to figure out what we're up to. They don't know for sure that anyone cracked up. So why are we here?"

"Ran out of gas?"

"Maybe, or maybe they figure we're meeting someone. Either way I reckon they won't be too long coming—if our help comes they're sunk, and if they wait till night we can most likely slip off."

"Here's your gas sack," said Sangria huskily.

"Thanks. Listen, when the shit hits the fan, Professor, you keep your head down. If they cut around your side we'll use your hole and you use ours. Don't fire, or at least don't let them see you fire, 'cause if anything goes wrong and they get you they might be feeling savage if some of their friends have got dead, and they might take it out on you. This way you can say we forced you along. I guess I'm sorry it's turned out this way, but you can see how we feel, it's one on all with us."

Sangria nodded.

"Milt," Long Range went on, all the while stuffing an old rag into the throat of the gas-filled skin and binding it fast with cord, "when they come I'm going to ride around and try to stop the bug. That should draw out their bikes; you have to try and take them out with the carbine. If I get the bug stood still, you go in there with the fire-bolt."

"It should be my ass out there," muttered Milt. "Why risk the bike that runs?"

"Because only speed is going to make it this time, and you know yours is liable to die on you any time. And no one gets to ride my bike."

"Johnny Angel, eh? Asshole."

"Flower-fucker."

"Gah, ya pitiful piece of chickenshit, I'll let you go just to see you get your ass shot off."

"I reckoned that was more your style. Come on, let's eat while we can."

Once more they passed food and water from one to the other, their dry mouths finding the meat cloying and difficult to swallow. Long Range looked at his friend's face and at the strained, fine face of Sangria. He wanted to take

170

care of them, but there was no way he wanted to die doing it. He looked around at the holy vastness of the landscape, the plains, the shivering tawny grasses and the burning blue sky, and he loved it with an intense love and longing, and he did not want to lose it.

He felt a grim excitement mounting in him; yeah, it was like leaning out over a big drop, there was no room for any falseness, just the exhilaration, the tension converted into power that took him surging up. Then he remembered a chant that Black Horse Rider had told him:

> "I am a Fox
> I am supposed to die."

The elation rose in him and he repeated the words as:

> "I am a Hawk
> I am supposed to die."

He stared across at the enemy vehicles and muttered his song:

> "Reach the end
> Fly beyond
> Hawks fly on."

Throwing all the force of it at their enemies, fronting them, daring them to break the stand-off. Next he chanted Milt's song, then as an afterthought Belial's, bringing him back to them.

> "River run
> Gypsy blood
> Hawks fly on."

The other two sweated out the wait, bellies down on the hard dusty earth, craning their necks awkwardly to watch the truck; but there was no wait for Long Range, just the power rising and directed, and the battle lust. He had sung

Belial's song to himself for the third time when he thought he saw the truck move. Then he was sure. He felt breathless and fought to control his excitement.

"They've done waiting," he called to the Professor; then, thinking quickly, to Milt, "Glitch, you got any matches?"

Milt tossed him a box, and fingers fumbling, he taped three bundles of four matches each together and put them in the pocket of his red shirt.

"Snap it up, they're getting close," yelled Milt. "One bike off to each side."

"All right, I take the right one, you try for the other," said Long Range breathlessly, slinging the strap of the gas-bomb once around the left-hand side of the handlebars; last he checked the breech of the scatter-gun and shoved it deep into his right-hand saddlebag, with the butt where he could reach it. He bent to heave the big bike upright and grunted over his shoulder to Milt.

"And don't shoot me, asshole."

"It's as good as done," said Milt shakily.

As he heaved the bike upright a shot snapped out, and then a burst of automatic fire kicked up flurries of dust lower down the hill. The other two plunged their heads behind the mounds of earth and squirmed their bodies closer to the ground. Suddenly for Long Range it was all gone, and he did not want to leave the hill at all. For a moment he stood paralyzed, then another burst of fire forced him to push-start the bike over the far edge of the knoll. As soon as he was in the familiar saddle, bumping down the rocky slope and concentrating fiercely on handling his machine and picking his line, his nerves had passed and the joy was rising again. For a terrible moment his motor faltered, and just in time he leaned over and switched on the gas tap; then heeled the bike over to the left and swung in a tight descending curve to keep the hill between himself and the truck and bring himself face to face with one of the enemy bikes.

As he hit level ground and came round the hill the first thing that registered was the truck itself on his left, shockingly close, close enough for him to make out the shiny rows of rivets where the dun-colored camouflage paint had worn away, see the small red and blue unit insignia painted on one side, see even the stupid expression of surprise on the face of the gunner, his head and shoulders perched above the cab behind an armored shield, who next instant was swiveling his weapon toward the biker. And the enemy bike he had meant to fight was nowhere to be seen. By instinct he gunned the motor and hauled back on the front wheel as a storm of bullets walked across the ground between them and seemed to pass beneath his machine; shaking his head in a maze of dust and gravel kicking up around him he jerked the bike left, swerving behind the truck's tail and out of the gunner's field of fire. Snapping a glance behind he saw the truck already turning to its left to give the gunner a clear shot at him, and at the same moment realized that the ground fell away to his right in a shallow arroyo, so instantly flung the bike that way, and, bumping down into the draw, rode crouching back in the direction of the knoll, out of sight of the truck.

Then ahead of him he saw another motorcycle picking its line along the sunken way, and realized why he had been unable to see the enemy bike. He pushed his own machine forward fast; the roar of the big V-twin must have reached the enemy rider beneath his domed helmet, as with seventy yards between them Long Range saw him glance over his shoulder, catch a glimpse of the Angel tailing him, slam on the brakes and, still straddling his immobile machine, begin to unsling the carbine across his shoulders. But Long Range had grabbed behind him for the shotgun; cocking it with his thumb, now he took both hands off the handlebars, steered with his knees, took aim with the stubby weapon, and at thirty yards let the enemy soldier have both barrels in the head.

The man fell head over heels and his bike crashed on top of him; Long Range had to drop his weapon and grab the bars as he bumped his heavy bike over the tangle blocking the arroyo and, crouching, rode on. When he glanced up he just had time to be aware of the truck perched to the right on the lip of the draw ahead of him, the gunner jerked his weapon downwards to get a shot at him, and then he was simultaneously braking desperately and throwing the machine up the left-hand wall, heeling over hard back across the draw and completing his turn up the far right wall, in seconds bumping away in the opposite direction back down the gulley, with no time to stop for his weapon as he felt the violence of the fire at his unprotected back, wove wildly and then jumped the bike up the arroyo wall and back on to the plain.

The automatic fire stopped for long moments—a jam or an empty clip, he flashed—and he looked about quickly. Ahead of him over the plain he saw the second Eastern biker, who saw him at the same moment and slowed, groping for his carbine. The firing from the truck reached for him again, dust kicking in spurts around his turning wheels, and recklessly he headed for the last enemy bike. Not realizing that he was unarmed the man gunned his machine forward, and Long Range was able to pull in about twenty yards behind him as both of them turned hard left, crossing diagonally in front of the hill. The firing from the truck ceased abruptly as he pulled closer to the enemy bike and the gunner feared to hit his own man.

For long moments the two bikes ran along together, Long Range still behind and to the left, the enemy rider running in terror of the shot from behind. It could not last; eventually, turning across the front of the hill again, Long Range saw him snap a glance back and realize his pursuer was unarmed. As he slowed to stop and unsling the carbine, Long Range lunged at him with the big bike, threatening to ride him down if he halted. The lighter machine shot forward again, the Eastern trooper reaching behind him and unslinging the carbine left-handed, hefting it toward Long Range who slowed frantically to stay behind, kicking down through the howling gears; but his momentum was too great and he slid in front of the enemy bike, ducking down over the tank as in slow motion he saw the trooper, visored head levelled, begin to take aim. He dropped the bike left, then

174

reversed it, with no hope, and a shot slammed out. Nothing happened: so he began a wide very fast right turn and slipped a glance behind him, to see, incredulously, the enemy bike spinning after him with no rider in the seat; turning again he saw the bike fall over, and as, far behind, the prostrate rider threshed in the dust, he realized that the pursuit had brought his enemy close enough to Milt on the hill for him to get a clear shot.

Elation rose again, then hammering from behind snapped him back to reality and he saw the truck firing at him from well over a hundred yards' range. Kicking into top gear, he shot the bike to the right of the hill to put this obstacle between them again, glimpsing from the corner of his eye the shape of the truck lurching forward to meet him on the far side. Thinking quickly, once he was out of sight he slammed on the brakes once more, skidded into a 180-degree turn and shot out from behind the hill the way he had gone in; tilting fast around the base he saw the truck churning slowly away from him, traveling in the same direction, apparently unaware of his presence. Trembling with excitement he unhooked the skin full of gas dangling from the left of his bars, once more removed both hands from the steering, and, reaching into his top pocket for the taped matches, struck them on the tank and lit the cloth fuse of the bomb. Reaching forward with his right hand to the throttle he gunned up level with the back of the lumbering truck; a shot spat out hopelessly from one of the rear slits of the bouncing vehicle, and with no second to spare he hurled the fire-bomb as far as he could beneath the roaring wheels.

But the driver had been alerted by the shot and hurled the truck to the left, and Long Range just had time to see the gas flare harmlessly behind it before he was riding across the front of the truck, passing with inches to spare. He had time to realize he had failed before the shooting began again and he heeled right and tore round the hill once more, his mind a blank—his luck had run out?— and he rode steadily, almost mechanically round the hill, still not taking it in, and rounded an escarpment to find the truck had played his own trick on him and reversed its turn and he was riding straight at it, not fifty yards distant, and his vision was slow-motion again, seeing the hunched gunner behind his armored plate slap home a fresh clip and bend to sight on him, and in the suspended instant when he knew what he must do and opened the throttle wide, faces flashed in his mind—there was time, almost leisurely, for them all: Lila, Belial, Sky—and he got one leg up almost to the saddle, the dun armor of the truck's front filling all his field of vision, and there was time even for a wave of affection for his black bike as he kicked clear of it and fell, rolling; but as the deafening impact of bike and truck came he rolled head-first into a rock and blackness.

HE NEVER SAW THE TRUCK GRINDING TO A HALT WITH his bike stoved into its engine, never saw Milt leap to his feet on the hill, shoot the gunner and run screaming down to the wreck, leaving Sangria to remember the bolt-gun and follow with it in the wake of the Angel's battle rage.

At forty yards Milt shot the first man who piled out of the armored doors at the back of the truck, and the man fell dead between the doors, jamming them open, Milt running ahead, yelling and weaving, at twenty yards blowing down the driver as he scrambled from the front, but sprinting on was gunned down himself through a slit in the armor by one of the two troopers left alive in the back of the truck.

So it was the tall Professor, crouching by Milt's body with burning lungs and trembling hands, who put a match to the tip of the fire-bolt, and, as a shot kicked up dust by him, in the first act of violence of his life fired the flame-tipped bolt through the open doors into the back of the truck, where in a sheet of white flame the gas inside ignited instantly, lifting the bulky vehicle three feet clear of the ground before it crashed back, settling, enveloped in fierce flames, a wreck and a funeral pyre for the men inside.

Sangria was blown off his feet by the concussion and lay

winded on the rocky ground, watching the black smoke rise with wide-open eyes, until the stench came to him and he looked to see the dead driver with his hair burning. Sangria's stomach heaved; he threw up on the dry earth, his insides continuing to contract long after everything was gone.

An hour later he had carried the two Angels back to the top of the little hill. He sat there breathless, though they had not been heavy burdens. It was their pitiful lightness, he thought, that made him weep, the tears trickling down cheeks cracked by the sun, and falling to the dust.

STRANGE LONG HOURS PASSED FOR HIM THAT AFTERNOON. Milt had lost a lot of blood from the wound in his shoulder; Sangria bandaged it as best he could from the kit in the tool-bag. Long Range lay, pale beneath the stubble and the sunburn, his breathing shallow and his pulse feeble; all Sangria could do was cover him with his coat, trickle water on to his cracked lips and down his throat from time to time, and keep the insects away. For the rest he sat in the sweltering heat, staring out over the plains.

The sun was well down in the sky when he became aware of the faint sound, shifting with the prairie wind, of motors far off. Clenching his teeth he took up the carbine, found the catch that released the magazine, took off the empty one and, pushing a full one home, made the weapon ready.

They would come to the pillar of smoke. But they weren't going to get his friends. Or him, come to that. Before the last fight he had always had the possibility of surrendering and returning east, knowing he was too valuable for them to punish. Some time during the afternoon that possibility had ceased to exist for him.

He crouched, listening to the motors approach. Something puzzled him; and then a great wave of hope swept over him as he realized that what he could hear was not the high two-stroke whir, or the rumble of trucks, but the sharp, deep, explosive roar of heavy motorcycles.

Five riders swept into view, racing to the base of the hill and fanning out around the smoldering wreck. Already Sangria could make out the winged death's heads on their backs, the flowing hair and the somber brilliance of the dark and silver machines. He leapt to his feet, yelled and waved the rifle; and came within a hair of getting shot for his enthusiasm.

They rose up the hill as he walked from the summit, stopping halfway down. He found himself scrutinized impassively by a dark man, his black hair secured by a headband of knotted leather cord.

"Who are you?" said the dark one at last.

"My name is Carlos Sangria."

There were slight exclamations.

"We've been looking for you," said the leader.

"You're Angels, aren't you?"

The man nodded. "Some boys were sent to get you. When they didn't come back we came ourselves."

But at that moment a voice sounded from the summit of the hill and they all looked up to hear Milt calling hoarsely:

"Glitch, Frank, what took you so long?"

V   THE VALLEY BATTLE

It was very dark now, and all the roaring west was streaked fearfully with swift fire.

— Black Elk Speaks

THEY LAY UP WITH THE ANGELS IN THE HILLS NORTH OF Harmony, while two of the bikers rode a tanker back to the Fief to let Eliot know that they had the Professor, and find out what he would give them in exchange.

As they recovered and rested, Long Range and Milt pieced together the situation—or rather followed the changes, for the country was now convulsed as never before.

As soon as his concussion and exhaustion passed, Long Range borrowed a bike and rode to the site of the Lakota camp by the river. It was deserted; nothing but some faded circles of grass betrayed that there had been a camp there at all. No one saw a sign of the Lakota in the weeks that followed.

When Long Range got back the two messengers had returned. Eliot had accepted their demands for coin, guns, bikes and dope; only in the matter of an annual tribute of Fief virgins had he suggested an alternative arrangement, permanent unlimited credit at the brothels of the City. Frank allowed that that would do.

But what rocked them all was the news that there were no more Gypsies.

As soon as the Professor had made his escape from the Iron Mountain, the warlike factions in the Eastern Seaboard Federation had had their way. The East moved without warning against their neighbors, striking straight for the Cartel oilfields to the south, and occupying the southern statelets in their path; not merely passing through these small states and plundering them, but replacing their councils with military government (though many of these had been willing to cooperate with the East in the first place) and announcing their absorption into the bosom of the Federation.

The great drive west had begun.

In the Fief, Eliot had responded to this news with decisive action. Using as an excuse a coup within the Peregrine Fief (which he himself had engineered), the Fief in turn had moved on their neighbors, where resistance had been confined to desperate fighting in the streets of the Peregrine city. It was there that the last of the Gypsy Jokers died, or burned their colors and faded away.

As they heard of this in the hills above Harmony, the Angels were deeply confused. After a century of warring with the rival band, total victory had finally come. But as Frank put it later, riding the tanker that took the Professor back to the city: "What do we do now?"

For the moment, however, there was immediate employment for the Hell's Angels' talents.

The Fief, when they occupied the Peregrine Fief, merely took over control of their military, whose officers were mollified by the prospect of immediate action against the East. They left the government without interference to the rebel Peregrine party which they had supported, so there was little resentment among the people there and no call for an occupying force. Eliot had thus secured the Juice Route, taken over the Peregrine's stockpiled fuel, prevented the Fief's neighbors helping the East against them, and doubled his own armed forces.

Realizing all this, the East moved with even greater determination. Under the military leadership of General Robert "Red-eye" Crocker, more cautious or moderate opinions were overridden, and by mid-July the entire Eastern force was committed to a lightning mechanized drive west, with Crocker's First Army streaking across the plains, parallelled further south by a similar move westward along the Juice Route by the Third Army under General Stroud; the two armies were to converge on Harmony, link and drive on, west and north along the Juice Route, to the Fief itself.

All this would have to be accomplished during the remaining months of summer, in view of the available fuel stocks, the extended lines of communication and the difficulties of winter campaigning. But Red-eye reckoned himself man enough for the job, and certainly no one at the time could be found to dispute his assertion.

The first stages of the campaign amply justified him. The Indian resistance on the frontier was swept aside, the rivers bridged with pontoons, and within a week his columns were scaling the mountain passes to the west of the great plains. Here resistance was stiffer; the Indians regrouped and were joined by regular Peregrine troops, and by citizen levies from Harmony and other southern towns who did not relish the prospect of a fate similar to the southern statelets already occupied by the Federation.

However, these forces were outnumbered three to one by Red-eye's five First Army divisions, and although they mauled his vanguard and held him for three days, soon the speed and dash of his men (and the presence of several batteries of mobile mountain artillery) turned the tide in his favor, and the arrival of elements of the Third Army in the enemy's rear sealed the victory. The irregulars were smashed and dispersed, and General Crocker triumphantly entered Harmony, just two weeks after the drive had begun, and a day ahead of General Stroud and the Third.

Some members of his staff pointed out that the casualties sustained by the enemy forces in the passes had not been considerable, and that there was every possibility

181

that they would regroup and harass the East's extended lines of communication along the Juice Route; they even had the temerity to suggest that Crocker should consolidate his position around Harmony, clear his rear during the winter and postpone the attack on the Fief until the following spring. Still more disturbing was the fact that Crocker's colleague Stroud, an older man and a veteran of much border skirmishing, was inclined to lend support to this view; and had been reported to remark that the engagement in the passes had merely increased the First Army's confidence while diminishing their resources.

Red-eye called Stroud a pick-nose (but not to his face), and attributed his timidity to the fact that there was gas enough for only one of their armies to drive on the Fief, and Stroud didn't want him, Crocker, to get all the glory. Publicly he continuously urged the necessity of maintaining the momentum of the attack, and the probable cost of holding back now and giving the Fief time to organize, on account of the presence of a few irregulars in their rear. As ranking officer, he had his way.

Ten days later, in the full heat of August, the sweltering columns of the First Army left Harmony, crossed the Rio Grande and moved up the road into the mountains.

IT WAS NEARLY FOUR WEEKS AND FOUR HUNDRED MILES later that the spearhead of Crocker's column came down onto the Colorado River, in surprisingly good order, considering the rigors of climate they had endured. Water had been pegged to one gallon per man per day for all purposes. There had been sporadic harassment—night raids and dynamiting of the road—by small bands of local Indians, mostly Apache with some Navajo and Zuni, obviously incited and equipped by the Fief; but the engineers had coped well with the damage to the road. More disturbing perhaps were the attacks on the supply columns back along the Route; some of the officers had noticed that these had seemed almost selective, concentrating on the artillery ammunition and fuel, so that by the time they reached the river the mountain guns still had only a few rounds each and the army was down to about a full week's supply of gas, which was enough to go either forward or back, but not both. There were also the usual difficulties with the radios, so that by and large units could communicate with each other, but not with the commander-in-chief or head-quarters.

Among the groups harassing the army there had been several bands of Hell's Angels; some officers noted that these were the only troops directly connected with the Fief that they had encountered so far. Two of the bikers had been captured by skirmishes off the road. One of them was the Hulk, Long Range's foster father. The two revealed nothing to their interrogators. General Crocker paraded as many of his men as he conveniently could in the boiling heat to watch the ''renegades'' hang. Some of the men were chilled by the silence with which the glaring bikers met their end.

The first unit of regular Fief troops that the army saw was the company guarding the bridge on the Colorado. The First Army scouts observed them without being observed, took note that it seemed a light detachment only and re-ported back. General Crocker came to see for himself, guessed it was a demolition detail and personally super-vised the lightning night assault which took the bridge within two hours. One of the defenders did indeed reach the detonating mechanism, but through a fault in the wiring the charges failed to explode.

The bridge stood; the First Army poured across and deployed among the palms and tamarisks on the western side. Off to the south they could see needlelike spires of rock. After breakfast that morning General Crocker as-sembled the troops again and told them that there could now be no question of turning back; one more effort on the desert road ahead and they would reach their goal, the fertile and degenerate Californian valleys. The busi-ness at the bridge showed two things clearly: they were a magnificent army, and God was on their side. (Some of his staff added the silent aside that they were also a

183

damned lucky army; while others were oppressed by the way in which the war was being drawn further and further westward.) A few of the men cheered, hoarsely, from raspingly dry throats, but cheers nonetheless, and "Redeye" Crocker was seen to blink once or twice before gruffly dismissing them.

The columns of dun-colored vehicles were on the move again, with the infantry flankers plodding in the dust and motorcycles riding up and down the road. It was a stirring sight to see the implacable line winding through the low bleached hills, with only the far glisten of salt flats spacing the distance to the mountains, bristling dull blue in outline all around them.

The road ran northwest parallel to the river for about thirty miles, then swung in a wide loop through west to southwest, running for thirty miles through a broad valley before veering right to climb west again through the desert proper.

The next day Crocker's scouts reported that at this point, the bottom of the valley where the road turned west, there lay a large camouflaged dump, fairly heavily guarded by Fief regulars, which closer observation revealed to be principally a fuel depot; the scouts had got near enough to actually see the five-gallon cans being filled from the big drums.

Crocker was hard put to it to contain his raptures. If they could snatch this unsuspecting depot, they would likely double their fuel reserves, and ensure their successful passage through the desert. He could only guess that news of the capture of the bridge had not reached the bulk of the Fief forces, which he surmised they would encounter somewhere in the desert ahead. His speed had caught them; at times it had even surprised himself; he was well ahead of his own estimates. If they had the dump, the First Army was home free.

It was the morning of 30 August when the First Army assault force swept through the depot at dawn. They found it deserted. When one of the officers unscrewed a can to check the fuel, the stench that arose told him at once that the liquid the scouts had seen was the only one not in demand among men in the desert. And at that moment the dump blew up in their faces.

Concealed charges ignited; mortar bombs rained down, and from camouflaged firing pits a withering fire raked the assault group. They were virtually wiped out, and the cover sections severely mauled. Ten miles back on the road the sound of the heavy firing galvanized the units at the van of the armored column. But they had roared forward only a few hundred yards when the road itself erupted as hidden charges were detonated and the mortar bombs whistled in once more. The leading vehicles were wreathed in flames or blown on their sides, the road torn up and blocked. Those following gunned their heavy vehicles off the road, only to plunge some way off into concealed pits, whose camouflaged tops had taken the weight of the infantry already passed but now hurled the juggernauts into the axle-breaking drops and onto mines. Within seconds the orderly relief column was in a shambles. And there was no way of letting command know what the bursting bombs and burning vehicles represented.

General Crocker reacted quickly, after resourcefully taking a command buggy close enough to the front of the column to see the situation for himself. He ordered fire laid down at the enemy batteries concealed on either side of the wide valley, though the drifting smoke and their concealment made accurate shooting difficult; he deployed the bulk of the column well back from the firing line in positions that could quickly turn offensive or defensive as the situation demanded; he detailed a section of his staff to work out the best available positions should the action prove to be the major one he had been longing for and he used the high-power radio to outline the situation to General Stroud back in Harmony and urge him, if gas supplies permitted, to send a relief column up and if possible command it himself; he was thinking in terms of exploiting the situation after "the big one," rather than rescue, but either way it made sense.

Then he concentrated once more on the problem of relieving the men of the assault and support groups, ambushed at the dump eight or ten miles further down the road. Radio contact with them had been lost, so Crocker had to gamble that the sound of distant firing meant that they were fighting their way back. He quickly marshaled three crack tank companies and sent them in a wide curve leftward off the road and toward the depot, covering them as best he could where they passed near the enemy batteries on the south side of the valley. But they had not gone far before a column of vehicles was sighted coming down the road toward them; they took this to be the support column which must have fought its way out of the dump. It was only when the vehicles were well within range (and the advantage of the East's larger-caliber tank guns was lost) that some realized the oncoming vehicles were an unfamiliar shape—not their own support column at all, but the Fief attacking.

In the confusion that followed, Crocker's crack tanks did as well as could be expected, but the Fief self-propelled guns had concealed positions to take up, which the speed of the Eastern advance had allowed to pass unnoticed; the movement of the Eastern tanks was hampered by the hills on one side and the blocked road and tank pits on the other; they were still coming under fire from the southern wall of the valley; and the Fief force was fresh and had surprise on its side. Within an hour, less than a third of General Crocker's tanks were still in action, covering each other as they limped back down the valley to the main force; leaving behind a waste of burning vehicles and drifting smoke, thick and oily. Some chola cacti also burned fiercely where they stood. Everything else that burned in the desert was a vehicle. The Eastern troopers saw many fires.

IT WAS BY NOW LATE AFTERNOON, AND CROCKER, DESPITE his silent rage at the day's events, had sense enough not to commit more men at this point. His staff had come up with a position for the army to fall back on; halfway back to its northeastern end, the valley narrowed and the road passed

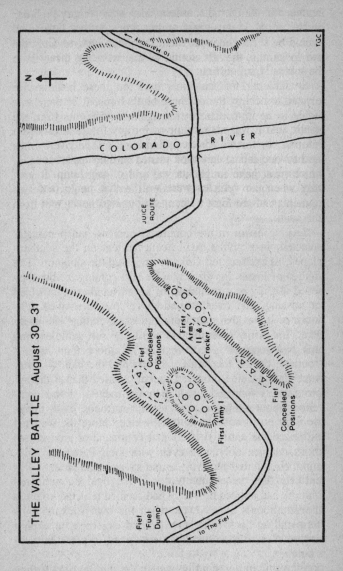

THE VALLEY BATTLE August 30–31

to Harmony

N

COLORADO RIVER

JUICE ROUTE

Fief Concealed Positions

First Army II & Crocker

First Army I

Fief Concealed Positions

Fief 'Fuel Dump'

to The Fief

TGC

between bluffs on the southern side and a solitary high hill to the north. If these high points were occupied the road would be secure between them; although unfortunately the two positions, the hill and the bluffs, were too far apart to be mutually supporting.

So Crocker fell his units back on these heights. He elected to occupy the southern bluffs himself, as there was liable to be immediate action against infiltrators from the south, and it was also the pivot for any future advance on his part, or for his forces falling back on the river. Once he had decided all this and started pulling back his men, he sent a detachment back to the bridge itself (radio contact had once again been lost) to alert them of the day's developments and reinforce them against a possible attempt from the south.

Settling down in the command post he had personally selected, in a ravine giving concealment on the southern slopes, as evening fell Crocker reviewed the situation. The figures of losses for the day were still coming in, but they stood already at a minimum of seven hundred men killed or missing, and over a hundred vehicles destroyed. The worst of it was that they were almost all combat elements. The First Army columns had had to be self-sufficient and this had required a composition of about four support troopers, cooks, mechanics, drivers and the like, to every three fighting men proper; Crocker guessed that of the approximately four and a half thousand men left in his command, about a third were now combat troops. Still, things were by no means black. Intelligence before the war had estimated the entire Fief combat command at around two thousand men only, and even with their Peregrine allies and their infernal motorcycle and savage auxiliaries it was unlikely that the enemy forces in the field outnumbered him: he had noticed how they had seemed reluctant to press the afternoon's attack even when his own forward units were falling back fast; such lack of eagerness to exploit argued weakness to him; he determined to press hard tomorrow.

With this in his mind he was in the middle of parceling

out the non-combatant troops among the fighting units, when shouts announced the arrival of the detachment he had dispatched to the bridge. Or rather a remnant of it. With a sinking heart he guessed they had been jumped on the way there, which meant the enemy was present in his rear.

But the truth was worse still.

Back at the bridge, at midday the same day, the Eastern troops on guard had sighted dust on the road coming from the east. They had stood to, but it turned out to be a column of prisoners, forty ragged and filthy Hell's Angels whom the escort explained they had bagged wandering ten miles further back in the hills, their water gone, and had marched to the bridge in the midday sun to take the starch out of them.

But once the column of bikers had reached both ends of the bridge, without warning they snatched their escorts' weapons, which had been empty, slapped home full clips and attacked the troopers on the bridge with guns and cold steel. It was so sudden that the guards were dead before they had thought of demolition. Immediately the Angels had succeeded they let off a flare and were reinforced by a battalion of Peregrine assault troops who appeared upriver in flat-bottomed boats and dug in at both ends of the bridge, after taking the Eastern covering detachments in the rear and capturing most of their heavy equipment. Some men from these covering detachments had escaped, and it was they who had explained the situation to the column Crocker had sent; which had made the mistake of attempting to retrieve the situation by attacking, and for their pains had been shot up by Peregrine troops manning their own guns.

"The idiots," snarled Crocker when he heard this, "they might have blown up the bloody bridge on us!"

Since the original guard on the Angels had definitely been Eastern troopers, it was evident that they themselves had been the captives, and acting under duress; possibly hostages were involved. But however it had been achieved, the bridge was lost. Crocker felt a terrible sinking feeling in the pit of his stomach, unfamiliar since childhood. He had been caught.

When one of his staff suggested an immediate determined assault on the bridge, Red-eye roared at him. "They'd blow it up, you imbecile! It's no use to them! And while we attack that way the rest of them will be up our asses!"

There were no more suggestions. For many minutes Crocker sat in silence. All the nagging whispers he had experienced during the thrust forward—the ease of it, the sketchy reconnaissance, the lack of solid intelligence information or secure flanks—all returned to mock him now. He was reminded fleetingly of a particularly infuriating chess opponent at college; that feeling. But this was so much worse, with thousands watching his humiliation; the First Army itself, his army; together with the whole of the East, and probably History itself.

Eventually he stirred himself, deputed a staffer to continue the parceling out of the service troops to the combat units, and issued detailed orders strengthening the army's defensive positions as best he could. (Some members of his staff felt that this meticulous placement should have been left to the company commanders, and would have the effect of freezing the defense.) He then ordered radio contact to be made with General Stroud again, and prepared to make the hardest request of his life. In the meantime he cursed the fact that he had made his dispositions before hearing about the loss of the bridge, for since he was now surrounded, the possession of the road meant little, and he had divided his forces on the two mountainsides for nothing. But night was about to fall, and it was too late to remedy now.

The conversation with Stroud was as unpleasant as he had foreseen, but the result was that Stroud agreed; next morning he and the Third Army would drive up the road westward and if all went well, relieve them within three or four days. Stroud would try to snatch the bridge, and failing that, would get Crocker and the First out by amphibian and dinghy lower down the river. Crocker reasoned that the Fief, to contain his army effectively and hold the bridge, must have fielded all their forces against him here, west of the Colorado; there would be little or nothing left to impede Stroud. And the First Army had supplies enough to hold out for a week or longer. It was galling to be relying on Stroud, but he felt that by swallowing his pride and acting promptly, he had prevented defeat becoming rout or massacre. Further remarks to his staff had the theme of defense as "the stronger form with the negative object."

The shadows lengthened over the First Army as they sweated, digging in on the hill and the southern slopes. The night brought little relief after the rigors of the heat-stricken day; the temperature the night before had been recorded at 108 degrees at midnight; water was going to be a problem.

Most of the men in the army were unaware that their retreat was cut off; but they were oppressed by the heat and the halting of their advance, though most had yet to see the enemy. That evening there were various alarms. About an hour before dark a Fief motorized column was sighted to the north, in the desert behind the hill. The men stood to wearily, but the column, after some maneuvering, roared off northwards once more. The same thing happened twice more; nothing came of it in each case, but the continual alarms exhausted the men still further.

Just before nightfall something disturbing happened. From the direction they had come, the mountains across the river behind them, came a low dull rumble, an ominous mutter, like the sound of the darkness itself gathering about them.

ELIOT COCKED HIS HEAD AT THE SOUND, THEN TURNED slowly to smile at a short Indian in a white collarless tunic, a headband securing his gleaming black hair, who looked back expressionlessly. They exchanged a few words and the Indian ducked out of the command tent.

Eliot stood in silence listening to the low muttering in

the distance until a Literate aide, wearing the dark blue fatigues and red and white patches of the Fief forces, announced himself and entered.

"Who was that leaving, Eliot? Apache?"

"No, Hopi," said Frank.

"They don't fight, do they?"

"No, Fred, they don't fight. But that one came to tell me that something they said was going to happen, happened."

He remembered the journey to the mesa, the rocky trail; the terraced pueblos of slab rock perched high on the plateau overlooking the shifting hues of the painted desert, silhouetted against the harsh blue sky; the hours of silence in the deep shadows of the stone room with the savage secret faces of the snake dancers. He still did not know why they had finally told him. But told him they had; given him the date of the rains.

"It should do us some good," was all he said.

"How did it go out at the hill?"

"Well from what I saw and what the other scouts say, it's a straight split; something like half Crocker's strength is dug in around the hill, and the guns are up in the caves, as you guessed. The rest are on the bluffs to the south of the valley. They can't support each other, of course. I tell you, Eliot, I wouldn't want to be those Easterners on the hill tonight. When I got up as close as I could to their positions just now, I suddenly felt someone grab me. He had a blade to my throat; I got ready to die, of course, but then his free hand started feeling my face, like a blind man, and he touched my badges, and a voice started muttering very low in my ear, I couldn't make out the tongue but I got the distinct impression it was baby-talk, you know, kind of '*Good* soldier, *nice* white soldier,' and whoever it was took me very gently by the wrist and led me back down to the men. Those Indians, they're really very scary."

"They are indeed, Fred; we're relying on that. But I don't envy you your experience. We have some strange allies."

The younger officer's face darkened.

"Have you heard about the ambulance, Eliot?"

"Another one?"

The younger man nodded. "It was this afternoon. Some of the Angels were on their way back from the bridge, riding round to the north, and they met one of our ambulances going up to the front."

"Did they get the morphine again?" said Eliot.

"And the benzedrine. But this time was worse. There were two nurses."

Eliot was silent for a while. Then he said without looking up, "Are they all right?"

"They're alive. But they won't be doing any nursing for a while; they need looking after themselves. The troops who found them have spread the word; if I was you I'd keep the Angels well-separated from our men tonight."

"It's already done; I knew there'd be some trouble or other. But this, now. . . ."

"Why do we have to use them?" the younger man burst out.

"Why do we have to fight at all? Why now, not in four or five years' time when we might have been ready? We use them because they're there and they're good. Look at the bridge this afternoon."

"But they represent the opposite of all we're fighting for. . . ."

"We're fighting to survive, at which they're specialists. No, I'm perfectly well aware of what you mean, Fred, and I know that when this is over, now that the Gypsy Jokers are gone, we'll have to consider their position very carefully. But for the moment we need them. And besides, after tomorrow's attack you may find the problem—diminished."

Fred looked at Eliot for a while.

"No one would be sorry," he said at length, "if it worked out that way."

"Except me," said Eliot. "Funny, isn't it?"

His next visitor was the Fief's military commander. They exchanged aphorisms. When the man began to complain of

193

the shortage of ammunition for the big guns, Eliot replied, "As we knew before we started this, the desert is the tactician's paradise but the quartermaster's hell."

"Who said that?" said the commander, smiling. "Moeltke?"

Eliot shook his head.

"Clausewitz?" the commander ventured.

Eliot shook his head again. "Von Ravenstein. Those mid-twentieth-century desert commanders repay study, you know. That was where I got the idea for our bit of business with the hill and the bluffs." And, Eliot thought, as this is the first major military engagement we've been involved in, we're relying fairly heavily on the book, or books. But he said nothing, for fear of appearing to belittle the military commander.

"But how did you know Crocker would bite, Eliot?" the man asked.

"Well I couldn't be sure of course, but I studied him, and their military in general, and it seemed like a fairly good bet. It's the old game; be ready for any move of theirs, while keeping the ability to develop your tactics in accordance with your own idea. I was guessing that they'd do it the way they fought the Indians, the way regular armies always tend to fight irregulars; unimaginatively, because there's not enough real threat to make them think. So what they do is play safe and carry on like a parade ground, executing maneuvers they've practiced already, with little or no reference to the terrain or their enemies' tactics.

"Back on their 'frontier' they're used to hill fighting, you see, so they know all about taking to the high ground; which we dutifully presented them with. But by dividing their forces they put themselves on the defensive, and ignored that 'tactician's paradise' we were speaking of, where Red-eye's tanks could really hurt us.

"I really shouldn't be speaking like this so early on in the game," he went on, "but if your men do as well tomorrow as they did today, I have little doubt as to the outcome."

194

"Well," said the military man slowly, "we're in position north and east of the hill; we played around out there when the light was going and then pulled out, only as we planned, two thirds of our forces stayed behind in the pits, with the guns. And we set up the 'shooting gallery' along the base of the bluffs: if Crocker tries to come out and help their men on the hill he'll get a bloody nose. But. . . ."

"Go on," said Eliot.

"Well you know what it is as well as I do. We've only enough shells for the big guns for two more days at the most. And that's not because of any quartermaster's hell. That's because we just don't have them."

"If it's any consolation, Crocker's in a far worse position," said Eliot, "our intelligence has made sure of that. But I know what you're driving at; we didn't go on a war footing two or three years ago. And you know my answer; that was not our way, and it never can be our way. Beyond a certain point, force doesn't maintain the Fief: it has to be the benefits of what we discover and rediscover, and our position itself. If we fear our enemies past a certain point, we take on their worst characteristics, we become them. While I had any say in it I was not prepared to let that happen.

"Certainly now it all rides on tomorrow, but as I say," he concluded with a belated attempt at geniality, "if the men's performance today was any indication, we shall have no problem."

"I'm flattered by your confidence," said the military commander stiffly, "but I wish I could say that all my brother officers were as happy as you are with our position."

With that he left. Eliot sighed and drank a glass of water, and then his next visitor entered with no announcement; a tall thin man in his forties who shrugged off a civilian coat to reveal a dusty Eastern uniform.

"How was it, Vincent? Are you all right?" inquired Eliot warmly.

"It had its moments," said the thin man. "But listen, I

195

saw Sangria waiting outside; can we have him in while I debrief? I'd be glad of his comments.''

Sangria was called and Eliot sat the two tall men on camp stools and sent for coffee.

The spy began a detailed report of the information he had gleaned, first among the Third Army in Harmony and then after the capture of the bridge where he had infiltrated Crocker's forces.

Eliot's eyes lit up when he heard that it was common knowledge in Harmony that the East's oil stocks were down to two weeks' supply, and chuckled when he heard of the success of the selective sabotage of the artillery ammunition convoys.

"But we weren't so lucky with their communications,'' Vincent went on. "Crocker is still in touch with Stroud.''

"That would work for us,'' said Eliot; "it was principally the First Army internal net I wanted out, and that seems to have happened. What I mean by working for us is that Stroud, and therefore the government back East, is going to know more or less in detail what happens to Crocker's army, if all goes well for us tomorrow. They're going to know, without being able to do much about it, anything at all about it, in fact. The way I see it that's going to put the anti-expansionist elements back East, among whom I believe Stroud himself can be numbered, in a position of some strength.''

"But I thought the whole of the East was sold on the Great Drive Westward at their mother's knee,'' said Vincent.

"No,'' cut in Sangria, "that's not altogether true. What you're exposed to is the talk of the army; they'd like to think it's that way, but back on the coast there are plenty of people who would give them an argument, if something happened to the military to suggest that their ambitions are impractical. Something like tomorrow, it is to be hoped.''

"And the beauty of it is,'' said Eliot, "it's exactly the right size disaster; not national disaster—Crocker is so cocky that lots of Eastern people think he's riding for a

196

fall; not an annihilation which would leave the door open for the south and the Cartel to move on the East; but just enough to stop them looking our way for a good while. During which time, courtesy of the Professor, we hopefully grow enough to discourage the idea altogether. In the meantime, too great a victory would be as disastrous to that kind of balance as no victory at all.''

AFTER VINCENT LEFT, ELIOT AND SANGRIA DRANK THEIR coffee and talked for a while about gardening, to which both were devoted.

Suddenly someone pushed past the guards outside and Frank, the Angel President, ducked into the tent, with Long Range at his heels.

"O.K., flower-fuckers, what is going on?" he stormed.

"What . . ." said Eliot, but went no further. Frank's eyes were bugged out and unblinking, his lips cracked and dry, his neck corded, his words hammering out and tripping over, his voice shaking. It was clear to Eliot where a massive dose of the benzedrine stolen from the ambulance had found its way.

"Somebody came to Long here," Frank rapped out, "says he has to make a meet across the river. A meet with the East but it'll do the Angels good he says, but I know better, man, I know what you're at, we'll go and it's a setup, you'll say ha, traitors, you'll try to put the Angels out of business. Well no day no fucking way, man, Frank's nobody's fool, right?"

"Let me understand you," Eliot cut in. "Somebody from the East has made contact with you? Now, tonight?"

"He said he was from there but I reckon he was from you, you slippery son of a bitch. Listen," said Frank, leaning over Eliot's table, "anybody that tries to get us, gets got, you know that?"

"Where is this person?" said Eliot, who had recoiled only slightly at the raw odor that rolled at him as Frank, bare-chested as usual beneath his colors, leaned across his table, splashing the Literate's papers with heavy drops of sweat.

197

"He split," sneered Frank, "naturally," as Long Range took his arm and steered him away from the desk. Sangria, as he nodded to the young Angel, was disturbed to note the air of tension about him, the dark rims under his eyes, the taut line of his mouth and haggard, thin, parched features. Now he was saying quietly to Frank:

"I think he's telling the truth. I think the guy really was from the East. I. . . ."

"What's up?" said Frank as Long Range clutched his head and moaned.

"I . . . aah, can't you feel it?"

"Feel what?" said Frank, as Sangria and Eliot stepped forward.

Long Range groaned, "Can't you feel it? My head . . . all day it's been like something's been clawing across somewhere soft in there. . . ." He shook his head and grunted.

"Is there something, did you get some feeling or knowledge," said Sangria quietly.

"It . . . ah, it's nothing, we're going to fight tomorrow, so . . . all right, I just felt the blood." He groaned again. "Frank, be careful."

The Angel leader was motionless for a moment before saying softly, "I surely will."

He turned to Eliot and said more slowly than before, "What we were talking about; someone came up to Long like I said, and if you're being straight then he was from the East. He said if Long and some other Angels went up the road back toward Harmony and met with them early tomorrow, we wouldn't be sorry. He said you were going to dump us after the fight tomorrow. He tried to give Long some coin, and then beat it."

"Trying to wean you away from us, by the sound of it," said Eliot, smiling and ignoring the hint of the Fief's intentions toward the Angels. "A not uncommon move on the eve of a battle; attempt to divest your enemy of his auxiliaries. It would be interesting to see what they feel they can offer you."

Frank nodded. "We'd get a look at their strength back

198

there, too. And I don't reckon they'd dare try anything with whoever went—they know we've got prisoners of theirs." He turned and said, "Long, what do you think?"

Long Range looked up from the stool he had slumped on, and said slowly, "If you ask me to, I'll go; but what about tomorrow?"

"We'll just have to start the party without you," grinned Frank.

"Are your men ready, Frank?" said Eliot.

"Ready?" Frank snorted. "Ready? Right now they're so stoned they'd ride into hell and piss on the flames if I told them to."

"But will they be in any shape to fight tomorrow?"

"Oh they'll be fine, we got something special for breakfast," said Frank, winking at Long Range.

"The mixture?" exclaimed Eliot in horror. "Now listen, Frank. . . ."

"No, you listen to me," shouted Frank, slamming the table with his fist. "We know what to do and when to do it, we were practicing that all last week."

"But do you know when to stop?" Eliot put in.

Frank was shouting, "How we do it is our business. And if you don't like it, take it up with whoever's left alive tomorrow night. Come on, Long." And the two Angels left the tent.

Eliot sat in silence for a while. Then he said in a low voice to Sangria, "In the world that we hope will come to be, what place will there be for that? That totally paranoid universe they inhabit?"

Sangria shrugged. "No gunpowder till now; no printing press; no Protestant religion; it's what you might call a model psychosis. But I fear," he went on, "that there will always be the unfavored son, the victim of cruelty, the runt; always minds with more hatred and rage at the world than words can express. The dark side of things."

SOLDIERS SWORE AT FRANK AND LONG RANGE AS THEY passed through the lines to the Angels' camp, the loud angry voices in the sweltering night hurling abuse and

199

threats. Frank simply ignored this and went on talking to the young Angel earnestly, an arm around his shoulder.

"Like I say, when you get back, see me first. I know, I know, you say we have to stick with the Fief and I'm with you, I don't like those Eastern bastards no more than you do, the fucking hangmen; but there might be something in it for us; you have to be a little sneaky if you want to stay alive in this world, you know? Business time is all the time."

Long Range made no reply. Frank went on, "Hey listen, you're still not looking too good. How about some uppers? Or I'll fix you a speedball with these and some of the shit from the ambulance? Or a smoke? You're still a little knocked out from that run East, I know. Listen, I'm glad you're making this trip tomorrow. It'll be a breeze, and you'll be out the way, you've done enough and more and anyway, hell, I like you." He laughed. "Listen, what did you mean when you told me to be careful?"

Long Range met his wide, speeding eyes briefly, and shook his head. "It was nothing."

But Frank wagged his head in disbelief.

They reached the Angels' camp. It was unusually quiet, with prospects working hard on the bikes, servicing, polishing and bolting on prized decorative extras, chromed panels and covers; beautifully patterned, lacquered and painted gas tanks, some with Fief runes painted underneath where they would not show, some glowing with black-rimmed painted eyes; fixing boldly welded sissy bars of chromed metal behind the curved seats, and at the front extravagant handlebars, pull-backs, Z-bars, cow-horns, all transforming the everyday working bikes into machines fit to be sung over when the story of the big battle went round, far in the future. As a last touch a prospect went round with a pile of helmets taken from the Eastern dead and lashed them in place on each bike where the headlamp would have been.

The Angels themselves for the most part lay around staring glassily into the fire or up at the stars. It was only noisy where Milt sat with Lila's father Fork, drinking bowls of beer and whisky, and singing. Fork jumped up when he saw Long Range, whom he now adored; since Belial had not returned, Half-Lugs and Rexit, without implicating themselves, had confirmed that it was Belial who got Lila pregnant; and Fork, childlike, had been trying to make it up to Long Range ever since. In the attack on the bridge the giant Angel's right arm had been nicked by a bullet. Now he wore it slung in a filthy sling.

"You two are in shape," said Frank, "so you'll do. You're going to take a run first thing tomorrow morning, back down the road, with Long Range and a big white flag."

Fork was pawing over Long Range, pouring beer down his throat from his own personal bowl.

"Groovy, groovy," he said happily.

31 AUGUST BEGAN EARLY FOR GENERAL CROCKER. AN hour before dawn his radio man shook him awake, and, instantly alert, he went to speak to Stroud.

Some of his aides said that it was only when they saw how he looked after that conversation that they realized quite how deep a hole the First Army was in.

Stroud spoke briefly and to the point. Reports had reached him from posts along the road up in the mountains. There had been a flash storm during the night. Crocker cut in to say that he thought that they had heard it beginning the night before. The weatherman had told them to expect something of the sort at the end of August; and the Hopi Indians up in the mountains performed their annual rain dance about this time every year.

Stroud continued impatiently that whether they had been prepared or not, this had been a disaster, unprecedented, a freak storm. About a hundred miles back from the bridge on the Colorado, a flash flood twenty feet wide had built up in the mountains and swept down on the road, which at the crucial moment had been weakened by a series of explosions; there had been reports of Fief men seen with the Hopis in the area earlier, but Stroud didn't know if that was significant. At any rate, what had happened was completely disastrous. A huge section of the road had been washed away down the mountainside; it would take at least a week to replace it and even that estimate was optimistic, since the equipment had to be assembled in Harmony and driven the three hundred miles to the chasm.

The best help Stroud could offer under the circumstances was to race as many men as he could to the spot by truck, disembark them, skirt the chasm and force-march a column to the bridge. It would take four or five days at least. Boats or amphibious equipment were out of the question. The problem of getting the First Army back across the river remained, and had deepened.

When he came away from the radio, General Crocker, in a low and halting voice, told his staff the news and immediately classified it top secret; if how he was feeling was any indication, it would have a disastrous effect on the army's morale. As dawn broke he gave the briefest of instructions to the officers to work out a withdrawal to the river commencing the following day, and went to sit on a rock off by himself; occasional phrases such as ''God help the First!'' reached the ears of nearby troops and had the effect of unnerving them still further.

Radio contact with the hill had been lost, but as the sun rose the men on the bluffs could see every detail of the scene in the valley; the dark line of the road and rising beyond it the hill, with the desert all around shimmering in the mounting heat.

BEFORE DAWN LONG RANGE AND MILT HAD MET IN THE half-light, passing Angel guards to get to the parked bikes. Milt's purple machine, with a new sidecar attached, gleamed dully. A military track ran along the edge of their parking area, and as they worked convoys of vehicles thundered past on the way to the front, bathing them in powdery dust. The soldiers in them spat and yelled abuse when they recognized the Angels' patches. Milt and Long Range tried to ignore this, checking the bike over in silence; they had agreed to make the run with Long Range riding in the sidecar.

As they straightened stiffly from the work Long Range picked up a light rucksack he had brought with him and placed it on the floorboards of the chair.

"What's that?" said Milt. "Lunch?"

"No," said Long Range, and sighed. "I guess I'd better tell you. Once we've made this meet, I'm not coming back."

"What?"

"I'm staying out there. You drop me off along the Route on the way back."

"Are you out of your skull? The Route and the hills are crawling with Eastern troops. You wouldn't last a day."

"I've made plans. You know I went to the Hopi pueblo with Eliot? While we were there I told them I needed help to get back east. They said I could stay with them, and when I was ready to move they'd hand me on. They told me where I could find them up in the hills. If I don't find them, they'll find me. I won't be long alone."

"But why in the hell do you want to go?" said Milt helplessly. "We've more than likely won here, we can go home."

"I'm going back to the Lakota," said Long Range. "I can't live with the memory, what we saw when the East hit their camp by Iron Mountain. The Angels' camp wouldn't be home for me now; even the Hulk's dead. I have to be out there."

"Look," said Milt, "if it's Rita you're missing, why don't you bring her back? I'd come with you. I've been cut in the ass, thumped hard in one shoulder and drilled clean through the other but I'd still come with you, just so long as you came back."

More trucks full of Fief troopers roared by, the men shouting and shaking their fists. Long Range reached out and clasped his friend's shoulder briefly.

"Thanks. But you know it's not just her. It's . . ." he gestured around at the shapes of the mountains vague in shadows before dawn. "What I felt out there. It was no more than hints, a feeling, even my vision was no more than that. But it was best. That's what I have to follow.

I'm pretty sure it won't be as good, as easy as it was with Black Horse Rider. There are going to be many times when I doubt what happened to me then, when I'm completely uncertain what I'm doing there. But that uncertainty, that gamble, is still better, for me, than what's going to go down here.''

"But you will try and see Rita again? So why not bring her back here where it's safer?''

"I love Rita as much as anything because she showed me things; she knew both worlds, so she could. She showed me that love isn't your own little safe area that you fence off, but something to help you be braver and more free. Now if I believe that, I can't think I'll ever possess her, like a bike or a blanket.

"I tell you, she showed me things; without her all this would be just a bunch of words, like it is to you; because of her it's the most important thing there is.''

"But Long,'' said Milt helplessly, "what's wrong with us and the Fief? You're always telling Frank that the Fief is O.K.''

"They are. They are a civilizing influence. Even us Angels were included, but as the opposite, the bogeyman: Eliot and the others were smart enough to see that they needed one. But with the Professor here now, the wheel turns. With the new numbers of people, the set-up will change. Before, they really were civilized; now they're going to start getting self-conscious about it; as they get richer and smarter, there's going to be a bad case of 'them' and 'us.' Do you think we stop the East, the East we saw in the cellar, if we defeat their army here? It could be we just bring the time closer when the Fief gets to be like them.''

"Then why go?'' said Milt angrily. "Why not fight it here?''

"Because I'm hooking up to something different,'' said Long Range. "Here's what I meant when I said the Fief was civilized. Eliot and the other Literates have tried to make a culture that's mentally united. Like I say, we were part of it too; our songs, our decoration, our machines, and more important, the way we speak and what we believe, and the way we think about ourselves, a lot of that comes from the Fief. Some of that tradition will survive. But the things that will finally break it apart begin now.''

"But," said Milt, "if we win and things really do change, think of the benefits, man. The Routes will be open; we can go anywhere we want. Machines will make life a lot easier. Finally a man will be able to choose what he really wants to do."

"Sure," said Long Range, "good times for a while, but what happens in the end? Pretty soon your free men are going to start colliding, and they won't be united mentally or any other way. That's why I'm going to try to get back to people that still are."

"All right, I'll tell you what I really think," Milt muttered angrily. "I think the Lakota are finished; Eliot won't be able to stand up for them, and the East will get them. And as for you and me and going home, I was just bullshitting before. For people like you and me, nowhere is home and nowhere ever will be. All we can do is try to have a good time before we bow out. That's what I'm going to do—I was hoping for your company. But I can get by without."

"Ah," said Long Range, grinning, "don't feel so fucking sorry for yourself. Like the Professor said, you have to dream it can be better."

"After the things we've seen?"

"Don't forget all the good people we met, too." He glanced up and said, "Listen, we better get going, it's close to light. Here's Fork. That's another reason I have to split; if I go back he'll throw me to his wives. Anyway first let's get this meet over. I got a funny feeling about it."

They ducked as the dust swirled around them from another column of trucks and the troopers cursed and spat on them again. Fork came up and yelled back mightily, "YOUR FATHERS ARE FAGGOTS. YOUR MOTHERS

SUCKED ANGELS' COCKS. GO GET YOUR BALLS SHOT OFF, IF YOU GOT ANY!''

Then he sang a few bars of "Running Down This Dry and Dusty Road," drank deeply from his bowl, belched, then spotted Long Range and Milt and sang out, "Hoo hoo hoo, Fork's got a brew. Come on, little brothers, let's haul ass out of this sorry shithole."

AT THE HILL ITSELF EVERYTHING THAT COULD BE DONE for defense had been carried out the previous night; wire strung, mines laid, foxholes dug and the vehicles placed hulls down; listening posts established and the guns laid on prearranged targets down the road. Although they were aware of the presence of the enemy in their rear at the bridge, the weight of the defense naturally faced the road to the southwest. This had been assisted by a feature of the terrain—some ledges and caves in the hillside where the mountain guns could be placed to command the road.

As day dawned, however, there was horrid evidence that the defense had been less than perfect. Something that looked like a cairn of stones had been piled on the plain a hundred yards off: it was in shadow as the sun had yet to rise from behind the hill, but inspection through glasses revealed the little pyramid to be a pile of helmeted heads. The listening posts had been overrun during the night and the soldiers there butchered to the last man.

As news of this outrage chilled the defenders, the sound of motors came to them on the hot morning breeze, and dust trails showed to the west. Most of the men had slept only fitfully in their new positions, away from their familiar vehicles, and now they stood to with no breakfast and nothing hot to drink. At a mile's distance, the sun glinting on polished chrome, the officers could make out a pack of between forty and fifty bikes approaching. They kept coming, in a loose spread-out line abreast; for most of the men it was their first sight of the enemy, and there were nervous shots fired while the bikers were still far beyond the range of small arms, which the officers
206

quickly stopped; orders had been passed that with their supplies cut, extremely sparing use of ammunition was to be enforced. For that reason the artillery and tanks held fire also.

The line of riders drew to a halt more than a third of a mile from the base of the hill, still in the shadow but close enough for the naked eye to make out the details of the shining machines, the weapons slung in saddle-boots, the Eastern helmets lashed in place up front, and on the riders' backs the white top-and-bottom rockers and the red flashes of the death's head patches. The dust settled and the soldiers on the hill, squinting over gun barrels mostly ineffectual at that range, saw the bikers passing food and wineskins along the line, occasionally pointing at the hill, jeering and giving their watchers the finger. The audacity of their breakfasting in full sight of their enemy's guns was somehow chilling, and the colonel in charge, in his command post halfway up the slope, worried what the purpose of this display was, simple harassment or something more.

During the next twenty minutes two more groups of riders joined the line, the wolf- and cougar-skins and the banners fluttering from the sissy bars of their leaders' machines. Dust rose again, the line shifted, gunners' calculations were made and remade. Engines revved and roared. There was fighting, French kissing and falling off among the bikers; the ride over had revived them after their heavy night and some amphetamines and the excitement had put them in high spirits. The patience of the machine-gunners on the hill was tested to the limit as one after another of their hairy foes ponderously dismounted, walked out in front of the line, turned to put their backs to the hill, lowered their pants to reveal calloused backsides, and relieved themselves in the faces of the enemy.

Then the line became perfect, and nearly two hundred bikers switched off their hammering engines and sat in absolute silence astride their machines. Two prospects bore a great wooden bowl to a figure at the center of the line. It was Frank who took it; and, as the sun came over the hill and struck the line of men and glittering metal, raised it in silent dedication to the disc of fire. Then he lifted it to his lips, drank, and passed it to his right-hand neighbor; taking a second bowl he repeated his actions and passed it along the line to his left. In silence each rider raised the bowl to the sun, drank, and passed the bowl to his neighbor.

Rumors of the Angels using drugs to induce a berserk battle-rage had already circulated among the Eastern troops, and it was ominously clear to those watching that the riders were priming themselves for a drug-crazed assault on the hill. The colonel knew he should be ebullient and tried to convey that impression, as there was no way the riders could hope to take on tanks and artillery; but he could not suppress a shiver down his spine as he watched the savage, silent bikers staring up at the hill. He tried to think what it could mean; unless it was the Angels' own initiative, what possible military purpose could a suicide attempt like this serve? Baffled, he could only conclude it was to draw their fire, and sent runners to all units (for the radios were out, and all the field telephone equipment had ended up at the bluffs) to repeat the orders for the men to hold fire until they were endangered themselves, or absolutely sure of their targets.

As the runners were leaving a strange sound reached the colonel's ears. From the Angel ranks came music; the somber pulse of drums, the twanging of a Jew's harp, the flute's wail. Prospects were playing as the sun rose and the riders waited. For the troops on the hill the music was the most unnerving and ominous thing to have happened so far. Some of them roared with nervous laughter at first, but as the minutes passed the sound of the drums wore away at them like dripping water.

AFTER HALF AN HOUR'S WAITING, THE MUSIC RISING AND falling in the growing heat and no visible sign given, the whole long line of riders kicked their machines into life and for a pulse-quickening second slowly began to creep forward, one and then another and another shooting forward whooping for a few feet, skidding to a trickle once more, falling back to the line. But after fifty yards or so of this one rider detached himself from the pack and, picking up speed, pulled steadily forward. It was Frank, his deep scarlet and silver machine a glistening minnow against the flat dun of the desert. At the head of a billowing cloud of dust he tore away from the now stationary line and headed straight for the hill.

Almost immediately there were nervous bursts of fire from the troops, most of which fell well short of the speeding bike. The colonel sent off another round of runners to stop this, but in the firing it went unnoticed for a while that several of these men were shot down. It was only when a trooper got up to aim at the biker and fell back with a hole in his face that his comrades realized there were snipers concealed somewhere close around the base of the hill who had awaited this opportunity to open up.

As Frank ripped in to less than a hundred and fifty yards, and, heeling over, wheeled full across the western side of the hill, the firing reached hysterical proportions; two of the tanks, hulls down at the base of the hill, joined in, blasting off with their cannon although by the time they did so Frank was clear of their trajectory. After endless seconds, as the ricochets finally kicked up closer to him, the outlaw leader reached the end of his run and suddenly disappeared, ducking into some dead ground and, re-emerging, headed back for the line of cheering, yelling Angels.

From then on the desert went mad. One after another the bikes streaked in, coming closer and closer to the hill. Still the troopers, especially the inexperienced, redistributed servicemen, blazed away, usually expending whole clips before the bikers were within useful range. Several of the runners and non-coms who tried to stop the panic were shot by snipers. One of the riders was shot off his bike and killed outright; a man who thought he had hit him leapt to his feet in triumph and instantly had his throat blown away by a sniper's bullet. Worst of all was the plight of the men on the eastern side of the hill, who were out of touch with the command post and could only sit listening to the mounting volume of fire a few hundred yards away on their flanks, not knowing the cause.

The Angels were riding immaculately, with the wind in their teeth and the blades of the drug working in their eyes and their blood; one by one, screaming their songs incoherently they tore in closer and closer to the hill, snaking their hips to weave the big machines through fire before it even hit. Soon dust billowed around the whole western side, obscuring much of what went on, riders flashing in and out of its protection; the soldiers saw one Angel swoop in to snatch a head from the pile at the base of the hill before disappearing into the dust again, laughing insanely.

Then came a lull, and as the dust settled, the shaken Easterners saw the line of bikers formed again, with Frank on the scarlet bike about ten yards in front, raising a wineskin to drink and then pour the rest of the liquor over his head and shake like a dog, tantalizing the thirsty men on the hill.

Frank shuddered with delight as he felt the wine trickling down his chest, smelled it mingled with the smell of warm oil, cordite and the sweating bodies of his brothers all about him. Staring ahead with eyes jammed wide he saw, suddenly, in the smoke billowing up from the Eastern guns, the shape of a huge crablike figure rearing above the hill, shaking its rattling claw arms at the Angels, threatening and taunting them. Not daring to take his eyes off it, Frank urgently gestured his Sergeant-at-Arms and the heads of the chapters to him and, speaking hoarsely, pointed out the beast in the air. Soon the whole line was mesmerized by the presence. There was silence once again; no one knew what to do; they all watched Frank. Slowly, not taking his eyes from the smoke, the Angel leader slipped his bike into gear and began to ease forward. Ten yards behind, the whole line, all two hundred Hell's Angels, followed suit as one man. For long moments the troopers on the hill were completely
210

still, unable to believe what was happening. Then the firing roared out, heavier than before.

Frank picked up speed. As shells began to burst behind them he kicked into third and tugged his shotgun from behind him. At two hundred yards, grinning grimly at the shock-blasts of hot air and the shrapnel whirring in the air around him, he raised the weapon very deliberately and pointed it at the hill.

A second passed, and then the caves and ledges where the Eastern mountain guns and command post had been sited disappeared in massive concussions. At Frank's signal, Fief demolition teams had pushed in plungers, and hidden charges on the hill detonated spectacularly, tongues of flame and streamers of smoke rocketing up into the azure sky. Some Angels were blown off their bikes by the unexpected force of the explosions. They were lucky; they were among the survivors.

On the hill the defense disintegrated; those on the lower slopes who lived through the detonation abandoned their positions in panic; those on the eastern slopes, unnerved by the blasts so close behind them, for which they had no explanation, and the firing that sounded all around them, either froze in their positions or milled around before taking up new and hastily chosen ones. And as this was happening, in the desert to the north and east, out from their concealment poured the bulk of the Fief troops; from the hidden positions they had taken up the evening before, less than a mile from the hill, armored trucks, self-propelled guns and lines of men drove at the northern side of the hill and quickly overran the lower slopes, blasting everything that moved.

As this was happening, the Angels according to plan should have wheeled and retreated. But as the survivors explained, they had got beyond the psychic point where this was possible. They charged on   intent on a death-combat with the Crab presence or his followers, and plunged into the dust and smoke surrounding the hill.

Here they ran head-on into three companies of Eastern tanks which had been in position in a ravine on the west of the hill. After the explosions and the panic all around, the tank commander, acting on his own initiative, had fired up and moved out as the first Fief troops had appeared on the hill behind him. As the tanks lumbered out over the lip of the ravine, the Angels' motorcycles were coming straight at them.

Carnage ensued. The Angels were cut down by machine-gun fire, blown up by the big guns firing at point-blank range. Several crashed head-on into the armored leviathans; one tank lost a track and was immobilized like that. Some of the Angels simply rode into the ravine and fell off; scrambling for their weapons, groups of these attacked the hill on foot. Most were killed in the fierce hand-to-hand fighting on the lower slopes. Half-Lugs was found with three Easterners dead of shotgun wounds around him, his hand still clenched around the knife he had plunged into the throat of a fourth as he himself died. Some of the bikers were shot in error by the waves of Fief soldiers coming in from the far side of the hill (although afterwards the Angels never believed it was error, for they knew that the Fief regulars hated them).

Within half an hour all the Easterners on the hill either surrendered or ran, heading pell-mell across the road and the dusty valley floor back to Crocker's force on the bluffs.

The three companies of Eastern tanks had split up; radio contact between them was fitful, and, acting individually, some turned to meet the Fief assault from the north, where they did considerable damage before being overwhelmed and knocked out. The rest fell back on the bluffs, but as they approached, the Fief guns that Eliot had ranged to the west covering the base of the cliffs opened up at the vehicles lumbering out of the dust cloud, with devastating effect. Only two tanks reached the bluffs; the oily smoke from the burned-out hulks thickened the dust at the base of the cliff; Red-eye's cutting edge was blunted for good.

From his command ravine, Crocker himself peered into the mist. It was half past ten in the morning, and a ground

212

haze was moving in from the east on a hot wind that filled the air with whirling sand particles and a low moaning sound. Crocker was desperate. The last view of the hill had disclosed the Fief attack closing fast. His aides spoke of "hostile debouchments to the north" and "apparent withdrawal of some elements of forces."

"Don't withdrawal me, you son of a bitch," shouted Crocker, "I know panic when I see it! They should be fucking shot!" He emphasized the point by pulling out his pistol. "In their yellow bellies!"

At this point several of his aides executed a strategic withdrawal of their own.

Crocker was correct in assuming that his combat command was collapsing. As the survivors from the hill ran in they became hopelessly muddled with the units on the bluffs. Individual commanders, hearing the guns to the west firing close, and sensing the Fief forces coming in ahead of them in pursuit of the troops from the hill, fell back further on the bluffs, in some cases demolishing their transport and heavy equipment to prevent it falling into enemy hands. The sound of these explosions so close at hand intensified the panic among the troops on the bluffs. These men, a large proportion of them inexperienced or non-combatant, exhausted by the harsh conditions of the night, in badly placed extemporized positions, with a nagging sense that the enemy was in their rear and the desert ahead, and with no superiors in touch, were ripe for capitulation; and as the explosions boomed around them and the hazy air was full of running figures, one by one and then in larger groups they broke and ran from the bluffs to surrender to the advancing troops in the valley.

Eliot, who had supervised the attack on the hill, now ordered his infantry to regroup and sweep straight on to the east end of the bluffs, while the motorized units kept up the pressure from in front. By half past eleven Fief infantry units were scaling the cliffs east of the bluffs and turning the flank of what remained of Crocker's defense.

* * *

RED-EYE HIMSELF HAD PULLED BACK HIGH ON THE SLOPES and was crouched in a large hollow behind a boulder, accompanied only by the radio man and a young and devoted aide who was paying so much attention to his own performance under pressure that he scarcely had time to be afraid, let alone to realize that he was on the losing end of a major military debacle. Red-eye found his company congenial. The general had used up some pistol ammunition on dun-uniformed figures fleeing past his command post, but to little effect.

Along the bluffs to their right small-arms fire was intensifying. Red-eye turned to his fuzzy-faced subordinate and directed him to run down the hill to the covering company and have a platoon brought up to cover their right. In the sporadic bursts of activity that interspersed his long silences, he declared that he was convinced the firing to their right was "a feint," and bent his energies to marshalling for a counterattack on the tank companies, whose whereabouts, however, no one could discover. A platoon would deal with "the feint" in the meantime.

The radio man rolled his eyes and hugged the rock. Crocker turned to him and ordered him to raise Stroud. He began to rehearse what he would say.

". . . First Army's present difficulties are directly attributable to your inexplicable refusal to provide close support . . . military incompetence aggravating personal jealousy . . . government will hear of it. . . ."

He was pursuing these pleasingly vindictive lines to the exclusion of the action all around, to the extent that the radio man had to hiss his name twice before succeeding in attracting his attention.

The man's pantomime agitation finally conveyed to his superior that something of interest was taking place further down the slope. Pistol in hand, Crocker leapt on top of the rock to see for himself. Below him he found his young aide with his hands raised straight up in the air, under the guns of two Hell's Angels.

Crocker flushed, shouted, "Drop!" to his aide and snapped a shot at the Angel on his right. He missed. The

214

Angel looked up incredulously at the figure on top of the rock silhouetted clearly against the sky, and then let go with his shotgun.

Red-eye found himself on his back. His right shoulder was numb; he looked around for his pistol, and drew his breath in with a hiss when he saw the blood. He wondered irrelevantly what the radio was doing on its side—he would need it to tell Stroud what he thought of him. Later.

He was aware of someone standing beside him. He looked up, squinting into the sun, and made out the Hell's Angel who had shot him. Suddenly he came to himself. He was afraid.

He tried to speak, croaked, finally managed to say, "I'm General Robert Crocker." He coughed, blood dribbling down his dirty chin. "Tell your superior . . . I wish to surrender."

The Angels stared at one another, then Crocker heard one say, "Well, praise the Lord," and the other say to him, "Surrender my ass, hangman." He broke out in sweat.

"Snap it up, man, there's Fief troops coming up the hill," he heard.

Cold metal touched each temple and he looked up at the gun barrels; started to say something in a breaking voice, then recovered some part of the self-image he had cultivated all his life. He cleared his throat and said, "You wouldn't dare."

The Angels waited just long enough for him to realize that he had made his last mistake.

BY LATE AFTERNOON FIEF STRETCHER-BEARERS HAD GATHered all the Angels left alive, and taken them to a field hospital that the doctor had set up under canvas in the ravine at the foot of the hill. Signs of the fight were all around, including the twisted wrecks of several of their bikes. Out of the dusty haze of the late afternoon, one by one the survivors had come to assemble there, standing in silence around the litter where Frank lay with both legs broken and a gaping hole in his stomach. His bike had fallen on him when he collided with a tank; but to his

215

complete satisfaction the tank had lost a track, and as the crew bailed out he had shot them before passing out.

The men in the circle knew he was dying now, and he knew it himself. Still high on the battle brew, his unblinking eyes swept the faces about him.

About thirty. Two hundred had ridden out that morning.

Two more Angels pushed into the circle and handed something to the Sergeant-at-Arms. It was an Eastern helmet, with three stars painted on the front. The Sergeant-at-Arms knelt and showed it to Frank.

"Scumbag and Little Frank wasted Crocker," he said. "Took him off at the neck."

Frank nodded almost imperceptibly, then looking around croaked, "Not so many left, eh?"

"Hell, Frank," said the Sergeant-at-Arms, "it had to be, there was no other way."

Frank nodded again. Then he told them to fill the helmet with beer. No one stopped him as he drank deep, the liquid splashing over his beard and shoulders down onto the earth.

Next he asked where Long Range was, and when they told him that the party had not returned yet, he said, loud enough for most of them to hear, "If he comes back, follow him, do what he says. If not. . . ." He touched the Sergeant-at-Arms. "Stash some guns here, now," he went on. "Do what Eliot says but stay loose, stay tricky. Remember, more twists than. . . ." Here he was racked by coughing. But he recovered and lay staring slowly around the circle, his face very pale and radiant in the dusk, his look illuminated by the drug and the knowledge of his situation. A smile lit up his features and something like an electric shock passed round the circle of watchers; they shivered. The sun was dropping towards the lip of the ravine. He spoke again.

"They can't kill us. We're Angels. I'm not finished, it's just. . . ."

He was lost for words. He gestured to the Sergeant-at-Arms and said something quietly. The man straightened and began to chant. They all recognized Frank's song and their voices rose and swelled with it, the cadence carrying over the battlefield, ringing up into the sky. The doctor was weeping. Once Frank opened his eyes, saw him, beckoned him close and whispered something.

They sang on until the sun dropped, and they had sung him out of life. There was no wood for the pyre there, so four Angels carried him to the trucks with the other dead Angels for the long run home.

As they walked away the Sergeant-at-Arms took the doctor aside and asked him what Frank had said the last time.

The doctor chuckled hoarsely.

"He said if he met Crocker in hell he'd hang him. By his dick. He may only have been trying to cheer me up; but either way he's got to be the meanest motherfucker in the Valley."

UP IN THE MOUNTAINS EAST OF THE RIVER, AFTER THE rains a thorny mantle of delicate-hued vegetation had burst into flower.

Long Range sat back in the sidecar, a white flag fluttering from a staff behind, while Milt drove them bouncing along the road winding higher into the mountains. It was a glorious morning and Long Range twisted and turned continually, taking in every detail of the miracle of the desert in flower; feeling the exaltation of the pure upper air, and an obscure but stirring knowledge that something crucial was at hand. From behind as the sun rose, occasionally they caught above the rumble of their engines the distant poppings and thump of gunfire.

Beside them on his bike Fork rode, grinning hugely and singing out, reaching across solicitously to hand Long Range the wineskin, mostly steering with his body and his good left hand and letting his bandaged right one rest in his lap, raising it only to give the finger to the few foot detachments of Eastern troops they passed.

By about eleven in the morning they had ridden more than a hundred miles, and rounding a shoulder of mountain which continued to fall away dizzily below them on their right, they saw their destination. Like a vast white gash in the violet gray of the mountainside, the fall of rock had cut vertically, making a cross with the line of the road, a stark scar above and below it; they could make out the antlike figures of men and vehicles on the far side of the fall. As they wound closer, each new view emphasized the awesome scale of the landslide. Long Range judged that at least thirty yards of road were gone. On the far side a white flag stirred lazily.

Closer to the divide big boulders lay in the rubble on the cracked road, and Milt drew the sidecar to a halt in the shade of one of them; Fork threaded his bike through the rocks and rubble to the edge of the gap where he stayed astride his machine. The other two joined him, and they stood looking over the scree slope of the rockfall at the group opposite them.

They counted ten men in full Eastern battle-gear, their visored helmets bearing the markings of an elite motorcycle unit, and their bikes parked behind them. Then as they watched, one of the dun-clad figures straddled his bike and rode forward to the edge of the abyss.

When he switched off, as the dust settled there was silence for long moments. Then the figure across from them lifted his visor.

Long Range and Milt started to say something, but then stopped. The rider called across expressionlessly, motioning behind him at the other troopers.

"Don't worry, they know who I am."

It was Belial.

The three of them stared in silence until the redheaded Angel laughed harshly and said, "What's the matter, seen a ghost? You're hard to get hold of," he went on, addressing Long Range and Milt. "I had us all set up at Iron Mountain, then you flew the coop. Same thing at the Lakota camp the next morning. Gone before I could let you know what was happening."

"You took the troops there?" shouted Milt.

"Sure," said Belial. "You're not going to cry for a

218

few dead skins?'' he sneered. ''Oh yeah, I forgot, your girlfriend there had something going with them. Sorry, Long Range. At least you have to admit it was quick for them.''

''Why did you do it?'' said Long Range steadily.

Belial laughed.

''Frank told me to.''

''What?'' screamed Milt.

''You heard me; Frank told me to. You think he'd tell a couple of little pricks like you everything—a couple of one-week Angels? And he was right—look at the way you lost your heads with the fucking skins.''

''What exactly did he tell you?'' said Long Range.

''He said to make the best deal I could for the Angels—''

''But we know that,'' cried Milt, ''we hung on to the Professor until we got a good trade from the Fief—''

''Yeah, but you didn't think what a *really* good deal would be. As soon as I saw the Easterners I knew that the Fief was just small-time. They won't last. We have to get with the winners. I couldn't do much in the cellar, so I got out and then let the officers know about our break—I needed something to get their ear, make them grateful. I couldn't get a message to you without the prisoners' getting suspicious. Then you broke. I had to get in with the East so I took them to the skins' camp during the night, to try and get the Professor back. Since then I've been doing nothing but try and contact the Angels to let them know the East will give them a good deal if they came over. That asshole Crocker had hung the Hulk and Weasel before I could reach them. So I sent for you because you know me. This way we do the Angels some good.''

''But why?'' said Milt helplessly.

''Are you blind or something, man? Because the East is the *power*, man. Didn't you get to see how many of them there are? Their guns, their tanks. . . .''

''Their road?'' sneered Milt, gesturing down at the shattered chasm between them. ''They're not so much, they can be beat. It's you that's really something, Belial; you fink on your brothers so they'll get dead, and you're still fooling yourself that you're doing *right*. Frank may be sneaky sometimes, but he'll know where that's at. And he knows throwing in with these butchers, these fucking *cops*, that's not what Angels are about. You're finished, man, this time you're done."

Belial smiled thinly. "Says you, sisters. I didn't reckon you'd see it. Let's see what a real Angel says. What do you think, Fork?"

Fork had sat staring silently at Belial. Now he said simply, "If I had a gun you're dead."

For the first time they saw Belial's composure slip. Milt laughed out loud and shouted, "Half-Lugs and Rexit blew the whistle on you for Lila, boy. If you come back now the Wolves are going to cut off all your little pieces, that's if Fork doesn't get to you first. Like I say, you're through. Better go and play with your new friends!"

Belial's face contorted with fury. He shouted hoarsely at the men behind him.

"Give me a gun!"

But a bulky sergeant shook his head solidly and said, "Our orders were to escort you to talk. There was nothing about shooting."

"Give me a gun, you rotten fucker!" Belial screamed.

The sergeant grinned and shook his head. "We have to ride with you, but there's no way we have to like it, animal. I understand how your friends aren't too happy with you—I guess the colonel won't be either. If your people won't listen to you, you're not much use to us that I can see. I guess you'll be going back to the cellar soon. Or the end of a rope. And believe me, we won't be crying, animal."

Belial blinked two or three times. He stared sightlessly across the chasm at Fork. The huge Angel rested his grimy bandaged hands on the handlebars and said hoarsely, "You scum-thing, Belial. You little piece of pus."

There was a moment's silence. Then before anyone realized what was happening both Fork and Belial had kicked their bikes into life, slammed into gear and shot forward

220

off the edges of the road on to the treacherous stretch of boulder-strewn scree. Snaking and sliding they were on each other in a second, the two bikes slamming deafeningly together; the watchers could see Fork's heavier machine knock Belial and his two-stroke into the air before the impact toppled Fork too, and the mass of metal and men began to tumble down the cliff-face, picking up speed, the rending crash of metal on rock only partly masking the cries of Fork and Belial as they fell, bouncing, far down the mountain's slope, plummetting to smash to their death somewhere far below, marked by a final cloud of dust alone.

From start to finish the others had stood stock-still. After a long minute one of the troopers swore. They stared across the chasm at the Angels. Then the sergeant mounted, kicked his machine into life, turned and without a word threaded his way back in the direction he had come. One by one, all the troopers followed.

As the whir of the engines died away Long Range and Milt walked back to the sidecar. Milt was shaking.

He started to speak, then simply kicked the bike into life, waited till Long Range scrambled into the chair, and pulled away.

They rode in silence in the midday heat for six or seven miles. Then Long Range leaned over and touched Milt's arm. Reluctantly, the scrawny Angel drew to a halt.

Long Range unwound his tall frame from the sidecar and clambered out, clutching his small sack of belongings.

Wordlessly, they looked at one another. Then Long Range slipped off his colors and held them out to his friend.

"Look after them for me. No good where I'm going."

"But man—they're your colors—"

Long Range smiled.

"Just cloth and thread."

"You know that's not it. . . ."

"I know," said Long Range, "there's more to it. But one day you'll see it my way."

His friend looked down, unable to answer. Long Range said, "You know I'll be seeing you, Milt. Either soon, or not so soon. But when the time's right I'll see you."

Milt nodded, a lump in his throat. Long Range clasped his shoulder, squeezed once and then turned and began to scramble up the slope with springy steps. Soon he was high above. Once he turned and, shading his eyes with one hand, looked back at Milt. To the Angel watching below, his figure, everything about him, seemed to be trying to communicate something, but Milt could not explain to himself what it was. Then he had passed from sight and was gone.

EPILOGUE:
THE OLD MAN AND THE ANGEL

"SO THAT WAS IT," SAID THE OLD MAN. "BELIAL WENT down the hill, Long Range went up the hill, I went back to what was left of the Angels, and we all went home.

"That's right," he went on. "I was the one called Milt. At your service."

The family, who had listened spellbound to the tale, stared at him. Outside it was still; the dead of night, the wind dropped, the snow lying silent under moonlight. Inside the cabin, slowly they came back to themselves; groggy from the dope and beer and the long hours lost in the tale, they became aware again of the cabin's musty smells, the fire burning low.

"So home we went," the gray-haired figure continued, "and at first it wasn't too bad—all those widows, see? And I was a hero. You can bet lots of them wanted to see my scar," he guffawed, slapping his backside.

"But right away that bastard Eliot stuck it to us. It was as gentle as you please, but we knew we were being screwed. We'd fought their war for them and once we were weak from doing that, they zapped us.

223

"Even with the prospects there were only about sixty riders left, so they suggested at the Fief that we come in from our camp and live in the City. No way we could refuse; we were low on everything. Well, that lasted about a couple of months. Brawls, hassles, the whole bit. So then they moved us out again, but close to the City, and they tried it another way—every time we spit they busted us, they made our kids go to their schools, stuff like that.

"The other thing was, as the Professor's shit began to work and they got more land, they eased us out of the cattle business. And they started passing laws about slaves and captives—I reckon I could point the finger at you for this boy Jimmy of yours: he looks like a slave to me, the way you work him, and that's against the law now. You ought to get out of here, son—get your ass down south and put in with us for a prospect. You should do it.

"Anyway that was another market gone. The Fief was getting a bad case of civilization.

"Then Eliot died—we were sorry to see him go, in a way; he may have screwed us at the end, but he understood us, I think. So, after that things looked up. The Fief was growing so fast they didn't know their ass from their elbow. They started fighting amongst themselves; even their priests got into it. Suddenly everybody wanted to know us. I was leader of the Hawk chapter by then. We had a fine time, playing them off one against the other, getting everything we wanted, brawling in the City for this one or that one.

"But then even hayseeds like you know what happened next. The East pushed again and the Fief fell into line behind this Literate bastard Hemingway, who thinks he's sort of a smart-ass version of us. It's been the same story as before—they use us and then clamp down after.

"But I got to ride to Harmony, with all the guys this time. Even looked up old Lizzy Gomez again—two hundred forty pounds and about thirteen children, but still game; Lord, there was a woman.

"While we were there I heard about the Lakota. Like I guessed, the East really let them have it after the first war;
224

from then on they were driven all over the plains, which the Fief couldn't do nothing about. The herds got smaller. But all the time we'd heard about this leader, who was a holy man as well as a great warrior, who rallied them, who they'd die for; Bad Hand, they said his name was, and I was the only one who knew who that was.

"It was while I was out to Harmony last year—there was some hassle with the East again, we hired out to the Cartel for the summer—while I was there I got a message, which is why I'm here now, enjoying your hospitality. The tail end of the year, the back end of the world. But I come, 'cause I got a fair idea who's going to meet me. And I dearly want to see him again once before I die."

He sighed, then continued bitterly, talking more to himself now than to the family of farmers. "Why not, anyway? What have I got better to do? The Fief uses us and then puts us down, like always. Now it's got so bad, the only way we can get it together is peddling off captive women to the houses in the City—they don't ask no questions. We're supposed to just sit on our asses in our camp, but most of the time half of us is out raiding—the Fief cops never know how many of us there are, and besides, they can't tell us apart. But it's not getting any easier. It's getting harder all the time. But we do all right. We do all right."

When he said that, something in the tone of his voice made the captive family look again at Milt. Suddenly he did seem old to them, an old, weary man.

"We do all right," he said once more, then stayed silent for a long while.

The fire crackled once, burning low; the cabin was in shadows.

Milt stirred himself looking to the fire, and reached for fresh wood to build it up. Then, suddenly, he was on his feet, whirling, his knife in his hand.

They were no longer alone in the cabin.

A tall figure was standing in the shadows. After a while Milt put his knife on the table and said, "Long?" peering forward. To the seated family, straining their eyes by the faint light of the dying fire, little could be discerned—a pale, spare shape, no more.

Milt was confused and made no move to go to his friend; he was still shaken by his sudden appearance; he had secured and bolted all the doors and windows of the cabin. Well, there's always a way round that; but Long had surely learned to move like an Indian. He turned again to his friend, trying to make out the expression on the familiar-unfamiliar taut features. Uncertain, he gestured behind him at the staked farmers and the captive wife and started to make some joke about it, when something extraordinary happened to him.

Very abruptly he was somewhere else and moving in a way completely unfamiliar to him, through silent billowing clouds of damp gray mist. His mind flashed to the moment before they had set out so many years ago, when they lay beside their bikes in the dark, listening to the barnacle geese winging north above them. Now he beat on through the rolling mist, aware of another bird-shape gleaming faintly ahead and to his right.

Suddenly below, there was a patch like an area lit by a spotlight, and looking down, he saw himself gesturing behind him, and the captive farmers, and the tethered woman. He saw the expression on his own face wheedling, almost cringing, trying to persuade whoever he was gesturing to, as well as himself, of the cleverness of what he had done, the wealth of his capture, the pleasure of his power—and failing utterly, appearing hopelessly abject, false and used-up. In the instant the feeling of his worthlessness overwhelmed him, he was back in the cabin making the very same gesture.

He jumped and stood speechless, staring helplessly at the pale figure in the shadows. The word "magic" exploded in his mind; but even as it did so, somewhere, just on the edge of his awareness, but forever beyond the reach of words, the true significance of the experience hovered, the meaning of his whole life.

Something made him look about him nervously, and he saw that the whole room had changed, been transformed;

every object and person in it had welded together some-how, become part of some presence of the room that ef-fortlessly included all, without division. His fierce regret that he had done violence here gave way to a bitter fear that he would lose the loveliness of what he was experi-encing now; the same crabbed, grasping, old feeling he had seen while looking at himself possessed him again, and he began to hug himself as if against great cold (and he was shivering now) and to sob incoherently, trying in spite of the long years of loneliness and bitterness somehow to shake off the stinginess and self-absorption and regain something of the generous nature he knew once to have been his. He appealed wordlessly to his friend, and for the first time the figure in the shadows moved, gesturing Milt to go to the fire, and with the gracious motion of his arm came a wave of warm kindness that Milt felt flowing sweetly through his being.

The family watching dumbly saw him turn and stumble to the fireplace where he threw on logs and sank to his knees as the wood crackled and caught and the flames rose.

To Milt the invisible currents uniting the room grew more intense as the flames rose. The heart of the mystery seemed to be in the colors of the fire and its connection to him, the saffron, orange, rose blooming at the bottom of the shuddering breaths he took; overwhelmed by it all, sensing through it all like a luminous aureola the presence of his friend behind him, over his shoulder. Trembling with bliss at the warmth and light bathing him, he then knew what he must do.

One part of his wizened, stingy present-self, which he now felt to be not his soul at all, but an accretion on it, drew back from the step. Must he sacrifice what meant so much? That one thing?

The long-forgotten force of love answered him, and with one rueful smile he slipped off his colors and dropped them on the living flames.

He seemed to see his friend's shape before him now in the center of the light of the fire, rainbow pulsations throb-bing from him steadily in comradeship, joy and love. Milt felt twitches, shivers, shudders rack him. A howl of helpless delicious ecstasy welled up in him, as over his knees, his genitals, his chest, in soaked cells stained with color, in waves, finally in a great fluid rush, upwards he went with the wash of the flames.

DAWN HAD COME AN HOUR BEFORE THE WOMAN, THE FIRST of the family to move, untied herself and stood stiffly.

No one said anything. She went to the windows and, lifting the crossbars securing the shutters, swung them open wide. Outside the cabin a dazzling expanse of whiteness, unstirred by the faintest breeze, lay beneath a deep blue sky.

The family looked about them, at the shattered beer-casks, the bolt-guns, the dying embers of the fire; but there was no sign of the Angel or his visitor. It had happened; but what had happened, and how, they did not know, and they instinctively withdrew from thinking of it. Though the men's hands were still stapled to the table, no one said anything.

The woman went to look for the boy, Jimmy, to help her with the job of freeing the men. With unaccustomed quietness she passed through the kitchen. The back door was open. She stood there in silence, slowly looking out over the glittering fields of snow. The sun warmed her.

At the bottom of the hill by the tree-line, birds sang. A single line of footprints, the slight imprint of the boy's boots that she knew well, ran down the hill to the trees; heading for the path and the crossroads, she knew, heading south as fast as he could go.

ABOUT THE AUTHOR

Steve Wilson was born in 1943. After leaving Oxford he traveled by motorcycle throughout Europe, by sea to South America, by hitchhiking and horseback up to Mexico and the West Coast, eventually returning to England. The author of such novels as 13, DEALER'S MOVE, DEALER'S WAR, and DEALER'S WHEELS, he now lives in Sussex, England.